ONCE FORSAKEN

(A RILEY PAIGE MYSTERY—BOOK 7)

BLAKE PIERCE

D1495623

BOOKS BY BLAKE PIERCE

RILEY PAIGE MYSTERY SERIES
ONCE GONE (Book #1)
ONCE TAKEN (Book #2)
ONCE CRAVED (Book #3)
ONCE LURED (Book #4)
ONCE HUNTED (Book #5)
ONCE PINED (Book #6)
ONCE FORSAKEN (Book #7)
ONCE COLD (Book #8)

MACKENZIE WHITE MYSTERY SERIES
BEFORE HE KILLS (Book #1)
BEFORE HE SEES (Book #2)
BEFORE HE COVETS (Book #3)
BEFORE HE TAKES (Book #4)
BEFORE HE NEEDS (Book #5)

AVERY BLACK MYSTERY SERIES
CAUSE TO KILL (Book #1)
CAUSE TO RUN (Book #2)
CAUSE TO HIDE (Book #3)
CAUSE TO FEAR (Book #4)

KERI LOCKE MYSTERY SERIES
A TRACE OF DEATH (Book #1)
A TRACE OF MURDER (Book #2)
A TRACE OF VICE (Book #3)

PROLOGUE

Tiffany was all dressed when her mother called out from downstairs.

"Tiffany! Are you ready for church?"

"Almost, Mom," Tiffany yelled back. "Just a few minutes."

"Well, hurry up. We've got to leave here in five minutes."

"OK."

The truth was, Tiffany had finished dressing several minutes ago, right after eating a delicious waffle breakfast downstairs with Mom and Dad. She just wasn't ready to go anywhere yet. She was really enjoying a bunch of funny animal videos on her cell phone.

So far she'd watched a skateboarding Pekingese, a bulldog climbing a ladder, a cat trying to play a guitar, a big dog that chased its tail whenever someone sang "Pop Goes the Weasel," and a herd of hundreds of stampeding bunnies.

Right now she was watching one that really made her laugh. A squirrel kept trying to get into a squirrel-proof birdfeeder. No matter how he approached the feeder, it would spin around and send him flying. But the squirrel was determined and wouldn't give up.

The video kept her giggling until her mother called out again.

"Tiffany! Is your sister coming with us?"

"I don't think so, Mom."

"Well, go ask her, please."

Tiffany sighed. She more than half wanted to yell back …

"Go ask her yourself."

Instead, she called back, "OK."

Tiffany's nineteen-year-old sister, Lois, hadn't come down to breakfast. Tiffany was pretty sure she had no intention of going to church. She'd told Tiffany yesterday that she didn't want to go.

Lois had been doing less and less with the family ever since she'd started college in the fall. She came home most weekends and on holidays and breaks, but either kept to herself or went out with friends, and almost always slept late in the mornings.

Tiffany couldn't blame her.

Life in the Pennington household was enough to bore a teenager to death. And church bored Tiffany more than almost anything.

With a sigh, she stopped the video and stepped out into the hallway. Lois's bedroom was upstairs from hers—a luxurious room that took up most of the attic. She even had her own private bathroom up there and a huge closet. Tiffany was still stuck in the smaller second-floor bedroom that had been hers for as long as she could remember.

It didn't seem fair. She'd hoped that she would inherit her sister's bedroom when she went to college. Why did Lois need all that space now that she was only home on weekends? Couldn't they trade bedrooms at long last?

She complained about it often and loudly, but nobody seemed to care.

She stood at the bottom of the stairs that led up to the attic and called out.

"Hey, Lois! Are you coming with us?"

She got no reply. She rolled her eyes. This often happened whenever she had to fetch Lois for one thing or another.

She climbed up the stairs and knocked on the door to her sister's room.

"Hey, Lois," she yelled again. "We're going to church. Are you coming?"

Again, she got no reply.

Tiffany shuffled her feet impatiently, then knocked again.

"Are you awake?" she asked.

There was still no reply.

Tiffany groaned aloud. Lois might be fast asleep or listening to music on headphones. More likely, though, she was just ignoring her.

"OK," she yelled. "I'll tell Mom you're not coming."

As Tiffany made her way back down the stairs, she worried a little. Lois had been a bit down during her most recent visits—not exactly depressed, but not as cheerful as usual. She'd told Tiffany that college was harder than she'd expected, and the pressure was getting to her.

At the bottom of the stairs, Dad was standing in the foyer checking his watch impatiently. He looked ready to go, warmly clad in an overcoat, a fur cap, a scarf, and gloves. Mom was putting on her own coat.

"So is Lois coming?" Dad asked.

"She says no," Tiffany said, lying a little. Dad might get mad if Tiffany said that Lois wouldn't even answer her knock on the door.

"Well, I'm not surprised," Mom said, putting on her gloves. "I heard her car pull in late last night. I'm not sure what time it was."

Tiffany felt another pang of envy at the mention of her sister's car. Lois had so much freedom now that she was in college! Best of all, nobody cared very much what time she came home at night. Tiffany hadn't even heard her come in at all last night.

I guess I was fast asleep, she thought.

As Tiffany started putting on her own coat, Dad grumbled, "The two of you are taking forever. We're going to be late for the service."

"We'll be there in plenty of time," Mom said calmly.

"I'll go out and get the car started," Dad said.

He opened the front door and stomped outside. Tiffany and her mother quickly got bundled up and followed him.

The cold air hit Tiffany hard. There was still snow on the ground from a few days ago. She wished she were still in her warm bed. It was a lousy day to have to go anywhere.

Suddenly, she heard her mom gasp.

"Lester, what is it?" Mom called out to Dad.

Tiffany saw Dad standing in front of the open garage door. He was staring into the garage, his eyes wide and his mouth hanging open. He looked stunned and horrified.

"What's going on?" Mom called out again.

Dad turned to see her. He seemed to be having trouble saying anything.

Finally, he blurted, "Call nine-one-one."

"Why?" Mom replied.

Dad didn't explain. He headed into the garage. Mom darted forward, and when she reached the open door, she let out a scream that paralyzed Tiffany with fear.

Mom rushed inside the garage.

For a long moment, Tiffany stood frozen in her tracks.

"What is it?" Tiffany called out.

She heard Mom's sobbing voice call out from the garage, "Go back inside, Tiffany."

"Why?" Tiffany yelled back.

Mom came running out of the garage. She grabbed Tiffany's arm and tried to turn her around to go back to the house.

"Don't look," she said. "Go back inside."

Tiffany wrestled loose from Mom and rushed into the garage.

It took her a moment to take everything in. All three cars were parked there. In the back corner to the left, Dad was wrestling clumsily with a ladder.

3

Something was hanging there by a rope tied to a roof beam.
It was a person.
It was her sister.

CHAPTER ONE

Riley Paige had just sat down to dinner when her daughter said something that really startled her.

"Aren't we just the picture-perfect family?"

Riley stared at April, whose face reddened with embarrassment.

"Wow, did I just say that aloud?" April said sheepishly. "Was that corny or what?"

Riley laughed and looked around the table. Her ex-husband, Ryan, was sitting at the far end of the table from her. To her left, her fifteen-year-old daughter, April, was sitting next to their housekeeper, Gabriela. To her right was thirteen-year-old Jilly, a newcomer to the household.

April and Jilly had just made hamburgers for Sunday's dinner, giving Gabriela a break from cooking.

Ryan took a bite of his hamburger, then said, "Well, we *are* a family, aren't we? I mean, just look at us."

Riley didn't say anything.

A family, she thought. *Is that what we are really?*

The idea took her just a little bit by surprise. After all, she and Ryan had separated almost two years ago, and had been divorced for six months now. Although they were spending time together again, Riley had avoided giving much thought to where that might lead. She had put aside years of hurt and betrayal in order to enjoy a peaceful present.

Then there was April, whose adolescence had been anything but easy. Would her desire for togetherness last?

Riley felt even more uncertain about Jilly. She'd found Jilly in a truck stop in Phoenix, trying to sell her own body to truck drivers. Riley had rescued Jilly from a terrible life and an abusive father, and now she hoped to adopt her. But Jilly was still a troubled girl, and things were touch-and-go with her.

The one person at the table Riley felt surest about was Gabriela. The stout Guatemalan woman had been working for the family since long before the divorce. Gabriela had never been anything other than responsible, grounded, and loving.

"What do you think, Gabriela?" Riley asked.

Gabriela smiled.

"A family can be chosen, not just inherited," she said. "Blood isn't everything. Love is what matters."

Riley suddenly felt warm inside. She could always count on Gabriela to say what needed to be said. She gazed with a new sense of satisfaction at the people around her.

After being on leave from BAU for a month, she was enjoying just being here at home in her townhouse.

And enjoying my family, she thought.

Then April said something else that surprised her.

"Daddy, when are you going to move in with us?"

Ryan looked quite startled. As she often did, Riley wondered whether his newfound commitment was too good to last.

"That's kind of a big topic to take on right now," Ryan said.

"How come?" April asked her father. "You might as well live here. I mean, you and Mom are sleeping together again and you're here almost every day."

Riley felt her face redden. Shocked, Gabriela gave April a sharp poke with her elbow.

"¡Chica! ¡Silencio!" she said.

Jilly looked around with a grin.

"Hey, that's a great idea," she said. "Then I'd be sure to get good grades."

It was true—Ryan had been helping Jilly get up to speed at her new school, especially with social studies. He'd actually been very supportive of all of them in recent months.

Riley's eyes met Ryan's. She saw that he was blushing too.

As for herself, she didn't know what to say. She had to admit that she found the idea appealing. She'd grown comfortable with Ryan spending most of his nights here. Everything had fallen into place so easily—perhaps too easily. Maybe some of her comfort came from not having to make decisions about it.

She remembered what April had called everybody just now.

"A picture-perfect family."

They all certainly seemed like that at the moment. But Riley couldn't help feeling uneasy. Was all this perfection just an illusion? Like reading a good book or watching a pleasant movie?

Riley was all too aware that the world outside was full of monsters. She'd devoted her professional life to fighting them. But for the past month, she'd almost been able to pretend they didn't exist.

A smile slowly crossed Ryan's face.

"Hey, why don't we all move into my place?" he said. "There's plenty of room for all of us."

Riley stifled a gasp of alarm.

The last thing she wanted was to move back to the big suburban home that she had shared with Ryan for years. It was too full of unpleasant memories.

"I couldn't give this place up," she said. "I've gotten settled in so comfortably here."

April looked at her father eagerly.

"It's up to you, Daddy," she said. "Are you moving in with us or not?"

Riley watched Ryan's face. She could tell that he was struggling with his decision. She understood at least one reason why. He belonged to a law firm in DC, but fairly often worked at home. There wasn't room for him to do that here.

Finally Ryan said, "I'd have to keep the house. It could still be my local office."

April was almost bouncing from excitement.

"So are you saying yes?" she asked.

Ryan smiled silently for a moment.

"Yeah, I guess I am," he finally said.

April let out a squeal of delight. Jilly clapped her hands and giggled.

"Great!" Jilly said. "Please pass the ketchup—Dad."

Ryan, April, Gabriela, and Jilly all started chattering happily as they continued eating.

Riley told herself to enjoy this happy glow while she could. Sooner or later, she would be called upon to stop another monster. The thought sent a chill up her spine. Was some evil already lurking, waiting for her?

*

The next day, April's school had a shortened schedule to allow for teacher meetings, and Riley had given in to her daughter's pleas to let her cut the whole day. They decided to go shopping together while Jilly was still in school.

The rows of stores in the mall seemed endless to Riley, and many of the shops looked very much alike. Skinny mannequins in stylish clothes held impossible poses in every window. The figures they were passing right now were headless, adding to Riley's impression that they were all interchangeable. But April kept telling her what each store carried, and which styles she'd loved to wear. April apparently saw variety where Riley only saw sameness.

A teenage thing, I guess, Riley thought.

At least the mall wasn't crowded today.

April pointed to a sign outside a store named Towne Shoppe.

"Oh, look!" she said. "'AFFORDABLE LUXURY'! Let's go in for a look!"

Inside the store, April pounced on a rack of jeans and jackets, pulling out things to try on.

"I guess I could use some new jeans myself," Riley said.

April rolled her eyes.

"Oh, Mom, not mom jeans, please!"

"Well, I can't wear what you wear. I've got to be able move around without worrying that my clothes are going to burst or fly off. No wardrobe malfunctions for me, thank you."

April laughed. "A pair of *slacks,* you mean! Good luck finding anything like that here."

Riley looked around at the available jeans. They were all extremely skinny, low-waisted, and artificially ragged.

Riley sighed. She knew of a couple of stores elsewhere in the mall where she could buy something more her style. But she'd have to endure all kinds of teasing and nagging from April.

"I'll look for mine another time," Riley said.

April grabbed a bundle of jeans and went to the changing room. When she came out, she was wearing the kind of jeans that Riley loathed—skin-tight, ripped in places, with the navel fully in view.

Riley shook her head.

"You might want to try mom jeans yourself," she said. "They'd be a lot more comfortable. But then, being comfortable isn't your thing, is it?"

"Nope," April said, turning and looking at her jeans in a mirror. "I'm getting these. I'll go try on the others."

April returned to the changing room several times. She always came back with jeans that Riley hated but knew better than to forbid her from buying. It really wasn't worth a battle, and she knew she'd lose one way or another.

As April posed in the mirror, Riley realized that her daughter was almost as tall as she was, and the T-shirt she was wearing revealed a well-developed figure. With her dark hair and hazel eyes, April's resemblance to Riley was striking. Of course, April's hair didn't show the streaks of gray that had appeared in Riley's. But even so …

She's becoming a woman, Riley thought.

She couldn't help but feel uneasy about the idea.

Was April growing up too fast?

She'd certainly been through a lot just during the last year. She'd been taken captive twice. One of those times she'd been kept in the dark by a sadist with a blowtorch. She'd also had to fight off a killer in their own home. Worst of all, an abusive boyfriend had drugged her and tried to sell her for sex.

Riley knew that it was all too much for a fifteen-year-old to have had to deal with. She felt guilty that her own work had put April and other people she loved in mortal danger.

And now here April was, looking remarkably mature despite her efforts to look and act like a normal teenager. April seemed to be over the worst of her PTSD. But what kinds of fears and anxieties still troubled her deep down? Would she ever really get over them?

Riley paid for April's new clothes and wandered out onto the mall balcony. The confidence in April's walk made Riley feel less worried. Things were getting better, after all. She knew that right then Ryan was moving some of his own things into her townhouse. And both April and Jilly were doing well in school.

Riley was about to suggest that they find a place to eat when April's phone buzzed. April abruptly walked away to take the call. Riley felt a flash of dismay. Sometimes that cell phone seemed to be a living thing that demanded all of April's attention.

"Hey, what's up?" April asked the caller.

Suddenly April's knees wobbled, and she sat down on a bench. Her face went pale, and her happy expression collapsed into pain. Tears began to roll down her face. Alarmed, Riley rushed over to her and sat down beside her.

"Oh my God!" April exclaimed. "How could—why—I can't—"

Riley felt a jolt of alarm.

What had happened?

Was someone hurt or in danger?

Was it Jilly, Ryan, Gabriela?

No, someone would surely have called Riley with such news, not April.

"I'm so, so sorry," April said over and over again.

Finally, she ended the call.

9

"Who was it?" Riley asked anxiously.

"It was Tiffany," April said in a stunned, quiet voice.

Riley recognized the name. Tiffany Pennington was April's best friend these days. Riley had met her a couple of times.

"What's the matter?" Riley asked.

April looked at Riley with an expression of grief and horror.

"Tiffany's sister is dead," April said.

April looked as though she couldn't believe her own words.

Then in a choked voice she added, "They say it was suicide."

CHAPTER TWO

Over dinner that evening, April tried to tell her family what little she knew about Lois's death. But her own words sounded strange and alien to her, like someone else was speaking.

It doesn't seem real, she kept thinking.

April had met Lois several times while visiting Tiffany. She remembered the last time clearly. Lois been smiling and happy, full of tales about being away at school. It was just impossible to believe that she was dead.

Death wasn't a complete stranger to April. She knew that her mom had faced death and had actually killed when working on FBI cases. But those had been bad guys, and they'd had to be stopped. April had even helped her mother fight and kill a sadistic murderer after he had taken April captive. She also knew that her grandfather had died four months ago, but she hadn't seen him in a long time and they had never been close.

But this death was more real to her, and it made no sense at all. Somehow it didn't even seem possible.

As April talked, she saw that her family was also confused and distressed. Her mom reached over and took her hand. Gabriela crossed herself and murmured a prayer in Spanish. Jilly's mouth hung open with horror.

April tried to remember everything that Tiffany had told her when they had talked again that afternoon. She had explained that yesterday morning Tiffany and her mom and dad had found Lois's body hanging in their garage. The police thought it looked like suicide. In fact, everybody was acting like it had been suicide. Like that was all settled.

Everybody but Tiffany, who kept saying she didn't think so.

April's father shuddered when she finished telling them everything she could think of.

"I know the Penningtons," he said. "Lester's a financial manager for a construction company. Not exactly wealthy, but comfortably well off. They've always seemed like a stable, happy family. Why would Lois do such a thing?"

April had been asking herself that very question all day.

"Tiffany says nobody knows," April said. "Lois was in her first year at Byars College. She was kind of stressed out about it, but even so …"

Dad shook his head sympathetically.

"Well, maybe that explains it," he said. "Byars is a tough school. Even tougher to get into than Georgetown. And very expensive. I'm surprised the family could afford it."

April drew a deep sigh and said nothing. She thought that Lois had been on scholarships, but she didn't say so. She didn't feel like talking about it. She didn't feel like eating, either. Gabriela had fixed one of her specialties, a seafood soup called *tapado* that April normally loved. But so far she hadn't taken a spoonful of it.

Everybody was quiet for a few moments.

Then Jilly said, "She didn't kill herself."

Startled, April stared across at Jilly. Everybody else was looking at Jilly, too. The younger teen had crossed her arms and was looking very serious.

"What?" April asked.

"Lois didn't kill herself," Jilly said.

"How do you know?" April asked.

"I met her, remember? I could tell. She wasn't the kind of girl who would ever want to do that. She didn't want to die."

Jilly paused for a moment.

Then she said, "I know how it feels to want to die. She didn't. I could tell."

April's heart jumped up into her throat.

She knew that Jilly had been through her own share of hell. Jilly had told her about how her abusive father had locked her out of the house one cold night. Jilly had slept in a drainpipe, and then she had gone to a truck stop where she tried to become a prostitute. That was when Mom had found her.

If anybody knew what it felt like to want to die, Jilly sure did.

April felt a flood of grief and horror ready to erupt inside her. Was Jilly wrong? Had Lois felt that miserable?

"Excuse me," she said. "I don't think I can eat now."

April got up from the table and rushed upstairs to her bedroom. She shut the door, threw herself down on her bed, and sobbed.

She didn't know how much time passed. But after a while, she heard a knock at the door.

"April, can I come in?" her mother asked.

"Yes," April said in a choked voice.

April sat up, and Mom walked into the room carrying a grilled cheese sandwich on a plate. Mom smiled sympathetically.

"Gabriela thought this might be easier on your stomach than

tapado," Mom said. "She's worried that you'll make yourself sick if you don't eat. I'm worried too."

April smiled through her tears. This was very sweet of both Gabriela and Mom.

"Thanks," she said.

She wiped her eyes and took a bite of the sandwich. Mom sat down on the bed beside her and took her hand.

"Do you want to talk about it?" Mom asked.

April gulped down a sob. For some reason, she found herself remembering how her best friend, Crystal, had moved away recently. Her father, Blaine, had been badly beaten right here in this house. Even though he and Mom had been interested in each other, he'd been so shaken that he'd decided to move.

"I've got the weirdest feeling," April said. "Like this was my fault somehow. Terrible things keep happening to us, and it's almost like it's contagious or something. I know it doesn't make sense but …"

"I understand how you feel," Mom said.

April was surprised. "You do?"

Mom's expression saddened.

"I feel like that a lot myself," she said. "My work is dangerous. And it puts everybody I love in danger. It makes me feel guilty. A lot."

"But it's not your fault," April said.

"So how come you think it's *your* fault?"

April didn't know what to say.

"What else is bothering you?" Mom asked.

April thought for a moment.

"Mom, Jilly's right. I don't think Lois killed herself. And Tiffany doesn't think so either. I knew Lois. She was happy, one of the most together people I've ever known. And Tiffany looked up to her. She was like Tiffany's hero. It just doesn't make sense."

April could tell by her mother's expression that she didn't believe her.

She just thinks I'm being hysterical, April thought.

"April, the police must think that it was suicide, and her mother and father—"

"Well, they're wrong," April said, surprised by the sharpness in her own voice. "Mom, you've got to check it out. You know more about this kind of thing than any of them do. More even than the police."

Mom shook her head sadly.

"April, I can't do that. I can't just go in and start investigating something that's already been settled. Think how the family would feel about that."

It was all April could do to keep from crying again.

"Mom, I'm begging you. If Tiffany never finds out the truth, it will ruin her life. She'll never get over it. Please, please do something."

It was a huge favor to ask, and April knew it. Mom didn't reply for a moment. She got up and walked over to the bedroom window and looked outside. She seemed to be deep in thought.

Still looking outside, Mom finally said, "I'll go talk to Tiffany's parents tomorrow. That is, if they want to talk to me. That's all I can do."

"Can I come with you?" April asked.

"You've got school tomorrow," Mom said.

"Let's do it after school then."

Mom fell quiet again, then said, "OK."

April got up from the bed and hugged her mother tightly. She wanted to say thank you, but she felt too overwhelmed with gratitude to get the words out.

If anyone can find out what's wrong, Mom can, April thought.

CHAPTER THREE

The next afternoon, Riley drove April to the Penningtons' house. Despite her doubts that Lois Pennington had been murdered, Riley felt sure that this was the best thing to do.

I owe it to April, she thought as she drove.

After all, she knew what it felt like to be positive about something and not have anyone believe her.

And April certainly did seem positive that something was very wrong.

As for Riley, her instincts hadn't kicked in one way or the other. But as they drove into a higher-class section of Fredericksburg, she reminded herself that monsters often lurked behind the most peaceful of facades. Many of the charming homes they passed on the way surely held dark secrets. She'd seen too much evil in her life not to know that all too well.

And whether Lois's death had been suicide or murder, there could be no doubt that a monster had invaded the Penningtons' seemingly happy home.

Riley parked on the street in front of the house. It was a large home, three stories tall and filling a fairly wide lot. Riley remembered what Ryan had said about the Penningtons.

"Not exactly wealthy, but comfortably well off."

The house confirmed what he'd said. It was an attractive upscale home in a nice neighborhood. The only thing that seemed unusual about it was the police tape across the doors of the detached garage where the family had found their daughter hanging.

The cold air bit sharply as Riley and April got out of the car and walked toward the house. Several cars were parked tightly in the driveway.

They rang the front doorbell, and Tiffany greeted them. April threw herself into Tiffany's arms, and both girls started sobbing.

"Oh, Tiffany, I'm so sorry," April said.

"Thank you, thank you for coming," Tiffany said.

Their shared emotion brought a lump into Riley's throat. The two girls seemed so young right now, barely more than children. It seemed horribly unfair that they should have to undergo such a terrible ordeal. Even so, she felt an odd hint of pride in April's heartfelt kindness. April was growing up to be caring and compassionate.

I must be doing something right as a parent, Riley thought.

Tiffany was a little shorter than April, with a bit more teenaged awkwardness about her. Her hair was strawberry blond, and her skin was pale and freckled, which made the redness around her eyes from crying look more pronounced.

Tiffany led Riley and April into the living room. Tiffany's parents were sitting on a couch, separated from each other slightly. Did their body language reveal anything? Riley wasn't sure. She knew that couples dealt with grief in many different ways.

Several other people were hovering around, speaking to each other in hushed whispers. Riley guessed that they were friends and family who had come to help out however they could.

She heard low voices and the rattling of utensils in the kitchen, where people seemed to be preparing food. Through an arch that led into the dining room, she saw two couples arranging pictures and memorabilia on the table. There were also pictures of Lois and her family at various ages set up in the living room.

Riley shuddered at the thought that the girl in the pictures had been alive just two days ago. How would she feel if she had lost April so suddenly? It was a chilling possibility, and there had already been too many close calls.

Who would come to her house to offer help and comfort?

Would she even *want* anybody's help and comfort?

She shook off such thoughts as Tiffany introduced her to her parents, Lester and Eunice.

"Please, don't get up," Riley said as the couple started to rise to greet her.

Riley and April sat down near the couple. Eunice had her daughter's freckled complexion and brightly colored hair. Lester's complexion was darker, and his face was long and thin.

"I'm very sorry for your loss," Riley said.

The couple thanked her. Lester managed to force a small smile.

"We've never met, but I know Ryan slightly," he said. "How's he doing these days?"

Tiffany reached from her own chair to tap her father on the arm. She silently mouthed, "They're divorced, Dad."

Lester's face reddened a little.

"Oh, I'm very sorry," he said.

Riley felt herself blush.

"Please don't be," she said. "Like people say these days—'it's complicated.'"

Lester nodded, still smiling weakly.

They all said nothing for a few moments as a low buzz of activity continued around them.

Then Tiffany said, "Mom, Dad—April's mother is an FBI agent."

Lester and Eunice gaped, not knowing what to say. Embarrassed again, Riley didn't know what to say either. She knew that April had called Tiffany yesterday to say that they were coming over. Apparently, Tiffany hadn't told her parents what Riley did for a living until just now.

Tiffany looked back and forth at her parents, then said, "I thought maybe she could help us find out … what really happened."

Lester gasped, and Eunice sighed bitterly.

"Tiffany, we've talked about this," Eunice said. "We know what happened. The police are sure. We've got no reason to think otherwise."

Lester stood unsteadily.

"I can't deal with this," he said. "I just … can't."

He turned and wandered into the dining room. Riley could see that the two couples there hurried to comfort him.

"Tiffany, you should be ashamed of yourself," Eunice said.

The girl's eyes were brimming with tears.

"But I just want to know the truth, Mom. Lois didn't kill herself. She couldn't have done that. I know it."

Eunice looked at Riley.

"I'm sorry you got caught in the middle of this," she said. "Tiffany's having trouble accepting the truth."

"It's you and Dad who can't deal with the truth," Tiffany said.

"Hush," her mother said.

Eunice handed her daughter a handkerchief.

"Tiffany, there were things you didn't know about Lois," she said slowly and cautiously. "She was more unhappy than she probably told you. She loved college, but it wasn't easy for her. Keeping her grades up for her scholarships was a lot of pressure, and it was also hard for her to be away from home. She was starting to take antidepressants and was getting counseling at Byars. Your father and I thought she was getting along better, but we were wrong."

Tiffany was trying to bring her sobs under control, but she still seemed very angry.

"That school is an awful place," she said. "I'd never go there."

"It's not awful," Eunice said. "It's a very good school. It's demanding, that's all."

"I'll bet those other girls didn't think it was such a good school," Tiffany said.

April had been listening to her friend with great concern.

"What other girls?" she asked.

"Deanna and Cory," Tiffany said. "They died too."

Eunice shook her head sadly and said to Riley, "Two other girls committed suicide at Byars last semester. It's been a terrible year there."

Tiffany stared at her mother.

"They weren't suicides," she said. "Lois didn't think so. She thought something was wrong at that place. She didn't know what it was, but she told me it was something really bad."

"Tiffany, they *were* suicides," Eunice said wearily. "Everybody says so. Things like this happen."

Tiffany stood up, shaking with rage and frustration.

"Lois's death didn't 'just happen,'" she said.

Eunice said, "When you get older, you'll understand that life can be harder than you realize. Now sit back down, please."

Tiffany sat down in sullen silence. Eunice gazed off into space. Riley felt terribly uncomfortable.

"We really didn't come here to disturb you in any way," Riley told Eunice. "I apologize for the intrusion. Maybe it's best if we leave."

Eunice silently nodded. Riley and April showed themselves out.

"We should have stayed," April said sullenly as soon as they were outside. "We should have asked more questions."

"No, we were just upsetting them," Riley said. "It was a terrible mistake."

Suddenly, April trotted away from her.

"Where are you going?" Riley asked with alarm.

April headed straight for the side door to the garage. There was a strip of police tape across the doorframe.

"April, stay away from there!" Riley said.

April ignored both the tape and her mother and turned the doorknob. The door was unlocked and swung open. April ducked under the tape and into the garage. Riley hurried in after her, intending to scold her. Instead, her own curiosity got the best of her, and she peered around the garage.

There weren't any cars inside, which made the three-car space look eerily cavernous. Dim light shone in through several windows.

April pointed toward a corner.

"Tiffany told me that Lois was found over there," April said.

Sure enough, the spot was marked by strips of masking tape on the floor.

There were broad roof beams under the roof, and a stepladder leaning against the wall.

"Come on," Riley said. "We shouldn't be in here."

She led her daughter out and pulled the door shut. As she and April walked toward the car, Riley visualized the scene. It was easy to imagine how the girl could have climbed up on that ladder and hanged herself.

Or was that really what happened? she wondered.

She had no reason to think otherwise.

Even so, she was beginning to feel a faint tingle of doubt.

*

A short while later at home, Riley called the district medical examiner, Danica Selves. She had been friends with Danica for years. When Riley asked her about the case of Lois Pennington's death, Danica sounded surprised.

"Why are you so curious?" Danica asked. "Is the FBI taking an interest in this?"

"No, it's just something personal."

"Personal?"

Riley hesitated, then said, "My daughter is good friends with Lois's sister, and she also knew Lois a little. Both she and Lois's sister are having trouble believing that she committed suicide."

"I see," Danica said. "Well, the police found no signs of a struggle. And I conducted the tests and the autopsy myself. According to blood results, she'd taken a heavy dose of alprazolam some time before she died. My guess is she just wanted to be as out of it as she possibly could. By the time she hanged herself, she probably just didn't care about what she was doing. It would have been a lot easier to do that way."

"So it's really an open-and-shut case," Riley said.

"It sure looks that way to me," Danica said.

Riley thanked her and ended the call. At that moment, April came downstairs with a calculator and a piece of paper.

"Mom, I think I've proved it!" she said excitedly. "It couldn't have been anything but murder!"

April sat down beside Riley and showed her some numbers that she'd written down.

"I did a little research online," she said. "I found out that about seven point five college students commit suicide out of one hundred thousand. That's point zero zero seven five percent. But there are only about seven hundred students at Byars, and three of them are supposed to have killed themselves in the last few months. That's about point four three percent—which is fifty-seven times the average! It's just impossible!"

Riley's heart sank. She appreciated that April was putting so much thought into this. It seemed very mature of her.

"April, I'm sure your math is just fine, but …"

"But what?"

Riley shook her head. "It doesn't prove anything at all."

April's eyes widened with disbelief.

"What do you mean, it doesn't prove anything?"

"In statistics, there are things called *outliers.* They're exceptions to the rules, they go against the averages. It's like the last case I worked on—the poisoner, remember? Most serial killers are men, but that was a woman. And most killers like to watch their victims die, but she just didn't care. It's the same thing here. It's no surprise that there are some colleges where more students commit suicide than the average."

April stared at her and said nothing.

"April, I just talked to the medical examiner who did the autopsy. She's sure that Lois's death was a suicide. And she knows her job. She's an expert. We have to trust her judgment."

April's face was tight with anger.

"I don't see why you can't trust *my* judgment just this once."

Then she stormed away and went upstairs.

At least she's sure she knows what happened, she thought with a groan.

That was more than Riley could say for herself.

Her instincts still told her nothing at all.

CHAPTER FOUR

It was happening all over again.

The monster named Peterson held April captive somewhere just ahead.

Riley struggled and searched through the dark. Each step seemed slow and cumbersome, but she knew she had to hurry.

With her shotgun slung over her shoulder, Riley stumbled in the dark down a sharp, muddy slope toward a river. Suddenly she saw them. Peterson was standing ankle-deep in the water. Just a few feet from him, April was half submerged in the water, bound by her hands and feet.

Riley reached for her shotgun, but Peterson raised a pistol and pointed it directly at April.

"Don't even think about it," Peterson yelled. "One move and it's over."

Riley was seized with horror. If she even raised her shotgun, Peterson would kill April before she could fire.

She put the shotgun on the ground.

The terror on her daughter's face would haunt her forever ...

Riley stopped running and bent over, gasping.

It was early morning, and she had gone out for a run. But the horrible memory had stopped her dead in her tracks.

Would she ever forget that terrible moment?

Would she ever stop feeling guilty for putting April in deadly danger?

No, she thought. *And that's as it should be. I must never forget.*

She inhaled and exhaled the sharp, cold air until she felt steadier. Then she started walking along the familiar woodland trail. Pale early-morning daylight was filtering through the trees.

This city park trail was close to home and easy to get to. Riley often ran here in the mornings. The exertion was usually good for driving ghosts and demons of past cases from her mind. But today it was having the opposite effect.

All that had happened yesterday—the visit to the Penningtons', the peek into the garage, and April's anger at Riley—had brought back floods of ugly memories.

And all because of me, Riley thought, quickening her pace into a jog.

But then she remembered what had happened next in that river.

Peterson's gun jammed, and Riley shoved a knife between his ribs, only to stagger and fall into the cold water. Wounded, Peterson still managed to hold Riley under.

Then she saw April, wrists and feet still bound, raise the shotgun that Riley had dropped. She heard it crack against Peterson's head.

But the monster turned and charged April. He shoved her face down in the water.

Her daughter was going to drown.

Riley found a sharp rock.

She lunged at Peterson, smashing it into his head.

He fell, and she leaped on top of him.

She smashed the rock into Peterson's face over and over again.

The river darkened with blood.

Stirred by the memory, Riley ran faster.

She was proud of her daughter. April had shown courage and resourcefulness on that terrible day. She had been brave in other dangerous situations too.

But now April was angry with Riley.

And Riley couldn't help but wonder if it was with good reason.

*

Riley felt doubly out of place at Lois Pennington's church funeral service late that afternoon.

For one thing, she'd seldom gone to church over the years. Her father had been a hardened ex-Marine who never believed in anything or anyone but himself. She'd lived with an aunt and uncle during some of her childhood and teen years, and they'd tried to get her to go to church, but Riley had been too rebellious.

As far as funerals were concerned, Riley simply hated them. She'd seen too much of the brutal reality of death during her two decades in law enforcement, so as far as she was concerned, funerals were simply phony. They always made death seem so clean and peaceful.

The whole thing is misleading, she kept thinking. This girl had died violently, whether at her own hands or someone else's.

But April had insisted on coming, and Riley couldn't let her face this by herself. Which seemed ironic, because at the moment it was Riley who felt alone. She was sitting next to the aisle in the back row of the crowded sanctuary. April was up near the front, sitting in the row right behind the family, as close to Tiffany as she could get. But Riley was glad that April was near her friend, and she didn't mind sitting by herself.

Sunshine brightened the stained glass windows, and the casket at the front was layered with flowers and several large wreaths. The service was dignified and the choir sang well.

The preacher was droning on now about faith and salvation, assuring everybody that Lois was now in a better place. Riley wasn't paying attention to his words. She was looking around for telltale clues as to why Lois Pennington had died.

Yesterday she had noticed how Lois's parents sat slightly apart on their couch, not quite touching. She hadn't been sure how to read their body language. But now Lester Pennington's arm was around Eunice's shoulder in a warm gesture of comfort. The two of them seemed to be perfectly ordinary grieving parents.

If there was anything seriously amiss about the Penningtons as a family, Riley couldn't see it.

And oddly enough, that made Riley feel distinctly uneasy.

She considered herself a keen observer of human nature. If Lois had really committed suicide, her family life had most likely been troubled. But nothing appeared wrong with them—nothing other than normal grief.

The preacher managed to finish his sermon without once mentioning the supposed cause of Lois's death.

Then came a series of short, tearful testimonials by friends and relatives. They spoke of grief and happier times, sometimes relating humorous events that evoked sad chuckles from the congregation.

But nothing about suicide, Riley kept thinking.

Something seemed off to her.

Wouldn't somebody who had been close to Lois want to acknowledge something dark about her final days—a struggle against depression, a battle against inner demons, some unanswered cry for help? Wouldn't somebody suggest that her tragic death should be a lesson to others to get help and support instead of taking one's own life?

But no one said anything of the kind.

No one wanted to talk about it.

They seemed to be ashamed or baffled or both.

Perhaps they didn't even fully believe it.

The testimonials ended, and it came time for viewing the body. Riley stayed seated. She was sure that the mortician had done a skillful job. Whatever was left of poor Lois didn't look at all like she had looked when she was found hanging in that garage. Riley knew from hard experience what a strangled corpse looked like.

Finally the preacher offered a closing benediction and the casket was carried out. The family walked out together, and everybody else was free to go.

When Riley got outside, she saw Tiffany and April hugging each other tearfully. Then Tiffany saw Riley and hurried toward her.

"Isn't there anything you can do?" the girl asked in a choked voice.

Shaken, Riley managed to say, "No, I'm sorry."

Before Tiffany could plead further, her father called out her name. Tiffany's family was climbing into a black limousine. Tiffany joined them, and the vehicle drove away.

Riley turned back toward April, who refused to look at her.

"I'll take a bus home," April said.

April walked away, and Riley didn't try to stop her. Feeling terrible, she made her way to her car in the church parking lot.

*

Dinner that evening was hardly the cheerful occasion it had been just two days ago. April was still not speaking to Riley, and barely to anybody else. Her sadness was catching. Ryan and Gabriela were somber as well.

In the middle of the meal, Jilly spoke up.

"I made a friend at school today. Her name is Jane. She's adopted, like me."

April's expression brightened.

"Hey, that's great, Jilly," April said.

"Yeah. We've got a whole lot in common. A lot to talk about."

Riley's own spirits lifted slightly. It was good that Jilly was starting to make friends. And Riley knew that April had been worried about Jilly.

The two girls talked a little about Jane. Then everybody fell silent again, as somber as before.

Riley knew that Jilly wanted to break the dark mood, to cheer

April up. But the younger girl looked worried now. Riley guessed that she was alarmed by all this tension in her new family. Jilly was surely afraid she could lose what she had so recently found.

I hope she's not right, Riley thought.

After dinner, the girls went upstairs to their rooms and Gabriela cleaned up the kitchen. Ryan poured a glass of bourbon for Riley and another for himself, and they sat together in the living room.

Neither of them spoke for a little while.

"I'm going upstairs to talk to April," Ryan finally said.

"Why?" Riley asked.

"She's being rude. And she's being disrespectful to you. We shouldn't let her get away with it."

Riley sighed.

"She's not being rude," she said.

"Well, what would you call it?"

Riley thought for a moment.

"She just really *cares*," she said. "She's worried about her friend Tiffany, and she's feeling powerless. She's afraid that something terrible happened to Lois. We should be glad that she's thinking about others. It's a sign of growing up."

They both fell silent again.

"What do you think really happened?" Ryan finally asked. "Do you think Lois committed suicide, or was she murdered?"

Riley shook her head wearily.

"I wish I knew," she said. "I've learned to trust my gut, my instincts. But my instincts aren't kicking in at all. I just don't have any feeling about it one way or the other."

Ryan patted her hand.

"Whatever happened, it's not your responsibility," he said.

"You're right," Riley said.

Ryan yawned.

"I'm tired," he said. "I think I'm going to turn in early."

"I'll sit down here for a while," Riley said. "I'm not ready to sleep yet."

Ryan went upstairs, and Riley poured herself another large drink. The house was quiet, and Riley felt alone and strangely helpless—just as she was sure April was feeling. But after another drink, she started to relax and soon felt drowsy. She kicked off her shoes and stretched out on the couch.

A little while later she woke up to find that somebody had tucked blankets around her. Ryan must have come downstairs to check on her and make sure she was comfortable.

Riley smiled, feeling less alone now. Then she fell asleep again.

*

Riley felt a flash of déjà vu as April hurried toward the Penningtons' garage.

As she'd done yesterday, Riley called out.

"April, stay away from there!"

This time, April pulled the police tape loose before she opened the door.

Then April disappeared into the garage.

Riley ran after her and went inside.

The garage interior was much bigger and darker than it had been yesterday, like a huge abandoned warehouse.

Riley didn't see April anywhere.

"April, where are you?" she called out.

April's voice echoed in the air.

"I'm here, Mom."

Riley couldn't tell where the voice was coming from.

She turned slowly around, peering into the seemingly endless darkness.

Finally, an overhead light switched on.

Riley was stunned with horror.

Hanging from a beam was a girl just a couple of years older than April.

She was dead, but her eyes were open, and her gaze was locked on Riley.

And scattered all around the girl, on tables and on the floor, were hundreds of framed pictures showing the girl and her family at different times of her life.

"April!" Riley screamed.

No answer came.

Riley awakened and sat bolt upright on the couch, almost hyperventilating with terror at the nightmare.

It was all she could do to stop herself from yelling at the top of her lungs …

"April!"

But she knew that April was upstairs asleep.

The whole family was asleep—except for her.

Why did I have that dream? she wondered.

It took only a moment for her to know the answer.

She realized that her instincts had kicked in at long last.

She knew that April was right—something was very wrong with Lois's death.

And it was up to her to do something about it.

CHAPTER FIVE

Riley felt a distinct chill when she got out of her car at Byars College. It wasn't just from the weather, which was cold enough. The school had a weirdly unwelcoming vibe about it.

She shivered deeply as she looked around.

Students were wandering the campus, bundled tightly against the cold, hurrying to their destinations and barely speaking to one another. None of them looked happy to be here.

Small wonder this place makes students want to kill themselves, Riley thought.

For one thing, the place seemed to belong to a bygone age. Riley almost felt like she was stepping back in time. The old brick buildings had been kept in perfect condition. So had the white columns, relics of times when columns were required for this kind of setting.

The parklike campus was impressively large, given that it was planted right in the nation's capital. Of course, DC had grown up around it during the nearly two hundred years of its existence. The small, exclusive school had thrived, producing alumni who went on to success in the nation's most prestigious graduate schools, then into positions of power in business and politics. Students came to schools like this to make and maintain high-level connections that would last a lifetime.

Naturally, it was far too expensive for Riley's family—even, she felt sure, with the scholarship support they occasionally gave for excellent students from significant families. Not that she would ever want to send April here. Or Jilly, for that matter.

Riley went into the administration building and found the dean's office, where she was greeted by a stern-looking secretary.

Riley showed the woman her badge.

"I'm Special Agent Riley Paige with the FBI. I called earlier today."

The woman nodded.

"Dean Autrey is expecting you," she said.

The woman showed Riley into a large, gloomy office with heavy, dark wood paneling.

An elegant, somewhat elderly man stood up from his desk to greet her. He was tall, with silver hair, and he wore an expensive three-piece suit with a bow tie.

"Agent Paige, I presume," he said with a chilly smile. "I'm Dean Willis Autrey. Please have a seat."

Riley sat down in front of his desk. Autrey sat down and swiveled in his chair.

"I'm not sure I understand the nature of your visit," he said. "Something to do with the unfortunate passing of Lois Pennington, isn't it?"

"Her suicide, you mean," Riley said.

Autrey nodded and steepled his fingers.

"Hardly an FBI case, I would think," he said. "I called the girl's parents, gave them the school's heartfelt condolences. They were devastated, of course. The whole thing was so unfortunate. But they didn't seem to have any specific concerns."

Riley realized that she had to choose her words carefully. She wasn't here on an assigned case—in fact, her superiors at Quantico wouldn't approve of this visit at all. But maybe she could manage to keep Autrey from finding that out.

"Another family member has expressed misgivings," she said.

She figured there was no need to tell him she meant Lois's teenaged sister.

"How unfortunate," he said.

He seems to like using that word—unfortunate, Riley thought.

"What can you tell me about Lois Pennington?" Riley asked.

Autrey was starting to seem bored now, as if his mind were elsewhere.

"Well, nothing that her family hasn't told you, I'm sure," he said. "I didn't know her personally, but ..."

He turned toward his computer and typed.

"She seems to have been a perfectly ordinary first-year student," he said, looking at the screen. "Reasonably good grades. No reports of anything untoward. Although I see that she did get some counseling for depression."

"But she's not the only suicide at your school this year," Riley said.

Autrey's expression darkened a little. He said nothing.

Before leaving home, Riley had done a little research into the two suicides that Tiffany had mentioned.

"Deanna Webber and Cory Linz both allegedly killed themselves last semester," Riley said. "Cory's death was right here on campus."

"'Allegedly'?" Autrey asked. "A rather unfortunate word, I

think. I've not heard anything to the contrary."

He turned his face slightly away from Riley, as if to pretend she wasn't even there.

"Ms. Paige—" he began.

"*Agent* Paige," Riley corrected.

"Agent Paige—I'm sure that a professional such as yourself is aware that the suicide rate among college students has increased over recent decades. It's the third leading cause of death among people in the undergraduate age group. There are more than a thousand suicides on college campuses each year."

He paused, as if to let those facts sink in.

"And of course," he said, "some schools experience clusters in a given year. Byars is a demanding school. It's unfortunate but rather inevitable that we should get somewhat more than our share of suicides."

Riley suppressed a smile.

The figures April had researched a couple of days ago were about to come in handy.

April would be pleased, she thought.

She said, "The national average of college suicides is about seven point five out of one hundred thousand. But just this year, three of your students out of seven hundred have killed themselves. That's fifty-seven times the national average."

Autrey raised his eyebrows.

"Well, as I'm sure you know, there are always—"

"Outliers," Riley said, managing again not to smile. "Yes, I know all about outliers. Even so, the suicide rate at your school strikes me as exceptionally—unfortunate."

Autrey sat looking away in silence.

"Dean Autrey, I'm under the impression you're not happy to have an FBI agent poking around here," she said.

"As a matter of fact, I'm not," he said. "Should I feel otherwise? This is a waste of your time and mine, and of taxpayers' money as well. And your presence here might give the impression that something is amiss. There's nothing amiss here at Byars College, I assure you."

He leaned across his desk toward Riley.

"Agent Paige, what branch of the FBI are you with exactly?"

"The Behavioral Analysis Unit."

"Ah. Right nearby in Quantico. Well, you might want to keep in mind that many of our students come from political families.

Some of their parents have considerable influence over the government—the FBI included, I imagine. I'm sure we don't want this sort of thing getting back to them."

"This sort of thing?" Riley asked.

Autrey swiveled back and forth in his chair.

"Such people might be prone to register complaints with your superiors," he said with a significant look.

Riley felt a tingle of unease.

She sensed that he'd guessed she wasn't here in an official capacity.

"It's really best not to stir up trouble where no problem exists," Autrey continued. "I'm only making this observation for your benefit. I'd hate for you to run afoul of your superiors."

Riley almost laughed aloud.

Running "afoul" of her superiors was practically routine for her.

So was getting suspended or fired and then getting reinstated again.

It didn't scare Riley in the least.

"I see," she said. "Anything not to taint your school's reputation."

"I'm glad we see eye to eye," Autrey said.

He rose to his feet, obviously expecting Riley to leave.

But Riley wasn't ready to leave—not yet.

"Thank you for your time," she said. "I'll be on my way as soon as you give me the contact information for the families of the previous suicides."

Autrey stood glaring at her. Riley glared back without moving from her chair.

Autrey glanced at his watch. "I have another appointment. I must go now."

Riley smiled.

"I'm in a bit of a hurry too," she said, looking at her own watch. "So the sooner you give me that information, the sooner we both can get on with things. I'll wait."

Autrey frowned, then sat down at his computer again. He typed a little, and then his printer rumbled. He handed the sheet with the information to Riley.

"I'm afraid that I'll have to register a complaint with your superiors," he said.

Riley still didn't move. Her curiosity was mounting.

"Dean Autrey, you just mentioned that Byars gets 'somewhat more than its share' of suicides. Just how many suicides are we talking about?"

Autrey didn't reply. His face reddened with anger, but he kept his voice quiet and controlled.

"Your superior at BAU will be hearing from me," he said.

"Of course," Riley said with measured politeness. "Thank you for your time."

Riley left the office and the administration building. This time the cold air felt bracing and invigorating.

Autrey's evasiveness convinced Riley that she'd come upon a nest of trouble.

And Riley thrived on trouble.

CHAPTER SIX

As soon as Riley got into her car, she went over the information Dean Autrey had given her. Details about Deanna Webber's death began to come back to her.

Of course, she remembered, bringing up old news stories on her cell phone. *The congresswoman's daughter.*

Representative Hazel Webber was a rising politician, married to a prominent Maryland lawyer. Their daughter's death had been in the headlines last fall. Riley hadn't paid much attention to the story at the time. It seemed more like salacious gossip than real news— the sort of thing Riley thought was nobody's business but the family's.

Now she thought differently.

She found the phone number for Congresswoman Hazel Webber's office in Washington. When she dialed the number, an efficient-sounding receptionist answered.

"This is Special Agent Riley Paige, with the FBI's Behavioral Analysis Unit," Riley said. "I'd like to arrange a meeting with Representative Webber."

"May I ask what this is about?"

"I need to talk with her about her daughter's death last fall."

A silence fell.

Riley said, "I'm sorry to disturb the congresswoman and her family about this terrible tragedy. But we just need to tie up a few loose ends."

More silence.

"I'm sorry," the receptionist said slowly. "But Representative Webber isn't in Washington right now. You'll need to wait until she gets back from Maryland."

"And when might that be?" Riley asked.

"I couldn't say. You'll just have to call back."

The receptionist ended the call without another word.

She's in Maryland, Riley thought.

She ran a quick search and found that Hazel Webber lived in Maryland horse country. It didn't look as though the place would be hard to find.

But before Riley could start her car, her cell phone buzzed.

"This is Hazel Webber," the caller said.

Riley was startled. The receptionist must have contacted the congresswoman immediately after hanging up on Riley. She certainly hadn't expected to hear back from Webber herself, much less so quickly.

"How can I help you?" Webber said.

Riley explained again that she wanted to talk about some "loose ends" regarding her daughter's death.

"Could you be a bit more specific?" Webber asked.

"I'd rather do that in person," Riley said.

Webber was quiet for a moment.

"I'm afraid that's impossible," Webber said. "And I'll thank you and your superiors not to trouble me and my family any further. We're just now beginning to heal. I'm sure you understand."

Riley was struck by the woman's icy tone. She didn't detect the slightest trace of grief.

"Representative Webber, if you can give me just a little bit of your time—"

"I said no."

Webber ended the call.

Riley was dumbstruck. She had no idea what to make of the terse, awkward exchange.

All she knew for sure was that she'd touched a nerve with the congresswoman.

And she needed to go to Maryland right away.

*

It was a pleasant two-hour drive. Since the weather was good, Riley took a route that included the Chesapeake Bay Bridge, paying the toll in order to enjoy the drive across the water.

She soon found herself in Maryland horse country, where handsome wooden fences enclosed pastures, and tree-lined lanes led to elegant homes and barns set far back from the road.

She pulled up to the gate outside the Webbers' estate. A heavyset uniformed guard stepped out of his shack and approached her.

Riley showed the guard her badge and introduced herself.

"I'm here to see Representative Webber," she said.

The guard stepped away and spoke into his microphone. Then he stepped toward Riley again.

"The congresswoman says there's been some sort of mistake," he said. "She isn't expecting you."

Riley smiled as broadly as she could.

"Oh, is she too busy at the moment? That's okay, my schedule's not tight. I'll wait right here until she has time."

The guard scowled, trying to look intimidating.

"I'm afraid you'll have to leave, ma'am," he said.

Riley shrugged and acted as if she didn't take his meaning.

"Oh, really, it's all right. No trouble at all. I can wait right here."

The guard stepped away and spoke into his microphone again. After glaring at Riley silently for a moment, he went into his shack and opened the gate. Riley drove on through.

She drove through a broad, snow-patched pasture, where a couple of horses trotted freely about. It was a peaceful scene.

When she reached the house, it was even larger than she had expected—a contemporary mansion. She glimpsed other well-kept buildings just beyond a slight rise in the rolling landscape.

An Asian man wordlessly met her at the door. He was about as large as a sumo wrestler, which made his formal, butler-like suit seem grotesquely inappropriate. He led Riley through a vaulted corridor with a floor of expensive-looking reddish-brown wood.

Finally she was greeted by a small, grim-looking woman who wordlessly led her into an almost eerily neat office.

"Wait here," the woman said.

She left, shutting the door behind her.

Riley sat in a chair near the desk. Minutes passed. She felt tempted to take a look at materials on the desk or even on the computer. But she knew that her every move was surely being recorded by security cameras.

Finally, Representative Hazel Webber swept into the room.

She was a tall woman—thin but imposing. She didn't look old enough to have been in Congress for as long as Riley supposed—nor did she look old enough to have a college-aged daughter. A certain stiffness around her eyes might be habitual or Botox-induced or both.

Riley remembered seeing her on television. Normally when she met someone she'd seen on TV, she was struck by how different they looked in real life. Weirdly, Hazel Webber looked exactly the same. It was as if she were truly two-dimensional—an almost unnaturally shallow human being in every possible way.

Her outfit also puzzled Riley. Why was she wearing a jacket over her lightweight sweater? The house was certainly warm enough.

Part of her style, I guess, Riley figured.

The jacket gave her a more formal, businesslike look than just slacks and a sweater. Perhaps it also represented a kind of armor, a protection against any genuine human contact.

Riley stood up to introduce herself, but Webber spoke first.

"Agent Riley Paige, BAU," she said. "I know."

Without another word, she sat down at her desk.

"What are you here to tell me?" Webber said.

Riley felt a jolt of alarm. Of course, she had nothing to tell her. Her whole visit was a bluff, and Webber suddenly struck her as the kind of woman who wasn't easily bluffed. Riley was in over her head and had to tread water as hard as she could.

"I'm actually here to ask *you* for information," Riley said. "Is your husband at home?"

"Yes," the woman said.

"Would it be possible for me to talk with both of you?"

"He knows that you're here."

Her non-answer disarmed Riley, but she took care not to show it. The woman fastened her cold, blue eyes on Riley's. Riley didn't flinch. She just returned her stare, bracing herself for a subtle battle of wills.

Riley said, "The Behavioral Analysis Unit is investigating an unusual number of apparent suicides at Byars College."

"*Apparent* suicides?" Webber said, arching a single eyebrow. "I'd hardly describe Deanna's suicide as 'apparent.' It seemed plenty real to my husband and me."

Riley could swear that the temperature in the room had dropped a few degrees. Webber betrayed not the slightest hint of emotion at her mention of her own daughter's suicide.

She's got ice water in her veins, Riley thought.

"I'd like you to tell me what happened," Riley said.

"Why? I'm sure you've read the report."

Of course, Riley had done nothing of the kind. But she had to keep bluffing her way along.

"It would help if I could hear it in your own words," she said.

Webber was silent for a moment. Her stare was unwavering. But so was Riley's.

"Deanna was injured in a riding accident last summer," Webber said. "Her hip was badly fractured. It seemed likely that it would have to be replaced altogether. Her days of riding in competitions

36

were over. She was heartbroken."

Webber paused for a moment.

"She was taking oxycodone for the pain. She overdosed—deliberately. It was intentional, and that's all there is to it."

Riley sensed that she was leaving something unsaid.

"Where did it happen?" she asked.

"In her bedroom," Webber said. "She was snug in her bed. The medical examiner said she died of respiratory arrest. She looked like she was asleep when the maid found her."

And then—Webber blinked.

She literally blinked.

She had faltered in their battle of wills.

She's lying! Riley realized.

Riley's pulse quickened.

Now she had to really apply the pressure, probe with exactly the right questions.

But before Riley could even think of what to ask, the office door opened. The woman who had brought Riley here came in.

"Congresswoman, I need a word with you, please," she said.

Webber looked relieved as she got up from her desk and followed her assistant out the door.

Riley took some long, slow breaths.

She wished she hadn't been interrupted.

She was sure she'd been about to crack through Hazel Webber's deceptive facade.

But her opportunity wasn't gone.

When Webber came back, Riley would start in on her again.

After less than a minute, Webber returned. She seemed to have recovered her self-assurance.

She stood by the open door and said, "Agent Paige—if you really *are* Agent Paige—I'm afraid I must ask you to leave."

Riley gulped hard.

"I don't understand."

"My assistant just called the BAU. They have absolutely no investigation underway concerning suicides at Byars College. Now whoever you are—"

Riley pulled out her badge.

"I *am* Special Agent Riley Paige," she said with determination. "And I'm going to do everything I can to make sure that such an investigation gets underway as soon as possible."

She walked past Hazel Webber out of the office.

On her way out of the house, she knew that she had made an enemy—and a dangerous one at that.

It was a different sort of danger from what she usually faced.

Hazel Webber wasn't a psychopath whose weapons of choice were chains, knives, guns, or blowtorches.

She was a woman without a conscience, and her weapons were money and power.

Riley preferred the kind of adversary she could punch out or shoot. Even so, she was ready and willing to deal with Webber and whatever threats she could muster.

She lied to me about her daughter, Riley kept thinking.

And now Riley was determined to find out the truth.

The house seemed empty now. Riley was surprised to leave without encountering a single soul. She felt as if she could rob the place and not get caught.

She went outside and got into her car and drove away.

As she approached the manor gate, she saw that it was closed. Standing just inside were both the burly guard who had let her in and the enormous butler. Both had their arms crossed, and they were obviously waiting for her.

CHAPTER SEVEN

The two men definitely looked threatening. They also looked a little bit ridiculous—the smaller of the two wearing his guard uniform, his much more massive partner wearing his ultra-formal butler's outfit.

Like a pair of circus clowns, she thought.

But she knew they weren't trying to be funny.

Riley pulled her car to a stop right in front of them. She rolled down her window, looked out, and called to them.

"Is there some sort of problem, gentlemen?"

The guard came closer, directly in front of her car.

The colossal butler lumbered toward her passenger window.

He spoke in a rumbling bass voice.

"Representative Webber would like to clear up a misunderstanding."

"And that would be?"

"She wants you to understand that snoops aren't welcome here."

Now Riley got the picture.

Webber and her assistant had come to the conclusion that Riley was an imposter, not an FBI agent at all. They probably suspected that she was a reporter getting ready to write some sort of exposé about the congresswoman.

No doubt these two guys were used to dealing with nosy reporters.

Riley pulled out her badge again.

"I think there *has* been a misunderstanding," she said. "I really am a special agent with the FBI."

The big man smirked. He obviously believed the badge was a fake.

"Step out of the car, please," he said.

"I'd rather not, thank you," Riley said. "I'd really appreciate if you'd open the gate."

Riley had left her door unlocked. The big man opened it.

"Step out of the car, please," he repeated.

Riley groaned under her breath.

This isn't going to end well, she thought.

Riley stepped out of the car and shut the door. The two men moved to stand side by side a short distance from her.

Riley wondered which of them was going to make the first move.

Then the huge man cracked his knuckles and strode toward her.

Riley took a couple of steps toward him.

As he reached out for her, she grabbed him by his lapel and the sleeve of his left arm and tugged him off balance. Then she pivoted all the way around on her left foot and ducked down. She barely felt the man's massive weight as his whole body flew over her back. He slammed loudly and upside-down against the car door and then landed head first on the ground.

The car got the worst of it, she thought with fleeting dismay.

The other man was already moving toward her, and she whirled to face him.

She landed a kick to his groin. He bent over with a huge groan, and Riley could see that the altercation was over.

She snatched the man's pistol from his hip holster.

Then she surveyed her handiwork.

The larger man still lay in a crumpled heap beside the car, staring at her with a terrified expression. The car door was dented, but not as badly as Riley had feared. The uniformed guard was on his hands and knees gasping for breath.

She held the pistol, handle first, toward the guard.

"You seem to have misplaced this," she said in a pleasant voice.

His hands trembling, he reached for the gun.

Riley pulled it away from him.

"Huh-uh," she said. "Not until you open the gate."

She took the man by the hand and helped him to his feet. He staggered to the shack and threw the switch that opened the iron gate. Riley walked toward the car.

"Excuse me," she told the enormous man.

Still looking quite terrified, the man scrambled sideways like a giant crab, getting out of Riley's way. She got into the car and drove through the gate. She tossed the pistol on the ground as she drove away.

They don't think I'm a reporter anymore, she thought.

She was also sure that they would let the congresswoman know that pretty quickly.

*

A couple of hours later, Riley pulled her car into the parking lot at the BAU building. She sat there for a few moments. She hadn't been here once during her month on leave. She hadn't expected to be back so soon. It felt really strange.

She turned off the engine, removed the keys, got out of the car, and went into the building. As she made her way toward her office, friends and colleagues spoke to her with varying degrees of welcome, surprise, or restraint.

She stopped at the office of her usual partner, Bill Jeffreys, but he wasn't there. He was probably out on an assignment, working with someone else.

She felt a slight pang of sadness—even jealousy.

In many ways, Bill was her best friend in the world.

Still, she figured maybe this was just as well. Bill didn't know that she and Ryan were together again, and he wouldn't approve. He had held her hand too many times during her painful breakup and divorce. He'd find it hard to believe that Ryan was a changed man.

When she opened the door to her own office, she had to double check to make sure she was in the right place. It all looked far too neat and well organized. Had they given her office to another agent? Had someone else been working here?

Riley opened a drawer and found familiar files, though now in better order.

Who would have straightened everything up for her?

Certainly not Bill. He would have known better.

Lucy Vargas, maybe, she thought.

Lucy was a young agent that both she and Bill had worked with and liked. If Lucy was the culprit behind all this neatness, at least she'd done it in a spirit of helpfulness.

Riley sat at her desk for a few minutes.

Images and memories came to her—the girl's coffin, her devastated parents, and Riley's terrible dream of the hanged girl surrounded by mementos. She also remembered how Dean Autrey had evaded her questions, and how Hazel Webber had outright lied.

She reminded herself of what she'd said to Hazel Webber. She'd promised to get an official investigation underway. And it was time to make good on that promise.

She picked up her office phone and buzzed her boss, Brent Meredith.

When the team chief picked up, she said, "Sir, this is Riley

Paige. I wonder if I could—"

She was about to ask for a few minutes of his time when his voice thundered.

"Agent Paige, get in my office right now."

Riley shuddered.

Meredith was plenty mad at her about something.

CHAPTER EIGHT

When Riley hurried into Brent Meredith's office, she found him standing by his desk waiting for her.

"Close the door," he said. "Sit down."

Riley did as she was told.

Still standing, Meredith didn't speak for a few moments. He just glared at Riley. He was a big man—broad-built with black, angular features. And he was intimidating even when he was in the best of moods.

He wasn't in a good mood right now.

"Is there something you'd like to tell me, Agent Paige?" he asked.

Riley gulped. She guessed that some of her activities that day had already gotten back to him.

"Perhaps you'd better start first, sir," she said meekly.

He moved closer to her.

"I've just gotten two complaints from on high about you," he said.

Riley's heart sank. By "on high," she knew who Meredith meant. The complaints had come from Special Agent in Charge Carl Walder himself—a contemptible little man who had already suspended Riley more than once for insubordination.

Meredith growled, "Walder tells me he got a call from the dean of a small college."

"Yes, Byars College. But if you'll give me a moment to explain—"

Meredith interrupted her again.

"The dean said you walked into his office and made some preposterous allegations."

"That's not exactly what happened, sir," Riley pleaded.

But Meredith steamrolled right along.

"Walder also got a call from Representative Hazel Webber. She said that you made your way into her home and harassed her. You even lied to her about some nonexistent case. And then you assaulted two members of her staff. You threatened them at gunpoint."

Riley bristled at the accusation.

"That's *really* not what happened, sir."

"Then what did happen?"

"It was the guard's own gun," she blurted.

As soon as the words were out of her mouth, Riley realized ...

That didn't come out right at all.

"I was trying to give it back!" she said.

But she instantly knew ...

That didn't help.

A long silence fell.

Meredith drew a deep breath. Finally, he said, "You'd better have a good explanation for your actions, Agent Paige."

Riley took a deep breath.

"Sir, there have been three suspicious deaths at Byars College, just during this school year. They were allegedly suicides. I don't believe that's what they were."

"This is the first I've heard of it," Meredith said.

"I understand, sir. And I came here just to tell you about it."

Meredith stood, waiting for further explanation.

"A friend of my daughter's had a sister at Byars College—Lois Pennington, a freshman. Her family found her hanging in the garage last Sunday. Her sister doesn't believe it was suicide. I interviewed her parents, and—"

Meredith yelled loud enough to be heard out in the hallway.

"You *interviewed* her *parents*?"

"Yes, sir," Riley said quietly.

Meredith took a moment to try to bring his temper under control.

"Need I tell you that this is not a BAU case?"

"No, sir," Riley said.

"In fact, as far as I know, this is not a case at all."

Riley didn't know what to say next.

"So what did her parents tell you?" Meredith asked. "Did *they* think it was suicide?"

"Yes," Riley said in a hushed voice.

Now Meredith didn't seem to know what to say. He shook his head with dismay.

"Sir, I know how this sounds," Riley said. "But the dean at Byars was hiding something. And Hazel Webber lied to me about her own daughter's death."

"How do you know?"

"I just know!"

Riley looked at Meredith imploringly.

"Sir, after all these years, surely you know that my instincts are

44

good. When I feel something in my gut, I'm almost always right. You've got to trust me. There's something wrong with these girls' deaths."

"Riley, you know that's not the way things work."

Riley was startled. Meredith seldom called her by her first name—only when he was genuinely concerned about her. She knew that he valued, liked, and respected her, and she felt the same about him.

He leaned against his desk and shrugged unhappily.

"Maybe you're right, and maybe you're wrong," he said with a sigh. "Either way, I can't make this a BAU case just because of your gut feelings. There'd have to be a whole lot more to it."

Meredith now gazed at her with a worried expression.

"Agent Paige, you've been through a lot lately. You've been on some dangerous cases, and your partner almost got poisoned to death on the last one. And you've got a new family member to take care of, and …"

"And what?" Riley asked.

Meredith paused, then said, "I put you on leave a month ago. You seemed to think it was a good idea. The last time we talked, you even asked me for more time away. I think that's best. Take all the time you need. You need more rest."

Riley felt discouraged and defeated. But she knew there was no point in arguing. The truth was, Meredith was right. There was no way he could take on this case on the basis of what she'd told him. Especially not with a bureaucratic creep like Walder breathing down his neck.

"I'm sorry, sir," she said. "I'll go home now."

She felt terribly alone as she left Meredith's office and headed out of the building. But she wasn't ready to put her suspicions aside. Her gut feeling was much too strong for that. She knew she had to do something.

First things first, she thought.

She had to get more information. She had to prove that something was wrong.

But how was she going to do that alone?

*

Riley got home about a half hour before dinner. She went into the kitchen and found Gabriela preparing another of her delicious

45

Guatemalan specialties, *gallo en perro,* a spicy stew.

"Are the girls home?" Riley asked.

"*Sí.* They are in April's room doing homework together."

Riley felt a bit relieved. At home at least, something seemed to be going right.

"How about Ryan?" Riley asked.

"He called. He will be late."

Riley felt a pang of unease. It reminded her of bad times with Ryan. But she told herself not to worry. Ryan's job was demanding, after all. And besides, Riley's own work kept her away from home much more than she would like.

She went upstairs and got on her computer. She ran a search on Deanna Webber's death, but didn't find anything she didn't know already. Then she looked for information on Cory Linz, the other girl who had died. Again, she found very little information.

She did a search for recent obituaries that mentioned Byars College, and soon came up with six. One of those had died in a hospital after a long battle with cancer. Of the others, she recognized the photos of three young people. They were Deanna Webber, Lois Pennington, and Cory Linz. But she didn't recognize the young man and the young woman in the other two obituaries. Their names were Kirk Farrell and Constance Yoh, both sophomores.

Of course, none of the obituaries stated that the deceased had committed suicide. Most of them were pretty vague about the actual cause of death.

Riley sat back in her chair and sighed.

She needed help. But who could she turn to? She still didn't have access to the techies at Quantico.

She shuddered at one possibility.

No, not Shane Hatcher, she thought.

The criminal genius who had escaped from Sing Sing had come to her aid on more than one case. Her failure—or was it her reluctance?—to recapture him had stirred considerable consternation among Riley's superiors at the BAU.

She knew perfectly well how to contact him.

In fact, she could do it right now, using her computer.

No, Riley thought with another shudder. *Absolutely not.*

But who else could she turn to?

Now she remembered something Hatcher had told her when she'd been in a similar situation.

"I think you know who to talk to at the FBI when you're persona non grata. It's somebody else who doesn't give a damn about the rules."

Riley felt a tingle of excitement.

She knew exactly whose help she needed.

CHAPTER NINE

Riley picked up her phone and dialed.

The answering voice said, "Roff here."

The socially inept computer geek was a technical analyst in the Seattle FBI field office. Van Roff had helped with her last case and, like other professional geeks she'd known, he positively relished any opportunity to bend or even break the rules.

Riley spoke excitedly.

"Van, I need your help. And I'm afraid it isn't exactly legitimate or sanctioned by the powers that be."

Before Riley could explain, Roff interrupted her very loudly.

"Hey, Rufus, old buddy! How's Cancún treating you? Listen, I hope you're staying safe, not catching any of them tropical diseases, if you know what I mean. You're wearing a condom, right?"

Baffled, Riley stammered, "Uh, what?"

Roff said, "Listen, Rufus, I'm sure you've got all kinds of raunchy stories, and I can't wait to hear them. Vicarious sex is pretty much all I get these days. But I can't talk right now. I'll get back to you later."

Then he hung up.

Riley stared at her phone. It took a moment for her to realize what had just happened.

Of course. He's not alone.

Higher-ups in the Seattle FBI tried to keep a close eye on Roff. Perhaps they were even listening in on his phone or monitoring his computer.

She was sure it was a game the computer geek enjoyed playing. He would be happy with the challenge of evading oversight and looking into whatever interested him.

Anyway, Riley felt sure that he would get in touch with her whenever he could. She hoped it wouldn't be very long.

*

A little while later, Riley joined Gabriela, April, and Jilly for dinner.

"How's the case going?" April asked eagerly as Riley sat at the table.

"Well, it's not exactly a 'case,'" Riley said.

"But you're working on it, right? Are you trying to find out what happened to those girls?"

Riley hesitated. How much should she tell April of her activities today?

"I'm working on it," she said. "But I'm not ready to talk about it yet."

April's smile made Riley feel a bit better. At least her daughter wasn't angry with her anymore. Riley just hoped that April wouldn't wind up disappointed. Although Riley was feeling sure that there was something to be investigated, she was a long way from making any progress. She would need to know a lot more in order to open an official case. And she suspected she was going to have to shed light on matters that some families wanted kept in the dark.

April and Jilly chatted cheerfully about one thing or another over dinner. At one point, April got out her cell phone and brought up questions for a test Jilly had coming up. April began to quiz her.

"Girls, not during supper, please," Riley said.

Riley was a bit surprised to hear Gabriela disagree with her.

"No, it is good. The girls studying is good, at the table or anywhere else."

Riley smiled. Yes, she supposed that this was good. She realized that Gabriela was keenly aware of Jilly's teetering on an edge between a desperate life and a happy one. And Gabriela would also know what kind of difference a good education could make.

So she said, "OK, study away. Anywhere, anytime."

Riley was pleased that the two girls were bonding wonderfully. And Jilly was getting truly excited about school.

The house phone rang during dinner. Riley got up and answered it. It was Ryan.

"Hi," she said. "Are you on your way? I can save some dinner for you."

"I'm afraid I won't get in until very late tonight," he said. "I've got a huge amount of work to do. I hope that's OK."

Riley stifled a sigh.

"It's OK," she said.

She ended the call and went back into the kitchen.

"Was that Dad?" April asked. "When's he getting home?"

"He says he'll be late," Riley said, sitting back down.

April's smile suddenly vanished.

Riley was sad to see April's change of mood. She knew that

Ryan was often overloaded with work. Like herself, he would sometimes have to be away.

But she and April both had too many memories of Ryan simply losing interest in his own family. Things had been so good lately, and Ryan had seemed like a changed man. Riley still hoped that this time would be different.

*

Later that night, Riley had a text message from Van Roff. It gave her his video address and said he was free to talk. Riley dialed him up. She was glad to see the hulking, overweight man appear on the screen.

"Hey, Rufus!" Roff said. "How's Cancún? Got lots of condoms handy?"

"Very funny," Riley said.

"So what are you up to that the powers that be wouldn't approve of?"

"I'm checking into suspicious deaths at a school near here. Byars College."

"I'm guessing this isn't an official investigation, since you're not using BAU services."

"The official word on three of them is that they're suicides. "If that's true, it's fifty-seven times the natural average."

Roff scratched his chin.

"An outlier maybe?" he asked.

"I've got a hunch it's not. "

Roff nodded.

"Well, outliers are outliers, hunches are hunches. I've learned to trust instincts over statistics most of the time."

Riley could see that Roff was already typing away.

"Byars College, you say? Right there in DC?"

"That's right. I interviewed Dean Willis Autrey about them, but he wasn't exactly forthcoming. I also talked to Congresswoman Hazel Webber, the mother of one of the victims. She was definitely hiding something. And she sicced a couple of her goons on me to teach me a lesson."

Roff was still typing.

"How did that work out?"

"Not too well—for them."

Roff chuckled as he worked.

"Wish I could have seen that!"

He stopped typing and said, "Okay, I see the obits you're talking about."

Riley said, "Pennington, Webber, and Linz are supposedly suicides. The two I don't know anything about are Kirk Farrell and Constance Yoh, both sophomores."

Roff typed for another few minutes, then stopped. He looked surprised.

"Holy smoke!" he said.

"What's the matter?"

Roff shook his head as if in disbelief.

"So that dean told you there had only been three suicides this year at Byars?"

"He didn't exactly *tell* me anything."

"Well, you'd better revise your figures. It's more like ninety-six times the national average."

Roff explained, "There have been five so-called suicides so far during this school year, not three. Kirk Farrell supposedly shot himself at his home in Atlanta. Constance Yoh hanged herself at her home near DC."

Riley's mouth dropped open. "Five, not three," she said.

"Well, suicides can be contagious. Especially among young people all living in the same environment."

"I know," Riley said. "But I don't think that's what this is."

"Then you have a very serious problem on your hands."

"Van, send me what you have. And can you get me contact information for the families of the students I didn't already know about?"

"Will do. I'll email them to you in a jiffy."

Riley thanked Roff for his help, and they ended the call. Riley sat for a moment poring over the new information. Did she now have enough information to persuade Meredith that this was an FBI case?

She sighed. Probably not. At least not now that Walder was complaining about her activities. She had to get more evidence. And she had to handle things delicately.

Anyway, the hour was late, and there wasn't anything else she could do right now.

*

Riley didn't sleep well that night. Ryan didn't come in at all. He had sent her a text message that he would spend the night at his house and go to his DC office this morning.

The next morning after the kids had gotten off to school, she sat down with the information that she had on the student deaths and thought about what to do next.

Should she try contacting any of the other families?

Riley shuddered at the idea. Her visits to both the Penningtons and the Webbers had been disasters. She had no reason to think she'd fare better with the others.

But what else could she do?

She summoned up her nerve, picked up the phone, and dialed the number for Cory Linz's family.

The man who answered the phone introduced himself as Conrad Linz.

Riley said, "Mr. Linz, this is Agent Riley Paige with the FBI, and—"

Conrad Linz interrupted before she could finish her sentence.

"The FBI! Is this about our daughter's death?"

"Yes, it is. You see—"

"Just a moment, let me get my wife on the line."

Riley heard him call out, "Olivia, it's the FBI!"

In a moment, the woman was on the line.

"Oh, please, please tell us you're investigating what happened to poor Cory!"

Her husband added, "Neither the police nor the school have been any help at all."

Riley gulped. What should she say to them?

"It's a little hard to discuss this on the phone," Riley said. "Perhaps I could come by your house. How's this morning?"

Conrad said, "I was just getting ready to go to work, but I'll stay home to meet with you."

"I'll be here too," Olivia said.

"Good. I see that you live in Mirabel. I'm driving from Fredericksburg. I should be able to get there soon."

The couple thanked her frantically. They sounded as if they were in tears.

When Riley ended the call, she was almost in tears herself.

She scrambled around her room, getting ready to go. Meeting with these people might give her the break she needed.

But what was she going to tell them? Was she going to lie

again, pretend that she was working with the FBI? Or was she going to tell them the truth—that she was investigating on her own, in defiance of orders?

CHAPTER TEN

The interstate traffic on the way to Mirabel was heavy but moving fast. As Riley drove, she struggled with her decision.

What should I tell the Linzes? she kept wondering.

It was one thing to trick her superiors—she sometimes avoided the complete truth even with Brent Meredith. Her bosses and colleagues knew that she frequently worked outside the box and followed her own rules. And she knew and accepted that there could be professional consequences for her willfulness— reprimands and even suspension. It was all part of how she did business. And her maverick methods had paid off with a high rate of success.

But could she lie to a grieving couple?

That was a line that she couldn't remember crossing before.

And yet, the more she thought about it, the more she felt that she had no other choice. If she admitted that she was going rogue in any way, the Linzes would be baffled, perhaps horrified.

If she could get enough information from them, maybe she could finally persuade Meredith to take the case.

Riley hoped that the end wound up justifying the means.

When Riley drove into Mirabel, she saw that it was a community of brand new homes with carefully manicured lawns and gardens already in place. Even with scattered patches of snow, the whole area seemed strangely toylike. Like many of the other houses, the Linzes' home was of a brick Colonial style with a wide, welcoming front porch.

I didn't know they built them like this anymore, Riley thought.

Olivia Linz welcomed Riley at the door. She was a tall, immaculately dressed woman with short, neatly arranged hair. She had a ruddy, healthy complexion, and Riley was startled to see a bright smile on her face.

"Oh, come in, come in!" she said before Riley had a chance to introduce herself or show her badge.

She led Riley into a high-ceilinged living room with a fire burning in the fireplace. Olivia's husband, Conrad, also tall and well-dressed with a glowing expression, stood up and shook Riley's hand. Like his wife, he was smiling pleasantly.

"Sit down, please!" he said.

"Would you like something to drink?" Olivia asked. "I've got some herbal tea ready—lemon, rosehip, and peppermint."

Riley was taken a little aback. The Linzes were treating her exactly as if she were here on a social visit. She wasn't used to this kind of hospitality from bereaved families. But for some reason, she couldn't refuse the offer.

"Yes, I would like some tea, thank you," she said.

Olivia went into the kitchen. Riley saw a pair of baby grand pianos sitting back to back at a far end of the room. Conrad noticed Riley's interest.

"Olivia's a piano teacher," he explained casually. "She performs her own recitals once in a while, and she's very good. I wish I had some musical talent. I wasn't a bad saxophonist when I was a kid, but it never went anywhere. I'm not the least bit artistic—not like Olivia. So I became an accountant. Numbers are boring, but so am I, I'm afraid."

He let out a self-deprecating chuckle.

Riley was feeling more puzzled by the moment.

Small talk? she wondered. *When I'm here to talk about how his daughter died?*

Riley almost wondered if she'd come to the right address. Maybe this was all a bizarre and embarrassing misunderstanding.

Nevertheless, Riley forced herself to smile.

Olivia came back with a silver tray holding a teapot and three china cups. She sat, setting the tray down where everyone could reach it. Riley poured herself some tea and sipped. It was delicious, but she'd really have preferred something with caffeine.

"But tell us," Olivia said eagerly. "Why did the FBI get interested in what happened to poor Cory?"

"Yes, we're surprised," her husband chimed in. "The police were so closed-minded. And we were under the impression that the FBI usually takes on cases only when local police ask them to."

They both seemed upbeat and excited.

The whole situation struck Riley as surreal. She remembered how frantic the couple had sounded on the phone. So where were those feelings now?

"Yes, that's usually true," Riley began uncertainly. "But this situation is …"

Her voice drifted off.

The couple's bright, alert eyes—Olivia's blue, Conrad's green—took her completely off guard.

Riley suddenly realized something.

However odd the Linzes emotional reactions might strike her
…

They're completely sincere. Completely honest.
She simply couldn't lie to them.
"Mr. and Mrs. Linz—"
"Conrad, please," the husband said.
"And Olivia," the wife added.

Riley fell silent for a moment, considering the best way to tell them the truth. She took out her badge and showed it to them.

"I think I'd better explain something," she said. "First of all, please believe that I really *am* an FBI agent, from the BAU in Quantico. But the truth is, your daughter's death is not an official BAU case. Not yet, anyway. And I'm—I'm not here in an official capacity. In fact …"

Riley gulped. For some reason, she felt compelled to be completely honest.

"I'm not *supposed* to be investigating your daughter's death at all."

Olivia and Conrad tilted their heads with curiosity. But neither of them seemed the least bit alarmed or upset.

"I'm not sure I understand," Olivia said.

"Nor do I," her husband said.

Riley thought carefully about what to say.

"Well, you might say I'm here in a strictly personal capacity. I found out from my daughter that a girl—not your daughter—hanged herself last weekend. She was also a student at Byars College. I looked into it and found out that a total of five Byars students—including your daughter—have supposedly committed suicide so far during this school year."

Olivia and Conrad glanced at each with amazement.

"That doesn't sound like it could be coincidence," Olivia said.

"I don't think so either," Riley said. "But I can't prove anything—not yet."

"What can we do to help?" Conrad said.

Riley was starting to relax a little. It felt good to know that the Linzes were on her side.

"Well, so far, I've not had any access to official records about the deaths. I don't know many details. For example, what can you tell me about your daughter's death?"

A cloud of sadness passed over the couple's faces—the first sign of grief Riley had noticed from them so far.

"It didn't make any sense," Olivia said. "We got a call from the school. It was the dean—Willis Autrey. He said that Cory had hanged herself in the gym locker room."

Riley's interest sharpened.

Another hanging—just like Lois Pennington and Constance Yoh!

Olivia continued, "Dean Autrey seemed to think she'd been bullied or something, and it had gotten to be too much for her. But that's just not—"

She choked on a sob and couldn't finish her sentence. Her husband gave her a handkerchief.

He said, "Cory told us that she didn't fit in especially well at school. She was different, and people can be mean. But that's been true all her life. And she never let it bother her. She was her own person. She got blue every now and then—who doesn't? But she never suffered from depression. She was always very happy."

Olivia had recovered some of her composure.

"The dean also said she'd taken a high dose of some kind of painkiller," she said.

"Alprazolam?" Riley asked, remembering what the medical examiner had told her about Lois Pennington's death.

"Why yes," Olivia said. "But that's impossible. She never touched drugs of any kind. Not even aspirin."

Conrad squeezed his wife's hand and said, "You see, she was a Scientist. We're all Scientists in this family."

Riley was puzzled.

A scientist?

Hadn't she just learned that Conrad was an accountant and Olivia a piano teacher?

But after a moment's thought, she understood.

"You're *Christian* Scientists," she said.

"That's right," Olivia said.

Suddenly, the couple's behavior seemed less strange to Riley.

Riley hadn't known many practicing Christian Scientists. But she'd heard that they could be extremely positive and optimistic, to the point of seeming otherworldly. After all, they believed that the material world was an illusion, and that death itself wasn't real.

Grieving just wasn't their style.

But these people were hurting nevertheless.

They felt that a terrible injustice had been done to their daughter.

Riley couldn't help but sympathize completely. Even so, she had to take into account the possibility that the couple had misjudged Cory.

"Olivia, Conrad, forgive me for suggesting this, but … well, I'm raising two teenage girls myself, and they can be hard to deal with at times. Are you absolutely sure that your daughter might not have, well, strayed from your beliefs? I mean, alprazolam is sometimes abused as a recreational drug. And kids sometimes do rebel."

Olivia shook her head slowly.

"Oh, no," she said, with no trace of defensiveness in her voice. "That really is impossible."

"Let me show you something," her husband said.

Conrad led Riley over to a wall filled with pictures of Cory throughout her life, looking as bright-faced and cheerful as her parents in all of them. Surrounding each picture were framed, handwritten letters that Cory had written to her parents—from clumsy block printing when she was just learning to write, to the beautiful handwriting she had now.

Riley almost gasped in amazement.

Did children even do this anymore—handwrite letters to their parents, or to anyone else for that matter?

How many letters had April handwritten to Riley over the years?

Hardly any. And the truth was, Riley hadn't even expected it—not in this information age, when communication was all about phones and computers.

But Riley was equally amazed that Cory's parents had framed so many letters with so many pictures, forming a sort of shrine to their daughter.

Had Riley ever known such a close-knit family before?

She doubted it.

Conrad silently directed Riley's attention to recent photos and letters, all from since Cory had gone to college. Cory had sent selfies of herself from all over the campus, always smiling and cheerful. Riley hastily skimmed some of them. All were upbeat about classes and grades and everything else in her life. Cory remarked here and there that she didn't fit in especially well among the other students, but she seemed to take even that in good humor.

Riley certainly found it unsurprising that a girl so cheerful and otherworldly might not connect with her peers. It was probably the story of her life. But somehow, Cory had never let it get her down. She was as emotionally secure as a young person could possibly be.

It was like Conrad had said a few moments ago.

"She's her own person."

Riley sat back down with Conrad and Olivia.

Olivia said, "You told us that five students supposedly committed suicide. Have you talked with any of the other families?"

Riley hesitated. How much should she tell the Linzes about what she knew so far?

As she looked at their open, friendly faces, she decided she'd better tell them everything that she could.

"Well, like I said, I first got wind of this from my own daughter. Her friend's sister was found hanging in the family garage. I talked to the girl's parents, but they completely believed the suicide story. My daughter's friend didn't believe it, though. And my daughter didn't either. That was when I started looking into it."

Riley thought for a moment, then asked, "Did you happen to hear about Deanna Webber's death last fall? Congresswoman Webber's daughter?"

"Oh, yes," Olivia said. "It happened shortly before … before what happened to Cory. Cory wrote to us about it. She knew Deanna a little. She was quite upset about it."

"I talked to the congresswoman about it," Riley said, choosing her words carefully. "She tried to convince me that Deanna's death really was a suicide. She said that Deanna deliberately overdosed and died in her bed asleep."

Olivia and Conrad looked at each other.

Olivia said, "I'm not sure whether we should say this, but—"

"Please tell me anything you can," Riley said.

Olivia hesitated.

"I don't think the congresswoman told you the truth."

CHAPTER ELEVEN

Riley was breathless with anticipation as she studied the Linzes' faces. By then, she knew that Olivia and Conrad were honest to a fault. She had no such feelings about Hazel Webber. She was already sure that the congresswoman was hiding something.

"This is so important," she said to Conrad and Olivia. "Please tell me whatever you know."

After a moment, Conrad said, "Maybe it would be better if we *showed* you," Conrad said.

He walked over to a bureau and pulled out a letter. He handed it to Riley. It was another handwritten letter from Cory. At a glance, Riley saw that it was not the kind of letter that her parents had wanted to frame and put on the wall.

Dear Mom and Dad,

Something awful has happened. Deanna Webber, the congresswoman's daughter, killed herself yesterday. Or that's what we've been told. I don't know if that's true. I knew her a little, and I talked to her a few times. She didn't seem like a very happy girl. Even so, she seemed to be looking forward to lots of things. She rides in equestrian competitions, and she was excited about one that was coming up this summer ...

Riley stopped right there. She remembered what Hazel Webber had told her. She'd said that Deanna's hip had been badly fractured and would probably have to be replaced.

"Her days of riding in competitions were over," she'd said. *"She was heartbroken."*

Had that been a lie?

Riley resumed reading.

Something else seems odd. A couple of family employees came to pick up her belongings—a man and a woman. I stopped by Deanna's room, where the woman was boxing up her stuff. I told her I was awfully sorry about Deanna, and I asked her how it had happened. She told me she'd drugged herself and hanged herself in the family stables.

I carried a box out to their van where the man was packing things up. I told him I was sad and shocked, that I never would have thought Deanna would do something like hang herself.

Then he got mad. He asked who told me that, and I said the woman inside. He said that Deanna did not *hang herself, that she'd overdosed and died in her sleep, and that I'd better not tell anybody otherwise.*

Mom, Dad, it sounded almost like a threat!

Then the man went into Deanna's room and I could hear him yelling at the woman—something about how she knew better than to say a thing like that, and she'd better learn to keep her mouth shut.

I got a little scared and left. But I can't help feeling that something is really wrong ...

Riley saw that the rest of the letter was pretty routine, about classes and activities.

"When did Cory write this?" she asked.

"Just a couple of weeks before ... what happened to her," Olivia said.

Riley's heart was pounding with excitement.

"Did she ever tell you the name of the woman who spoke of Deanna hanging herself?"

"No," Olivia replied. "I don't think she knew the woman's name."

"Did she say what that woman looked like?"

"No, I don't remember Cory saying anything more about her."

"I hate to ask this," Riley told the couple. "But could I take this letter with me? It might help me to persuade my superiors to open the case."

"Of course," Olivia said.

"Anything we can do to help," Conrad said.

Riley thanked them and left their house. As she got into her car, she felt certain that the so-called suicides really were murders. But she also knew that she'd need even more information to persuade Meredith and Walder. She knew who might be able to help her. She made a quick phone call to set up a meeting.

*

An hour later, Riley arrived in Manassas and pulled into the parking lot of the Northern Laboratory of the Virginia Department of Forensic Science. She headed straight for the office of her friend Danica Selves, the district medical examiner she'd called on

Tuesday. The stout, short-haired woman stood up from her desk to greet her.

"Hi, Riley. What's going on? When you called, it sounded very important."

Riley and Danica both sat down.

"Danica, a few days ago I called to ask about Lois Pennington's death," Riley began.

Danica nodded.

"You wondered whether it was really a suicide. I told you I was sure that it was."

"And now I'm sure that it wasn't," Riley said.

Danica looked surprised.

"Riley, I did that autopsy myself. I don't see how I could have been wrong."

Riley paused for a moment.

"Danica, I've been investigating a series of so-called suicides of students at Byars College, and—"

Danica gently interrupted her.

"'Investigating'? Riley, are you going rogue again?"

Riley smiled. Danica knew her all too well.

"Let's just say that my work hasn't been official—so far. That's why I want to talk to you. I need something more tangible to convince Meredith and Walder."

Danica was starting to look intrigued.

"Tell me what you've got," she said.

"Five Byars College students have committed suicide, just in this school year. Lois Pennington was one of them. So was Deanna Webber."

Danica's eyes twinkled with interest.

"The Maryland congresswoman's daughter?" she asked. "I'd read that she'd committed suicide. I didn't know that she'd gone to Byars too."

"I paid the congresswoman a visit—"

Danica let out a small laugh. "And she was delighted to see you, I'm sure."

"Not exactly. But I managed to interview her. And she told me, in no uncertain terms, that her daughter had deliberately overdosed on oxycodone and died in her bed asleep. She told me that Deanna had been depressed lately because she'd fractured a hip in a riding accident and couldn't compete anymore."

Riley took the letter she'd gotten from the Linzes out of her handbag.

She said, "But I just now interviewed the parents of another suicide victim—Cory Linz was her name. A couple of weeks before she died, she sent this letter to her parents."

Riley handed the letter to Danica. Her eyes widened as she read it.

"This certainly looks suspicious," Danica said. "And this would be a very high rate of suicides. I wonder—maybe I did come to the wrong conclusion about Lois Pennington's death."

Riley considered what to ask next.

Then she said, "One of the other five victims died near DC. Her name was Constance Yoh—another hanging, and another Byars student. But that's all I know about her so far. What can you tell me about her?"

Danica typed on her computer again.

"I don't believe I worked on that case myself …"

When the records came up, Danica's eyes widened.

"My God," she said. "Constance Yoh also took a high dose of alprazolam."

Danica shook her head.

"This is very strange," she said. "What do you know about what happened to the Webber girl?"

"Very little, except that maybe her mother lied to me."

Danica thought for a moment, then said, "I know the chief examiner in Baltimore—Colin Metcalf. Let's give him a call."

A moment later, Riley and Danica were talking to Dr. Metcalf on speakerphone.

"What can you tell us about the death of Deanna Webber?" Danica asked.

There was a moment of silence.

"Why do you want to know?" Metcalf asked uneasily.

Riley and Danica glanced at each other warily.

"Well, there seem to be some inconsistencies in the family's story," Danica said.

Another pause fell. Then Metcalf began to speak slowly and cautiously.

"I did the autopsy myself. It was pretty cut and dried. Her body had been found hanging in the family stable. But …"

"But what?" Riley asked.

"I got a call from the family lawyer. He told me to keep the fact that she'd hanged herself out of the news, to say nothing to the media about it."

Riley leaned toward the phone.

"Did it sound like a threat?" she asked.

"I wasn't sure. But that family has a lot of power, and I'd be lying if I didn't say it scared me a little. Anyway, so far I've had no cause to do otherwise. I haven't said anything at all to any reporters about it. But it's been bothering me ever since. And it's in the official report, if anybody wants to see it."

Riley thought for a moment.

Then she asked, "Did your autopsy reveal any serious injuries—fractured bones, for example?"

"Let me see," Metcalf said.

Riley could hear the clattering of computer keys as Metcalf found the information.

"Yes, it appeared that she suffered from a fracture. Actually it was a hairline fracture in the upper thigh, not the hip joint. It looked like it had happened two or three years ago. But it was a clean break and seemed to have healed perfectly. It probably wasn't bothering her at all."

Again, Riley remembered Hazel Webber's words …

"Her hip was badly fractured. It seemed likely that it would have to be replaced altogether."

Another lie!

Had the congresswoman told Riley the truth about anything at all?

"What else do you want to know?" Metcalf asked.

Riley replayed parts of her conversation with Webber and remembered something else she had said.

"She was taking oxycodone for the pain."

What pain?

Riley asked, "I understand that she was also using a drug. What was it?"

Again Riley heard the clattering of keys.

"Alprazolam," Metcalf said. "Not enough to be a fatal dose, but enough to knock her out pretty much."

Riley looked at Danica and asked, "Is alprazolam used as a painkiller?"

Danica wrinkled her brow a little.

"No," she said. "It's strictly a sedative, used for panic and anxiety. It wouldn't be of any use at all as a painkiller."

Riley felt a tingle of excitement. Surely she now had all the evidence she needed to persuade Meredith. Walder might be a harder sell, but she was determined to try.

Riley asked, "Dr. Metcalf, could you forward your entire autopsy report to me?"

"Of course," he said.

Riley gave him her contact information, and the call ended.

Then Riley asked, "Danica, can you give me a copy of your reports on Lois Pennington and Constance Yoh?"

Danica didn't respond for a moment. She looked uneasy.

"Riley, I can do that, but ..."

"But what?"

Danica shook her head worriedly.

"We didn't say a word to Colin about this not being an official FBI case ..."

Her voice trailed off for a moment. Then she added, "Now you're asking me for information on a case that isn't even open. I know Carl Walder. He's liable to have a fit about your going over his head. And Congresswoman Webber is a powerful woman—maybe even dangerous."

Riley's heart sank a little. It was bad enough that she was making trouble for herself. Was it fair to also put Danica on the spot? She couldn't think of any way around it.

"Danica, I'm sorry, but I really need your report. It's the only way I can get this thing going. And I'm sure you believe me. There have been five so-called suicides at one school, and at least four of the victims had the same drug in their system. There was another Byars student suicide that was said to be by gunshot, and I definitely want to check that out. Anyway, there's no way this run of deaths can be attributed to suicide. I really need your help."

Riley and Danica looked at each other for a moment.

Riley said, "Look, I promise to take the heat from Walder. I'll tell him that I tricked you, told you that I was here in an official capacity."

Danica sighed and shook her head.

"No, don't lie on my account. You're in enough trouble already." Then she added with a quiet laugh, "As usual."

Riley laughed a little too. Danica started typing on her computer.

"Anyway, you've convinced me," she said. "And I'm ready to help however I can. I'll email the report to you right now."

Riley stammered her heartfelt thanks and left.

When Riley got home that afternoon, the girls weren't home from school yet, and Ryan was still at work. Gabriela was doing some housecleaning.

Riley checked the messages on her house phone. There were two, and one of them was from Ryan.

"Hey, honey," he said. "I'm sorry, but I'm backed up with work again. Don't know when or if I'll get in tonight. I hope you understand."

Riley sighed. She was afraid she understood all too well. It was an all-too-familiar pattern with Ryan. Riley was starting to wonder if she'd made a terrible mistake letting him back into her life. She was especially worried about April, who had been so happy since he'd been around. And Jilly truly needed a father right now.

But Riley warned herself not to jump to conclusions.

Maybe Ryan really was just busy and not losing interest in his family again.

The next message really startled her.

"Special Agent in Charge Walder here. Agent Paige, you've got some explaining to do. Call me as soon as you get in."

He sounded furious. Riley had a pretty good idea about why. She dialed his number. His voice was almost shaking with rage.

"Agent Paige, I just got a call from the Maryland medical examiner. He said he was just checking in with me about a case you were working on with Danica Selves. A case that I'm pretty sure doesn't exist."

Riley gulped. She knew she ought to apologize. But for some reason, the words just wouldn't come.

"You lied to him," Walder said.

"I didn't exactly *lie*," Riley said.

"Well, you certainly didn't tell him the whole truth. And I'll bet you weren't exactly forthcoming with Danica Selves, either."

Riley felt a slight ripple of relief. As long as she didn't deny it, Danica was off the hook.

"I can explain," Riley said.

"I'm not interested in explanations," Walder said. "After that stunt you pulled with Congresswoman Webber, I expected you to back off. But you just wouldn't quit. You've really gone too far this time. I want to see you in my office first thing in the morning."

He hung up.

Riley stared at the phone for a moment.

What was Walder going to do—suspend her or fire her?

Oddly, Riley couldn't get worried about it.

In fact, she found herself looking forward to tomorrow morning.

If Walder wants a showdown, he's going to get one.

CHAPTER TWELVE

By nine o'clock the next morning, Riley was ready for the confrontation. She was prepared and eager as she knocked on the office door.

"Come in," Special Agent in Charge Carl Walder said sternly.

With a noncommittal expression on her face, Riley stepped inside.

Walder's spacious office was quite a bit more impressive than the man himself. He was babyish and freckled-faced, with curly, copper-colored hair, and a voice that sometimes squeaked with petulance. But his authority at the BAU was very real, and Riley knew better than to trifle with him.

"Sit down, let's talk," he said, mustering a stern tone.

But Riley didn't sit down.

"Sir, if you don't mind, I think we might need more space for this."

Walder tilted his head back with surprise.

"More space?"

"Please join me in the conference room."

Without another word, Riley turned and left the office. She walked away down the hall, not hastily but purposefully.

Walder quickly followed. When they reached the conference room, Riley stopped and held the door open for him.

When Walder stepped inside, his eyes widened with shock.

Riley struggled to suppress a smile.

Walder had walked straight into the ambush she had prepared for him.

Five other people were already in the room, ready to do business. One of them was Brent Meredith.

"Glad you could join us, Agent Walder," Meredith said gruffly. "Have a seat."

Dumbfounded, Walder sat down.

Riley sensed that Meredith was enjoying having the upper hand over his boss, at least for the moment.

Riley's old partner, Bill Jeffreys, was there as well. He and Riley had been working together for two decades now, and Riley was glad he was here. He was grinning broadly at Riley, not even trying to hide his delight in Walder's discomfort.

Also present were the younger agents Lucy Vargas and Craig Huang. Riley thought very highly of Lucy's work. Huang had originally been overeager, often rubbing her the wrong way. But now he was starting to grow on her.

Sam Flores, a thin, nerdish lab technician with big black-rimmed glasses, was running the multimedia display that Riley had prepared at home the night before. At the moment, five faces were shown on the massive bank of screens.

"What the hell is all this about?" Walder muttered, struggling to regain his bearings.

"Just some information I think we should all be interested in," Riley said, taking the floor.

She pointed to the face at the far left.

"This is Deanna Webber, the daughter of Hazel Webber, the Maryland congresswoman. On October seventh of last year, her dead body was found hanging in the family stables. The official word is that her death was a suicide. An extremely high level of the anti-anxiety drug alprazolam was found in her system."

Riley leveled her gaze at Walder.

"But when I interviewed her mother, she told me that Deanna had died in bed in her sleep from an overdose of oxycodone."

Walder's face was reddening with anger.

"This is outrageous!" he said. "Hazel called and complained about your behavior. I've known the Webbers for years. I went to prep school with Hazel's husband, Heath. They're good people. They're not liars."

Meredith looked across the table at Walder.

In a calm, sensible voice, he said, "Then how do you explain the discrepancy? Are you suggesting that the Maryland medical examiner is lying? I think we ought to hear Agent Paige out."

Walder let out a wordless sound, somewhere between a growl and a whine.

Riley pointed to the next picture.

"This is Cory Linz. She was found dead, hanging in the gym locker room at Byars College on October twenty-first, just two weeks after Deanna Webber's death. She, too, had a lot of alprazolam in her system. I talked to her parents, who don't believe that Cory's death was suicide. For one thing, the girl was a devout Christian Scientist and never took prescription medication of any kind. She was unlikely to even consider killing herself."

Riley signaled Flores to bring up another visual—the letter that Cory had written to her parents, with crucial passages highlighted.

"And as you can see, Cory stumbled across the truth about how

Deanna really died. A female employee of the Webbers slipped up and didn't stick to the 'official' story that Deanna had died in her sleep. And it sounds like she caught hell for it."

After the group had enough time to read the letter, Flores took it down and brought up the pictures again.

Riley pointed to a photo of a young Asian woman.

"Now, this is Constance Yoh. She was found dead by hanging at home in DC on November twentieth of last year. Also a supposed suicide. Also with alprazolam in her system."

Then she pointed to a picture of a smiling young man.

"This is Kirk Farrell, found dead of a gunshot wound at his home in Atlanta on November twentieth. Also a supposed suicide."

Finally she pointed to the last picture.

"And this is Lois Pennington, found hanging in her family's garage last Sunday. Another supposed suicide."

Riley looked at all the faces in the group.

"Oh, and I haven't mentioned that *all* of these students were currently enrolled at Byars College, a school with only about seven hundred students. Sam, could you show us some stats?"

Sam Flores brought up a sheet of statistics that Riley had prepared.

Riley said, "It seems that the suicide rate at Byars College is ninety-six times the national average. I think it's time to stop calling them suicides. Something deadly is going on at Byars. We need to investigate."

Walder rolled his eyes.

"This is ridiculous. I talked to the dean at Byars, Willis Autrey. He assured me that there was nothing untoward going on at his school. In fact, I think we should call him right now. He can clear things up, and we can put this whole business behind us and stop wasting agency time."

Riley nodded. "Fine," she said.

"Flores, get Autrey on the line," Walder continued. "Put him on speakerphone."

Sam Flores put through the call. Autrey's secretary answered and quickly got Autrey on the phone.

"Willis Autrey here."

Walder smirked self-confidently.

"Dean Autrey, this is Special Agent in Charge Carl Walder, BAU. We talked on the phone yesterday."

Autrey chuckled.

"Oh, yes. About that rather batty dame who showed up here unauthorized. Most unfortunate. I hope you put her straight about things."

Then with a coarse laugh he added, "A good spanking was in order, I'd say."

Walder glanced up at Riley and blushed.

"Well, as it happens, I'm still trying to deal with her," he said. "You see, she still thinks—"

Autrey interrupted.

"I thought I'd made it pretty clear when you and I last talked—three suicides in a single school year is unusual, but not statistically improbable."

Walder's face grew pale. He didn't know what to say.

Riley cleared her throat.

"Dean Autrey, this is the batty dame speaking. Three suicides is what might be called an outlier. But as you know perfectly well, there have been two more suicides in the last few months. How interesting that you've neglected to mention those. Five suicides in a single year, four of them by hanging, really pushes the definition of 'outlier.'"

A silence fell, followed by stammering.

"Pardon me," Autrey said. "I have a rather urgent appointment."

Autrey ended the call.

Walder's mouth was hanging open.

He couldn't talk for a moment.

Finally he stammered, "This is crazy. You're accusing somebody of murder, but who? Who are your suspects? The Byars dean? His staff? The Webber family? None of that makes any sense."

Nobody in the group replied. They just sat waiting for the man who was supposed to be in charge to say something else.

Walder threw his hands up and said, "I'm through with this. I have other important matters to attend to. Meredith, use your best judgment. Whatever you do, don't screw it up. And keep Agent Paige on a tight leash."

He got up and stormed out of the room.

After a moment, Meredith looked around at everybody.

"Well," he said dryly, "looks like we can get to work."

Everybody chuckled. Riley's heart warmed. It was nice to know that she had good people on her side at last.

CHAPTER THIRTEEN

Everybody in the room breathed easier now that Walder was gone. But Riley told herself not to get relaxed. There was urgent work to do.

"This is *your* case, Agent Paige," Meredith said. "You own it now. So where do we start?"

Riley looked around at the five helpful faces.

"I'm open to ideas," she said. "Any thoughts?"

Lucy Vargas's deep, dark eyes seemed almost to sparkle with excitement.

"I say we follow the lies," she said. "We just heard Willis Autrey trying to evade the truth. And Congresswoman Webber lied to Agent Paige. The question is, why? What are they trying to hide?"

Craig Huang's brow crinkled in thought.

"Autrey doesn't strike me as a killer," he said. "Just some administrative stooge watching out for his school's reputation."

"Or covering up for somebody," Lucy said. "Like the Webber family. Maybe the victims knew something dangerous, something the Webbers didn't want to get out. Something dangerous enough to kill for. Then they hired somebody—a professional smart enough to make the deaths look like suicides."

Craig Huang shook his head.

"I don't know, Lucy," he said. "Are you suggesting that Hazel Webber had her own daughter killed?"

"It's possible. Have you ever seen that woman on TV? She's cold!"

Riley glanced at Bill. She could tell from his smile that he, too, was enjoying the younger agents' enthusiasm. But the team needed more than enthusiasm to get things underway. It was time for Riley to give some marching orders.

She said, "In her letter, Cory Linz said that a Webber family employee told her the truth about what happened to Deanna. She was at the college cleaning out the girl's room. Flores, we need to locate that woman."

"I'll get right on it," Flores said.

Riley looked at the pictures still on the screen.

"We've got two more families to interview," she said. "Constance Yoh lived here in DC. Kirk Farrell lived in Atlanta."

Riley thought for a moment.

"Huang, Vargas, you go visit the Yoh family."

"We should check out the odd one," Bill chimed in.

Turning toward Meredith, Riley asked, "Is the company plane available?"

"If you want it to be," Meredith said.

"Good," Riley said. "Agent Jeffreys and I will fly down to Atlanta as soon as it's ready."

Riley felt a surge of gratitude toward her supportive colleagues. It was too much for her to put into words.

"That's all for now," she said. "Let's get to work."

*

A short while later, Riley sat looking out the window of the FBI jet as Quantico slipped behind her. She needed to get her mind on the case, but other thoughts kept intruding.

She heard Bill say from beside her, "You're trying to work things out with Ryan, aren't you?"

Riley turned to look at him. He gazed at her with concern.

"What makes you think that?" Riley asked.

Bill smiled sadly.

"You're being awfully quiet about *something*," he said. "It's the elephant on the plane, so to speak. I had a hunch."

Riley smiled at the bizarre image.

An elephant on the plane.

Yes, that image seemed to fit. Bill's detective instincts were almost as good as Riley's. She hadn't wanted to talk to him about this, but of course he wasn't going to let it go.

He was too good a friend to do that.

"Maybe I am," she said.

"Maybe? That doesn't sound too definite."

Riley sighed.

"It's pretty definite. He's moving in with us—April and Jilly and Gabriela and me."

Bill sounded surprised.

"Wow, that's a big step. How's it going so far?"

Riley didn't reply. The truth was, she didn't really know. Before she'd boarded the plane, she'd called home to make sure everything was OK. Gabriela had assured her that Ryan was coming home soon and the girls would be well looked after. Riley didn't have any reason to think otherwise.

Still, things seemed to be touch-and-go right now.

"Riley, I worry," Bill said.

"I know, Bill. And you have every right. You did more than anyone else to get me through that damned divorce. And I guess you'd be stuck with the job all over again if things go south this time."

"That's not what worries me."

"I know."

They were both quiet for a moment. The only noise was the low rumble of the plane engines. Bill squeezed Riley's hand.

"I'm always there for you," he said.

Then he hastily let her hand go. Riley understood why. They had long felt a mutual attraction that never quite went away, however much they tried to deny it. Each had tried to act on that attraction at one time or another. Riley cringed whenever she remembered a late-night drunken phone call in which she'd tried to talk Bill, who was still living with his family then, into having an affair.

It amazed her that their relationship had survived moments like that—both personally and professionally.

Then it occurred to her that she was being selfish right now. She knew that Bill had troubles of his own. He was still waiting out his own difficult divorce. She'd been out of touch with him for much too long.

"How are *you* getting along?" she asked.

Bill stared straight ahead with a pained expression.

"It's rough," he said.

Riley looked at him with sympathy. She didn't want to push him to talk about it if he didn't want to. But she was ready to listen.

Finally Bill said, "It's not that I miss Maggie. And I'm sure she doesn't miss me either. It was over between us a long time ago. It's just …"

He stopped for a moment, overcome with emotion.

"Is she letting you see the boys?" Riley asked.

If Riley remembered correctly, Bill's sons were nine and eleven now.

"Yeah, she's being fair about it," Bill said. "But having them visit me in my crummy apartment just isn't the same. Neither is taking them on outings—movies, museums, whatever. Everything seems forced, unnatural. It doesn't feel like being a dad anymore.

And it's all so temporary. I really don't know what's supposed to happen next. I don't know … what to do."

Bill lowered his head miserably. He seemed to be on the verge of tears.

Riley felt an urge to put her arms around him.

But if she did, what would it lead to?

Instead, she simply said, "I'm sorry."

Bill nodded and regained his composure.

"Anyway, we've got a case to solve," he said. "Let's get to it."

Riley and Bill both took out notebooks to jot down ideas as they talked.

"Have you got any theories?" Bill asked. "The kids seem to think it's some kind of conspiracy."

Riley smiled. By "the kids," she knew that Bill meant Lucy Vargas and Craig Huang. She, too, felt a certain parental affection for the younger agents. They were turning out well, due in no small part to guidance from Riley and Bill.

"Well, that would be an interesting change," she said. "We haven't dealt with any murderous conspiracies for a while. But …"

She paused.

"But what?" Bill asked.

"It seems to me a conspiracy would be more thorough. For example, as far as we know, none of the victims left a suicide note. I'd think that conspirators would be sure to plant phony notes. I think it's possible that we're in more familiar waters. Rich or poor, powerful or weak, we might be dealing with a garden-variety psychopath. So what can we put together in the way of a profile?"

Bill scratched his chin thoughtfully.

He said, "Most serial killers are male. That poisoner we caught on our last case was an outlier. And most serial murders have a sexual component. We've got five victims—but only four are female."

Riley instantly understood what Bill was driving at.

"Maybe that means the killer's bisexual," she said.

Bill nodded.

"Either that, or confused about his sexuality," he said.

Riley thought about it for a moment.

Then she said, "Or we could be dealing with another outlier—a woman. Think about it. The victims all seem to have been of small build. Most, maybe all, of them were sedated before they were killed. That might indicate a killer who's not strong enough to overpower victims."

Bill added, "Once the victims were drugged, she could drag them up a ladder."

Riley remembered the Penningtons' garage—the only crime scene she'd been able to check out so far.

"It looked to me like Lois Pennington was hanged from a roof beam. There might have been similar beams in the Webbers' stable, and maybe in the Byars locker room. A killer without a lot of strength—male or female—could haul the victims up with a rope."

Bill was jotting down their thoughts.

"We need more information about the crime scenes."

Riley agreed. "I'll send a note to Flores to get the full police reports."

Bill stopped writing and fell quiet.

"There's one thing that really worries me," he said.

"What's that?"

"The only murders we know of were these particular Byars College students. How do we know there haven't been many more—at other colleges, or anywhere else?"

"It's true that we don't have a consistent pattern in terms of timing," she said. "That could just mean that this killer is erratic. Or that he's driven by specific circumstances."

"But it also could mean we still don't know about all the deaths," Bill added.

Riley's mind boggled at the thought.

How were they going to determine how many recent suicides in the DC area were actually murders? There were hundreds in any given year.

"First things first," she finally said. "We've got an interview coming up."

"What do we know about Kirk Farrell's family?" Bill asked.

Riley pulled up the information Flores had given her on their computer, and she and Bill spent the rest of the flight poring over it.

*

When they landed in Atlanta and got off the plane, Riley realized that she was too warmly dressed for the weather. It was balmy and warm outside, and Riley's jacket was too thick and heavy. She usually checked the weather before traveling. But this trip had taken her by surprise.

She and Bill were greeted on the tarmac by Agents Joanne Honig and Nick Ritter of the Atlanta FBI field office. The two agents escorted Riley and Bill to the car they could use during their visit.

Riley asked as they walked, "When can we interview the Farrell family?"

"You can drive there right now," Ritter said.

"I called just a little while ago," Honig added. "The boy's father is expecting you as soon as you can get there."

Riley and Bill looked at each other with surprise. They hadn't expected it to be so easy to set up an appointment.

"How did he sound when you talked to him?" Riley asked Honig.

"He sounded delighted," Honig said. "He says he's looking forward to—how did he put it?—having a 'pleasant little chat' with you both."

Riley was truly taken aback.

A pleasant little chat?

What could that possibly mean?

CHAPTER FOURTEEN

Riley knew that they were going to interview a rich family, but even so the sight of the Farrell mansion took her breath away. Bill, driving the borrowed FBI car, had followed GPS directions into a wealthy suburb north of Atlanta.

She asked him, "Are you sure this is the right place? It doesn't look like a home at all."

"Apparently this is it," Bill replied.

It was a palatial building with tile roofs and flawlessly manicured hedges, positioned on spacious grounds. It looked like it might serve as some kind of European museum.

From the information Flores had given her, Riley knew that the patriarch, Andrew Farrell, was the head and founder of Farrell Fund Management. Riley didn't really understand the nature of the business, except that it had something to do with high finance, possibly hedge funds.

Bill parked the car in the circular drive and they got out. As soon as they approached the front entrance, a tall, lean butler greeted them.

"Agents Paige and Jeffreys, I presume," he said in an obsequious tone. "Mr. Farrell is eager to meet you. Come with me."

The butler led them through decorative doors and rows of columns into a vast interior that made the Webbers' mansion look like a modest bungalow. They arrived in a massive room with marble floors and a broad staircase with curved, fancy banisters. Two people were standing at the bottom of the stairway.

One was a very young, elegantly dressed young woman. She had the face and figure of a model, although she was much too thin to be in good health. Riley was sure she was anorexic. She was also sure that she was much too young to be the mother of the murder victim. She stared at Riley and Bill with large, vacant eyes.

The other was a tall man standing squarely at the base of the stairs. He had chiseled, aristocratic features and carried himself with style. Riley might have considered him good looking, except that there was something slightly reptilian about his eyes and his thin, twisted smile.

His arms were crossed, and he didn't move as Riley and Bill walked toward him.

The butler announced the guests, bowed, and disappeared into the house.

Andrew Farrell said nothing for a moment, only smiled. He stared at Riley and Bill intensely.

He's nothing if not vain, Riley thought.

She had the feeling that Farrell wanted her and Bill to take some time to appreciate his considerable presence. Indeed, Riley observed him with fascination. She was most interested in the body language of the man and the woman—she clinging limply to the banister for support, he standing with his feet apart in a forceful pose.

It was obvious to Riley that the woman must be Farrell's wife. But the relationship was clearly one of dominance versus servility. Riley sensed that the woman scarcely ever did anything except at Farrell's bidding.

Farrell spoke in a dark, silky baritone.

"I was wondering how long it would take the law to show up," he said. "It's been, after all, some three months now. And they sent the big guns! The FBI! I'm flattered."

He looked at his wife and nodded—a wordless command to leave.

For a moment, the woman locked eyes with Riley.

Riley felt an icy chill.

She'd seen that look before.

But when and where?

Then she remembered.

It was back when she'd been working a case that involved murdered prostitutes. She'd seen that look in the eyes of a young hooker named Chrissy. It was a look of sheer terror that Chrissy felt toward her pimp/husband, who had been standing right next to her at the time.

It was a silent cry for help.

Riley managed to suppress a shudder.

This woman was no prostitute—not in the ordinary sense.

But her terror was identical to Chrissy's.

And the abuse she must be suffering was just as real.

The woman bowed her head and slunk silently away down a hallway, without ever having said a word to Riley and Bill.

"My wife, Morgan," Farrell said smugly when she was out of earshot. "A rather famous model when I married her—perhaps you've seen her on magazine covers. I married her last year—shortly before *it* happened. She was Kirk's stepmother for less than

79

a month. And yes, she's very young."

Then he added with a chuckle, "A stepmother should never be older than her husband's oldest children. I've made sure of that with all my wives."

Then he gestured up the stairs.

"But what are we waiting for? You've come to hear my confession of murder. And I'm more than happy to oblige. Come with me."

Farrell turned and walked up the stairs.

Riley and Bill exchanged stunned looks and followed him.

He escorted them through a pair of double doors into a huge room with paneled walls and chandeliers. There was a desk at one end. Riley realized that this enormous space was Farrell's office.

An office with chandeliers, she thought.

She'd never imagined such a thing. The effect was astonishingly garish and unpleasant.

There were only two chairs in the room—a leather-upholstered swivel chair behind the desk, and a straight-backed antique chair in front of the desk.

Indicating the antique, he said to Riley, "Please, have a seat."

Riley sat down uneasily, leaving Bill standing.

She was starting to understand at least part of the man's game. He wanted his law enforcement guests to feel as awkward and uncomfortable as possible. He probably had no reason or rationale for doing so—it was all just sport to him.

And he was definitely succeeding.

Farrell sat down behind the desk, clasped his fingers together, and swiveled slightly back and forth, glancing from Riley to Bill and back again.

The desk was covered with dozens of standing framed pictures. Many showed Farrell himself posing with famous, rich, powerful people, including US presidents. Arranged to the left were five portraits. For a moment, Riley thought they were all of the same woman. But then she realized that they were different, even though they shared the same basic, interchangeable fashion-model glamour.

They also shared the same hollow, cheerless expressions—just like Morgan.

His wives, Riley realized with a shiver.

He had them all on display right here.

Seeming to notice Riley's reaction, Farrell chuckled.

"Some folks call me 'Bluebeard,'" he said. "You know, after

the folktale of the nobleman who murdered his wives and kept their bodies in a secret room. Well, divorce is generally more my style. And I keep pictures instead of bodies."

He pointed to the last picture to the right—an especially melancholy face.

"Of course, death sometimes does intervene. You probably know that Mimi here—Kirk's mother—committed suicide last year. An overdose of barbiturates."

Although Riley didn't say so, she and Bill had read about the woman's suicide in the information they'd just reviewed.

Farrell picked up the picture and looked at the face mock-wistfully.

"I didn't see it coming," he said. "No foul play on my part, I assure you. She simply wasn't a serious person. It's odd how flighty, trivial, silly people are always the ones who kill themselves. At least that's been my experience."

Then he pointed to three portraits on the right, all of young men who shared a marked and rather disagreeable resemblance to Farrell.

"And these are my sons, all by different wives. Hugh, the oldest, is president of our company. Sheldon, the next oldest, is deputy chairman. The youngest is Wayne, our chief compliance officer."

"Where's Kirk?" Riley asked.

Farrell's expression darkened.

"I'm afraid he never quite belonged here," he said.

He held Riley's gaze for a moment.

Then he said to both Riley and Bill, "I suppose I ought to ask for my lawyers to be present. But I'm not in the mood."

After a pause, he added, "Now tell me the exact nature of your business. I think I have a pretty good idea, but humor me."

Bill said, "The BAU is investigating five alleged suicides—your son's included."

Riley added, "All were students at Byars College—and all of them have died during the current school year."

For the first time, Farrell seemed to be genuinely surprised.

"*Five* suicides?" he asked.

"Alleged suicides," Riley said.

Farrell threw back his head and laughed.

"Oh, I didn't see this coming!" he said. "Well, I'm sure you've got no proof—for four of them, anyway. Give me the dates, and I'm sure I can give you airtight alibis."

Riley had no idea what to think. She and Bill hadn't even considered Farrell suspect at all until now. Now he seemed to be offering himself up as one.

Then he said, "But Kirk's death—well, I'll own up to that."

Riley struggled to understand where all this was going.

"The official report said that he shot himself," Riley said.

"And so he did," Farrell said.

"Right here at home," Riley added.

"Indeed."

Riley felt a strange tingle of anticipation.

"Where in the house, exactly?" she asked.

Farrell's reptilian smile broadened.

"Why, right where you're sitting, Agent Paige. And I was sitting right where I'm sitting right now. Imagine that!"

Riley felt chills all over.

He'd staged this scene so perfectly—placing her in exactly the spot where he could cause her the most discomfort.

And of course, it was because she was a woman.

It was his way of asserting his dominance over her.

And at the moment, he had the upper hand.

Riley couldn't help but look at the floor. An extremely valuable-looking Persian carpet was spread out beneath her chair over the elaborate parquet floor. Of course, Riley didn't see a drop of blood. But she had no doubt that Farrell had told the truth. Kirk's brains had surely been spattered all over another equally priceless carpet. Farrell had then tossed it away as if it were a cheap throw rug and put this one in its place.

"Poor Kirk," Farrell said with a note of feigned sadness. "He never quite caught on to what it meant to belong to the Farrell dynasty. I sent him to the same schools as my other sons— including Byars College. But his education didn't quite take. I don't know why."

Farrell swiveled slightly again and looked up at the ceiling.

"And he took his mother's death rather hard, I'm afraid. Blamed me for it, although I have no idea why. Didn't like my remarrying so soon afterwards, as if that were any of his business. And he wasn't applying himself in school. Said he wanted to be a musician, had some sort of silly group that he practiced with. He wasn't serious about it, of course. Never took lessons. He wasn't serious about anything—just like his mother."

Farrell locked eyes with Riley again.

"One day he came in here with a gun. Told me he wanted to leave school, devote himself full time to his music, and if I didn't give him my blessings, he'd blow his brains out."

Farrell paused for a moment.

"I told him to go right ahead," he said.

He paused again.

"And he did just that."

He smiled silently for a moment.

"So there it is. My full confession. No, I didn't pull the trigger, which was probably what you expected me to say. But I *did* trigger something in that little brain of his. He wouldn't have done it without my say-so. Of course, people in my life seldom do anything without my say-so."

He chuckled a little.

"Are you going to read me my rights now? Probably not. You haven't got me even for some lesser degree of manslaughter. The law's odd like that—leaky as a sieve. What's the legal difference between murder and suicide? Something to do with dying on your own terms, I suppose—of your own free will. An odd thing, free will. Many people have it. Most people don't. I do. My son did not."

He sat gloating silently, waiting for some reaction.

Riley felt physically ill.

She had no doubt at all that every word Farrell had said was true.

Ironically, she also knew something else.

Kirk Farrell's suicide was completely unconnected with the other Byars deaths.

And his father had nothing at all to do with those deaths.

She took some comfort in knowing that she was about to hurt this man—not deeply or lastingly, but in the only way he could really be hurt.

She was going to hurt his ego.

She rose from the chair.

"Thank you, Mr. Farrell," she said. "You are of no further interest to us. I won't waste more of our time with you."

Bill added, "We'll show ourselves out."

Riley held Farrell's gaze for a moment, enjoying his punctured expression. After all, this little performance he'd given had been about nothing but asserting his power. He'd expected some

83

resistance from the agents—and lots of frustration. But now Riley was dismissing him as if his power meant nothing.

He sat there saying nothing.

Riley and Bill silently left the office and went back down the stairs. On the way through the massive room, Riley glimpsed the man's young wife standing off to one side, staring at her once again with an imploring expression.

A feeling of helplessness came over her.

It was her job to bring down monsters and killers, and she and Bill did the best they could.

But many monsters and killers were immune to them—perhaps most of them, and perhaps the worst.

Without breaking her stride, Riley veered in the woman's direction. She reached inside her coat and pulled one of her FBI contact cards from her shirt pocket.

She held the card out to Morgan Farrell.

The young woman glanced to see that her husband wasn't watching. Then she hastily took the card and tucked it into her bra.

Riley continued on her way. There was nothing she or Bill could do—right now. But if Morgan Farrell ever reached out to her, something would surely happen then.

She and Bill got back into the car, and Bill started to drive.

"That was a waste of our time," Bill said.

It was true, of course. But Riley saw no point in saying so.

"So what do we do now?" Bill asked.

"Get back to Quantico right now," Riley said. "We've still got work to do. There are some things in this world that we *can* change."

CHAPTER FIFTEEN

Riley was in complete darkness. She had no idea where, but she could hear a voice calling.

"Mom! Mom!"

April's voice!

But where is she? *Riley wondered.*

And where am I?

It dawned on her that she was in the Penningtons' garage again.

It was even darker than before, and it was a vast space with no walls in sight.

Then a light came on straight above her. She looked up and saw sparkling crystals arranged in elaborate clusters. It was one of Andrew Farrell's grotesque chandeliers.

A chandelier in a garage! *Riley thought.*

It was vulgar and weird. And the light didn't carry very far into the darkness.

But it did illuminate a circle of doors standing shut around her.

She heard April's voice again.

"Mom!"

Riley tried to reply, but no voice came out of her throat.

Where had April's voice come from?

Surely from behind one of the doors. She thought she knew which one.

She rushed forward and opened the door.

Instead of April, a strange girl was hanging dead by a rope. Dozens of family photographs were scattered at her feet.

Riley backed away with horror.

Then she heard April's voice again.

"Mom!"

The voice seemed to be coming from the opposite side of the circle of doors.

Riley turned and rushed over to that door and pulled it open.

Again, a girl was hanging there, with pictures below her dangling feet.

Then came April's voice from behind another door.

"Mom!"

Riley felt something seize her by the shoulder—

"Mom!"

Riley's eyes snapped open, then she squinted against the light. It took her a moment to realize that she was lying in bed at home. April was standing beside her bed, shaking her awake.

Riley looked blearily at her daughter.

"What time is it?" she asked.

"Ten o'clock. You were sleeping late—and really hard."

Riley realized it was Sunday. She wasn't expected at the BAU this morning.

April added, "You were moaning. Were you having a nightmare?"

Riley didn't answer the question. Looking around, she saw that the bed was quite rumpled.

She was starting to remember now.

She'd gotten home from Atlanta late last night. Ryan had been here, asleep in bed. But he'd woken up as soon as she'd climbed in with him.

And then ...

Riley smiled at the memory. Maybe things were going to work out with Ryan after all.

"Mom, you've got to get up," April said. "Something's happened."

Riley sat bolt upright with alarm.

"Are you OK? And your dad? Jilly? Gabriela?"

"It's nothing bad," April said. "Dad and Jilly are downstairs eating breakfast. But this is important. Tiffany just got here."

Riley rubbed her eyes, trying to remember.

Oh, yes. Tiffany. April's friend—and the sister of the dead girl, Lois Pennington.

April said, "Tiffany didn't want to go to church with her parents. It was a week ago today that ... they found Lois. She wanted to be here instead. So they dropped her off."

Riley was surprised. When she'd visited the Penningtons, they hadn't seemed happy with her. On the other hand, they did know Ryan and they surely had nothing against him or April.

April continued, "Anyway, Tiffany and I thought of something. You really need to hear about it. Come on downstairs. I'll get you some coffee."

"I'll get dressed," Riley said.

April left the room, and Riley heard her footsteps going down the stairs.

Riley went to the bathroom, splashed water on her face, and combed her hair. She pulled on a pair of jeans and a sweatshirt and looked at herself in the mirror.

She turned around and smiled. She liked what she saw.

Mom jeans suit me, she thought. *Comfortable and practical.*

Of course, after last night, she thought she could feel sexy wearing a burlap sack.

Just as Riley finished dressing, April came back into her room and handed her a hot cup of coffee. Riley took a few sips, then they went downstairs.

Tiffany was sitting on the living room couch. Riley could see that the girl looked tired, but not nearly as distraught as she'd been the last time she'd seen her.

Ryan stepped out of the kitchen and called out to Riley.

"Want to join us for breakfast? Gabriela's made fried plantain and eggs. Delicious!"

He leered at Riley and winked.

Riley smiled back, remembering last night.

Then she blushed.

She hoped everyone in the house hadn't heard their intense lovemaking.

April said, "We'll be there in a few minutes, Dad. Tiffany too."

"OK," Ryan said, then disappeared back into the kitchen.

Riley and April sat down with Tiffany.

April said to Riley, "I just told Tiffany that the FBI opened a case about her sister and the others."

"Thank you," Tiffany said weakly. "My parents still believe it was—"

She couldn't finish the sentence. Then she said, "So can I talk to you about it? Is that OK?"

"Of course," Riley said.

Tiffany looked relieved but anxious.

"Well, I remembered something this morning," she said. "Lois had a friend at school who lived in the same dorm. Her name is Piper Durst. I met her once or twice at Byars. She's very nice. She called me for a video chat last Tuesday to tell me how sorry she was. I thanked her, but I asked her some questions."

"What sorts of questions?" Riley asked.

Tiffany shrugged slightly.

"I just wanted to know how Lois had seemed shortly before it happened. I mean, was she really depressed? Did she *seem* suicidal?"

"What did Piper say?" April asked.

"She said that Lois had seemed fine. The whole thing came as a complete shock to her. She couldn't understand it. But she also said ..."

Tiffany paused for a moment, then said, "She said that Lois had told her about some strange sort of guy she'd been talking to. She didn't say anything else about him. But it seems kind of odd that she'd mention him at all."

Tiffany looked at Riley.

"Do you think that might mean anything?" she asked.

"It might," Riley said. "Have you got her address for video chats?"

"Sure," Tiffany said.

April rushed upstairs to get her laptop computer. Then Riley, April, and Tiffany gathered around it and made the call.

Piper Durst was an ordinary-looking girl with dark, curly hair. Behind her, Riley could see a disheveled-looking dorm room, much like the one she'd had herself at college years ago. Riley didn't think she looked old enough to be a college freshman. But then, Riley was feeling that way more and more about young people. As she got older, kids seemed younger.

The girl smiled when she saw Tiffany's face crowded between Riley and April.

"Hey, Tiff! I've been thinking about you. How are you holding up?"

"OK, I guess," Tiffany said. "Listen, this is my friend April. And this lady is April's mother, Riley Paige. She's an FBI agent. And she's investigating some of the suicides that have been happening at Byars—including Lois."

The girl's eyes widened.

"The FBI? Holy shit!" Then she put her hand to her mouth and said, "Pardon my language."

"It's OK, Mom's cool," April said.

Piper squinted as she struggled to comprehend what the callers were saying.

"But why would the FBI be investigating a bunch of suicides? I know it's weird that there have been so many of them, but—"

Then she grew pale.

"Oh my God! You don't think they're suicides! You think those kids were—"

She stopped talking.

"We don't know what to think just yet," Riley said. "But Tiffany told me you might know something important. Before Lois died, did she say something about a strange guy?"

Piper thought for a moment.

"Well, yeah. But she didn't say much about him."

"Was she scared of him?" Riley asked.

"No, I don't think so. He was a student, she said. She said she didn't know whether to like him or feel sorry for him. But she said he was nice, and she liked to talk to him. I just got the feeling that he was kind of uncool somehow, and maybe Lois was feeling weird about getting to know him. Like she was a little embarrassed."

Tiffany looked at Riley and said, "Lois used to get crushes on odd sorts of guys. They ranged from jocks to nerds and every type in between, but they were a little offbeat one way or another. People sometimes made fun of her for it. She used to tell me about guys like that when she was still in high school and living at home. Sort of like she was asking whether it was OK to date them. Sometimes she did, sometimes she didn't. Whenever I met them, I thought they were OK."

Riley was rapidly taking notes.

She asked Piper, "Did she say anything else about him? His name? What year he was in school? Anything about what he looked like?"

"Not a word," Piper said.

Riley realized that the girl had told her all that she knew.

"Thanks for talking with me, Piper," Riley said. "I've got to ask you to keep quiet about this for now. Don't tell anybody."

The girl looked startled.

"Are you kidding? With a killer loose on campus? Shouldn't we all be watching out for this guy? Are any of us safe?"

Riley understood the girl's alarm. But the last thing anybody needed right now was an outburst of uncontrolled panic on the Byars campus.

Riley said, "I'll make sure the BAU releases a warning as soon as possible. But please, for the time being, don't say anything. Give me a chance to make it official."

Piper shook her head.

"Wow. OK, I guess. But I'll be scared to leave my room."

You're probably wise, Riley thought.

But she didn't say so aloud.

Riley thanked Piper again and they ended the call. Tiffany and April went to the kitchen for breakfast. But Riley didn't join them.

There's danger on that campus, she thought.

And she had to make sure that the students were warned about it.

CHAPTER SIXTEEN

For a moment, Riley couldn't think how to handle this. She had to get a warning out to Byars students as quickly as possible, and in a way that didn't cause a panic. Then she realized where she could get help.

Lucy Vargas was planning to work today. And Riley had meant to call her anyway to get an update. She picked up her phone and dialed Lucy's number.

"Hey, Riley. I'm glad you called," Lucy said. "I went to the Yoh residence yesterday and interviewed Constance's parents."

Riley listened eagerly. She knew little about Constance Yoh's death except that she'd been found hanging at home and had taken a high dose of alprazolam.

"What did her parents tell you?" Riley asked.

"They said they'd been worried about Constance's grades. They hadn't been *perfect,* they said—slipping below a 4.0 GPA. They said Constance had been worried too. Can you imagine that? Having your parents expect you to do everything perfectly? The pressure must have been awful."

Lucy's words made Riley wonder—had Constance Yoh committed suicide after all? And if she had, might Riley be wrong about all the other students? So far she hadn't proven that any of the deaths had been murders. Maybe she was wrong. Maybe she'd gotten this investigation underway over nothing.

If so, the last thing she wanted to do was cause a panic at Byars.

"What else did the parents tell you?" Riley asked.

"Well, it was kind of weird," Lucy said. "They're sure Constance didn't commit suicide. But it wasn't so much because they didn't think she *would* commit suicide. They just knew that she wouldn't do it that way. She would surely have left a note, they said, but she didn't. Also, it looked like she'd climbed a ladder to hang herself. But that was impossible, they said. She was too scared of heights—any kind of heights at all. She'd never been able to climb a ladder in her life."

"Not even if she'd been drugged up with alprazolam?" Riley asked.

"Well, that was another thing. She'd been taking anti-anxiety medication. But it was lorazepam, not alprazolam. There was no way she'd have deliberately overdosed on alprazolam instead."

So it was definitely murder, Riley thought.

But she didn't feel relieved about being right.

"Lucy, I need for you to do something," Riley said. "The students at Byars need to be warned about a possible killer. But we mustn't cause a panic. Can you get to work on that for me?"

"Sure," Lucy said. "What do you think we should say?"

Riley thought for a moment. Should she say that the killer might be a male student who didn't quite fit in?

No, she still didn't have enough information to be even that specific.

"Kids just need to watch out for any unusual interactions with other people on campus—either total strangers, or people they know who are acting strangely. And they should report anything strange immediately. They should especially avoid situations in which someone might deliberately slip them any kind of drugs."

"Anything else?"

Riley paused again. Yes, there was something that Lucy needed to know.

"To put out this warning, you're going to have to deal with Dean Willis Autrey. He's a jerk. He's liable to give you some resistance."

"I'm sure I can handle him," Lucy said.

Riley felt sure that Lucy was right. The young agent dealt with people better than Riley did. And this would be a good learning experience for her. Coping with hitches from people in power was an important part of the job.

Riley thanked Lucy and ended the call.

What do I do next? Riley wondered.

She realized that she was still sleepy. She needed to finish her coffee and get some breakfast. She went into the kitchen and joined her family.

*

After breakfast, Riley went to her office upstairs. She figured she was due for another visit to Byars College tomorrow, and she would have to meet again with Dean Autrey. Perhaps after talking with Lucy, Autrey would be more inclined to be helpful.

But Riley doubted it.

If he's given in on something, he's likely to get more stubborn than ever, she thought.

What could she do to change that?

Lucy would do her job right away. Riley also knew someone who might be able to help her.

She got on her computer and called up forensic psychiatrist Mike Nevins at home for a video chat.

"Riley!" Mike said when he appeared. "What a surprise! But I don't assume that this is a social call."

Riley was amused to see that the fussy, meticulous man looked as dapper as always, even on a morning away from work. It felt good to see him. He'd done a lot of consulting work on cases with her, and had counseled her through some of her own PTSD.

"Mike, have you heard about the Byars College case? The so-called suicides?"

"Yes, I heard that you managed to get the case off the ground with your usual panache. Poor Walder! You must drive him out of his mind."

Riley chuckled.

"I try," she said. "Anyway, I'm dealing with a serious psych case at Byars—a man who is paranoid and anal and pathologically uncooperative."

"Ah! A university administrator!"

Riley grinned. He'd picked up on her punch line.

"That's right. Willis Autrey is the dean of the college. He's been giving us a lot of pushback. He wasn't even straight with us about the number of so-called suicides there have been during this school year."

Mike stroked his chin thoughtfully.

"Well, he's got his own agenda. Reputation is everything for a prestigious school like that. It doesn't look good to have a homicidal maniac killing kids on campus. Try to see it from his point of view. And of course, he's too pathologically shortsighted to see that more murders aren't to the school's advantage. But first things first. Have the students been warned about the danger?"

"I've got Agent Lucy Vargas working on that," Riley said. "With luck, she'll get a warning out today. Autrey isn't going to like it, though. And he's liable to be in an especially bad mood when I go in to talk to him again tomorrow."

"Yessss, I suppose he will," Mike said.

He paused to think for a moment.

"Do you think the killer is a student?" he asked.

"I don't know yet. But it seems likely. All the victims that we

93

know about were students."

"If so, the killer may very well have a record at Byars for mental problems. You need to get that information from Autrey. Easier said than done, of course."

He thought again briefly.

"I could write a letter. You could take it with you tomorrow. I could say that I'm working as a consultant on the case, and that I'm requesting a subpoena to check the school's records for psychiatric problems."

"Can you actually do that?" Riley asked. "Ask for a subpoena, I mean, based on what little we know at this point?"

Mike chuckled.

"I don't know," he said. "But I doubt that he does either."

Riley laughed a little too.

Mike added, "Judging from my clinical knowledge of anal, paranoid college administrators, he won't want things to get that far. I've got a hunch that he'll be a lot more cooperative with you then. Who should I contact at the BAU to offer my services, making my involvement official? Walder, maybe?"

Riley shuddered slightly.

"No, not him. He wants nothing to do with this case. Right now Meredith's the man in charge."

"Ah. Meredith. Excellent. I'll write a letter right away and email it to you as a PDF."

"Thanks so much, Mike. I knew I could count on you."

Mike sat gazing at Riley for a few seconds.

"It's been a long time, Riley," he said. "How are you doing these days?"

Riley knew Mike's concern was both personal and professional.

"I'm better," she said. "The PTSD is really lifting."

"Do you still get nightmares?"

Riley hesitated.

"Sometimes," she said, downplaying the truth. She'd actually been having quite a few nightmares. "They tend to be about feeling helpless when people I love are in danger. April especially."

"That's understandable, considering everything you and your loved ones have been through. Maybe you should come by and talk about it sometime."

"I'll consider it," she said. "I appreciate your concern."

She thanked Mike for his help, and they ended the call.

Riley sat at her desk quietly for a few minutes. It began to dawn on her that there was a whole lot going on in her life that Mike Nevins knew nothing about—the adoption of Jilly, trying to put things together with Ryan.

But the truth was, she didn't want counseling about any of that. It would be nice to see Mike, but not if he was going to get all analytical. Maybe he really could help. But right now, Riley was determinedly putting one foot in front of the other, taking one day at a time. Talking to Mike would only make things more complicated.

There was a knock at the door, and April came in.

"Tiffany just left with her parents," April said. "Are you working on the case right now?"

"As a matter of fact, I am," Riley said. "I just talked to someone who's going to help. I'm going back to Byars College tomorrow. I'll call Bill—he's working on the case and I'm sure he'll go with me. Maybe we can find out more this time."

April smiled happily.

"That's so great, Mom! I can't tell you what it means to Tiffany. It means a lot to me too."

Then April's smile faded.

"I'm sorry I got so mad at you about it," she said.

Riley got up from her chair and put her arm around her daughter.

"Don't be," she said. "You were right. Sometimes it's good to light a fire under me."

April laughed.

"Well, with you and Bill on the case, the killer doesn't stand a chance."

Riley's spirits sank a little.

She could remember a few cases that she hadn't been able to solve, cases that had gone cold. Every FBI agent had faced some of those.

April didn't know about any of that.

And she couldn't bring herself to tell her.

Instead, she gave April a strong hug.

"What's that for?" April giggled, crushed up against her mother.

For luck, Riley thought.

But she didn't say so aloud.

She knew she was going to need a lot of luck to solve this one before someone else died.

CHAPTER SEVENTEEN

Murray clawed at the rope around his neck. The noose was tightening, and his consciousness was flickering. He was choking and gasping. Try as he might, he couldn't loosen the noose with his fingers.

I can't let this happen, he thought.

But he was dizzy from the loss of blood to his brain, and also from the drug.

He had seconds left before he'd fade away for good.

He struggled to think clearly.

He knew the ladder was nearby. Somehow he had to get to one of its steps to slacken the rope.

He swung toward the ladder, but then his weight carried him pendulum-like away from it, and the rope tightened more with the movement.

On his second swing, one foot hooked the ladder, and the other foot secured his hold on it.

The ladder rattled and lurched wildly with his moving body, its legs dancing on the concrete garage floor.

He couldn't let it fall over!

If that happened, it would be all over. He wouldn't stand a chance.

But to his own amazement, he managed to stabilize the ladder, then anchor both feet on one of its steps.

The rope slackened a little. But the pressure around his neck went unrelieved. The noose was still as tight as before. He continued to pull at the noose with his fingers, but the knot seemed to be stuck.

He could breathe just a little now, but the lack of blood flow made him increasingly dizzy.

He wasn't safe yet.

Far from it.

At this rate, he would still pass out.

When that happened, he'd tumble off the ladder to certain death.

Shelves full of garden tools were close by. He glanced sideways. Yes, there were the garden shears on the nearest shelf.

Could he reach those shears?

His arms flailed toward the shears. But they were just beyond his reach.

With his feet still on the ladder, he leaned toward the shelf. The swaying movement almost sent him into a fatal swoon. But now he was near enough to grasp the shears.

His hands and arms were tingling and numb. Even so, he managed to get hold of the shears, and he held them in front of him.

He knew what he had to do next.

He had to cut the rope above his head.

It ought to be simple and easy. The rope wasn't very thick, and the shears were sharp. A single swift slice ought to do it.

But his consciousness was waning, and he could barely feel the handles in his tingling grip.

Still, he managed to open the shears and raise them above his head.

With a great effort, he closed the shears, but they didn't seem to connect with the rope.

Panicked now, he sliced wildly, again and again.

Then came a moment of complete blackness.

He seemed to be sinking through space.

The next thing he knew, he lay on the cold garage floor, his body hurting from the blow. For a moment he wondered where he was. Then he realized that he'd cut the rope and fallen. The noose was too tight, and he still couldn't loosen it with his fingers.

He saw that the shears had fallen right next to him.

He picked them up, opened them slightly, and slid a sharp blade under the noose.

It took only one sharp slice this time.

The rope fell away from his neck.

He crouched on the floor on his hands and knees, coughing and gasping and retching.

Was he out of danger?

Almost, he realized, but not quite.

The drug was still in his system, and its effect was building.

If he didn't do something quickly, he'd pass out, and possibly slip into a coma, or even die.

He had to get out of the garage and get help from somebody.

One of the big doors that led to the street wasn't closed all the way. It had been left raised a couple of feet. He should be able to get under it.

He was so dizzy that he could barely tell up from down, but he summoned his strength and crawled toward the opening. Then he lay flat and rolled under the door.

He was out into the driveway.

His whole body felt the shock of exhilaration.

He tried to call out.

"Somebody help!"

But he could only make a hoarse, rasping sound.

He felt himself losing what was left of his lucidity.

Got to keep crawling, he thought dimly. *Keep crawling until I find somebody.*

He crawled and crawled. Then he heard the sound of an approaching car engine, and he was bathed in light. He was barely aware enough to understand what was happening. A car was approaching—and he was in the middle of the street!

He turned his head and saw a pair of blinding headlights. A car horn blasted through the night, followed by the screech of skidding tires.

Then he lost consciousness altogether.

CHAPTER EIGHTEEN

The next morning, Riley and Bill arrived at Byars College as early as the administrative offices would be open. As Bill drove into the campus, Riley saw that the students they passed were hunched against the cold, hurrying about and avoiding each other's eyes.

"Wow, these kids look scared," Bill commented. "The warning Lucy called in must have really had an impact."

Riley said, "Actually, they're acting pretty much the same as the last time I was here."

Bill shook his head.

"This place gives me the creeps," he said.

Riley felt exactly the same way. She felt sure that Byars was a miserable place to go to school, even when there wasn't a murderer stalking the campus.

Bill parked the car, and then he and Riley made their way to the dean's office, where they found the atmosphere as chilly as the weather outside.

The secretary greeted them coldly. Of course, she recognized Riley right away.

"Dean Autrey isn't on campus today," the woman said. "He can't be reached. He's attending a very important conference."

Riley was sure that the woman was lying and that she was following the orders of the dean. A glance at Bill told Riley that he thought so too.

"That's no problem," Riley said, pulling Mike Nevins's letter out of her bag. "I'm sure you can take care of this for us."

She handed the letter to the secretary. The woman's face grew pale as she read it.

Riley suppressed a smile. She knew that her psychiatrist friend was well known and respected in the nation's capital.

The letter stated Mike Nevins's concern that a mentally troubled killer was at large at Byars. It also said that Mike was requesting a subpoena for the school's records, and that he was sure that it would be granted.

It was, of course, written in Mike Nevins's inimitable style— formal and almost painfully polite.

And Riley knew that it was all the more effective because of its politeness.

It was like Mike had told her once …

"Politeness is scarier."

Sometimes Riley wished she could cultivate a little of Mike's brand of scary politeness. But it just wasn't her style.

The woman got up from her desk and went into the inner office. Riley and Bill could hear some noisy grumbling from in there. Soon the tall, silver-haired dean came stalking out, gripping the letter in his hand. He looked anything but pleased, and his customary formality was more than a little ruffled.

"You really don't give up, do you?" Autrey said.

Riley suppressed a smile. She wanted to say, *As a matter of fact, I don't.*

Instead, she introduced Autrey to Bill.

Then she said, "Sorry to trouble you. We were somehow under the impression that you weren't on campus."

"I'm not," Autrey sputtered confusedly. "I mean, I'm just on my way—somewhere important. First thing Monday morning, and you've already ruined my schedule."

Glancing toward the rattled secretary, Bill said, "Oh. Sorry for the misunderstanding."

Autrey said, "Well, if you came around to see if I complied about that silly warning, don't worry. The whole campus has been alerted about this imaginary killer of yours. Aside from causing a lot of undue worry, it's proven a great excuse to cut classes. Students are staying away in droves."

He peered at the letter through his narrow reading glasses, muttering.

"Such nonsense … Palpable baloney … A huge fuss about nothing …"

He looked up at Riley and Bill.

"I assure you that nobody has ever murdered anyone at Byars. Ever."

"So would you like us to get a subpoena?" Bill asked.

Autrey growled and shoved the letter at the secretary.

"Miss Engstrand, give them whatever they want," he said. "Sorry to put you to the trouble. I've got to go."

He grabbed his coat off the coat rack and stormed out of the office.

The secretary sat gaping at Riley and Bill.

"What do you want me to do?" she asked.

Bill began to explain.

"We need information on students, staff, graduates—anyone

who may have had major psychological issues …"

As Bill continued, Riley's phone buzzed. The call was from Meredith.

"Agent Paige, where are you right now?" he asked.

Riley gulped. Was she going to have to explain the gambit she and Mike Nevins had used to obtain records? She doubted that he would approve.

"I'm at Byars College with Agent Jeffreys," Riley said.

"I need the two of you to head straight over to Brandenburg Memorial Hospital."

Riley was surprised that he didn't seem the least bit curious about what she and Bill were doing.

"That's right here in DC, isn't it?" she asked.

"Right. It looks like someone survived an attack by our killer. He's in the ER there."

"He?" Riley thought.

After finding out that Kirk Farrell really had committed suicide, she'd assumed that the killer was only targeting females.

"His name is Murray Rossum, and he's a Byars freshman. He was found in the street outside of his home late last night, barely conscious. According to the police, he'd been drugged and hanged in the family garage. It was a miracle that he got away alive."

"Is he able to talk?"

"It's my understanding that he's conscious. I don't know whether he's talking or not."

Riley felt a tingle of excitement. This could be an unexpected break.

"We'll head right over there," Riley said.

She and Meredith ended the call. Bill had just finished explaining what he wanted to the secretary. She was already bringing up information on her computer.

"This will take some time," the woman grumbled.

"We need this as fast as you can get it," Bill said.

Riley took Bill aside.

"We've got to get to Brandenburg Memorial Hospital," she said. "Someone seems to have survived an attack—a guy this time."

Bill looked surprised.

"Sounds like my theory that he might be bisexual might have legs again," he said.

"Could be," Riley said. "Let's go."

As Bill drove, Riley exchanged text messages with Flores, who gave her as much information as he could put together about Murray Rossum. He was a very wealthy kid, the son of international real estate mogul Henry Rossum. The father had houses all over the world, but apparently Murray lived only in Georgetown. It seemed that Murray was Henry Rossum's only heir and offspring. Rossum had long ago divorced the boy's mother with a substantial settlement, and she had conveniently withdrawn from the scene.

Bill parked the car, and when they got out Riley could see that Brandenburg Memorial Hospital was a glittering glass tower of modern design, obviously a prestigious and expensive hospital.

They went inside and presented their badges to the receptionist, who directed them to the floor where Murray Rossum was being cared for. As they approached the room, they were stopped by a tall, distinguished-looking doctor.

"Hold it right there," he told Riley and Bill. "My patient isn't seeing any visitors."

Again, Riley and Bill showed their badges.

"We understand he was the victim of a homicidal attack," Bill said. "We have reason to believe it was part of a series of murders of Byars College students."

"Is Murray Rossum able to talk?" Riley asked.

The doctor wrinkled his brow with concern.

"He's in and out of consciousness," he said. "We expect a full recovery from his physical injuries and from the dose of alprazolam his attacker gave him. But the emotional trauma is another matter. That might take years."

"We understand your concern," Bill said. "But this is a matter of life and death. The killer is likely to strike again, and very soon."

The doctor thought for a moment.

"I'll allow it," he said. "But I want to be present. And I'll decide when to cut things short."

"That's fine," Riley said.

When they all walked into the room, the patient seemed to be asleep. But at the sound of their footsteps, he opened his eyes and looked at them.

He was a slight, sandy-haired young man with a soft, almost feminine face. His neck was bandaged, and he was on an IV line.

The doctor said, "Murray, you've got visitors from the FBI.

They're here to find out what happened to you."

Murray's large eyes widened.

"The FBI!" he said in a croaking voice. "Oh, thank God!"

CHAPTER NINETEEN

Murray Rossum looked on the verge of weeping.

Riley understood that the boy's anguished expression was from sheer relief at being able to tell his story. He seemed especially moved that he was able to talk to FBI agents. But he didn't seem to be quite able to actually cry.

He's too exhausted, Riley thought. She knew how that felt too. *Crying will come later.*

Her heart went out to him as she remembered her own long struggles against PTSD. She hoped that he had the emotional fortitude to pull through it. But as the doctor had said, that might take years.

She noticed how small he was—and at the moment, extremely fragile.

While the doctor stood to one side, Riley and Bill sat next to the bed in comfortable upholstered chairs. The room was plush and spacious. If it weren't for the adjustable bed, the IV stand, and other medical necessities, it might be mistaken for an expensive hotel room. Murray was obviously getting the best medical care possible and some extra comforts too.

At least he's lucky in that sense, Riley thought.

"We're here to find out what happened," Riley said.

"How much of it can you remember?" Bill asked.

Murray seemed to struggle with his thoughts.

"Sometimes I feel like I remember everything, then it all gets hazy," he said.

"Try to take us back to when it all started," Bill said.

"Take your time," Riley added.

Although the truth was, Riley was sure that time was in short supply. A killer was still out there, but she realized she couldn't rush this interview.

Murray's eyes roamed about, unfocused.

"There was a party last night at Pi Delta Beta, my fraternity," Murray said.

He fell silent. Riley wondered if he was going to be capable of putting together any kind of narrative. She and Bill needed to nudge him along.

"Was it for frat brothers only?" she asked.

"No, our parties are always pretty much open to anybody.

Keeps things from getting too boring, the guys say. And we get more girls that way."

He seemed to lose his train of thought.

"Was your attacker at the party?" Bill asked.

Murray nodded painfully.

"Yeah. He was by himself, off in a corner, with a six-pack of beer. I went over and said hello. He said his name was …"

He struggled to remember.

"Dane, I think. Something odd like that. But now I don't know if that was his real name. Maybe he just made it up."

Riley sensed that he needed encouragement.

"You're doing just fine. Can you remember what he looked like?"

Murray closed his eyes in concentration.

"Wow, that's tough. I just can't picture him. You'd think I could remember."

Riley understood. People often repressed the memories of an attacker's appearance, at least initially. But if she urged him on little by little, maybe more of what the guy looked like would come back to him.

"What did you talk about?" Bill asked.

"Well, he offered me a beer, it was open already, and I took it. He admitted he felt kind of out of place. He said …"

Then something clicked in Murray's expression.

"Oh, now I remember something about how he looked. He was overdressed for the party, wearing a suit jacket and a tie. That's how I knew he wasn't a rich guy. He was trying too hard to fit in, didn't quite know how to do it. And I … well, I don't know, I just …"

Murray looked oddly embarrassed.

"I guess I kind of made myself sound like a big shot. God, I hate it when people act all high and mighty because they're rich. Especially around people who haven't got a lot of money. But we all do that, I guess. When you go to a school like Byars, where almost everybody's loaded, you don't get a lot of chances to show off. Especially at a fraternity like Pi."

He made a hoarse, scoffing sound.

"I know this sounds weird, but being rich sucks sometimes."

Riley noticed that Bill flinched at this remark. It must have sounded awfully patronizing to him. But Riley could halfway understand what Murray meant. From being a lawyer's wife, she knew that life with a fair amount of money could be an empty life. You couldn't buy real friends. Perhaps that was a real problem for Murray.

But once again, Murray's mind seemed to be drifting. She had to keep him on topic.

"What happened next?" Riley asked.

"Well, it seemed like I really did impress him with my bullshit, and he asked me lots of questions about how I lived, and what my house was like. He said something like, 'Wow, it sounds like you live in a mansion or something.' I said, no, it was really just a really big townhouse, and I kept on describing it to him. He said he'd never even set foot in a place like that."

Murray paused a moment.

Riley said, "Try to relax. Let all the details come to you."

"Try to remember what happened from moment to moment," Bill added. "Try not to skip anything."

Murray nodded uncomfortably again.

"That was when I decided to take him to my house." He looked at them a little anxiously, as if to be sure what he was saying was all right.

"Go on," Riley said.

"I mean, the party was boring. He said something like he could swing either way. I thought well, why not. I'm not gay, you understand. But I'm not narrow-minded either. So I thought, what the hell, he could even stay the night if he liked."

"So you suggested he go home with you?" Riley prompted him.

"I knew that whenever I did go home that night, nobody would be there, just the live-in help, and they'd all be asleep. And I said, 'Let me finish my beer, and I'll drive you there.'"

Murray squinted and frowned.

"But he seemed to be in a hurry. He said something like, 'Why wait? We can drink our brewskies on the way over.'"

He looked a little embarrassed again.

"Look, I know it's illegal to drive with open containers in a car, let alone in your hand, and I don't normally do that. But I didn't want to seem uncool. So I said OK, and we headed out to my car. It's a big Lincoln, and he seemed really impressed. He said he drove around in a broken down old pickup."

Riley mentally seized on that detail. So far, it was the most valuable bit of solid information Murray had offered. Maybe she could coax more out of him.

"Can you remember anything else about what he looked like?" she asked.

His face flickered again with a memory.

"Yeah, maybe. He was a big guy. I don't mean fat, I just mean big, athletic, like a football player."

"How tall do you think he was?" Bill asked. "Six feet or so?"

"No, he wasn't that tall, maybe five nine or ten. It's just that he was … big."

Riley was slightly surprised. She'd been all but sure that the killer was smaller. The girls who had been killed had all been of slight build, and Murray himself looked scarcely larger than they'd been. Once again, she found herself wondering whether her instincts were starting to fail.

"Do you remember anything about his voice?" Riley asked.

Murray looked straight at her.

"Yeah, it was … well, kind of high-pitched, odd-sounding for a guy that big. And he had an accent, not like he was from around here. Maybe somewhere up north. Maybe New York or Boston or someplace like that."

"Did he say anything about where he lived or what he did for a living?" Bill asked.

Murray glanced back and forth between Riley and Bill.

"Just somewhere in DC, I think he said. I don't remember if he said anything about work except … oh, yeah. He said something about how he used his truck for his job. Maybe he said something else about it. I can't remember."

Bill was about to ask another question, but Riley silenced him with a gesture. If they pushed him too hard, he might not make it through his story.

Murray continued. "About the time I started driving, I was feeling really weird, like I was drugged. I hadn't drunk much of the beer yet, but I wondered if maybe he'd put something in it. And then I got scared. I wondered why he'd want to drug me. Then it occurred to me … maybe it was for sex."

Riley could see the alarm in Murray's eyes.

"I started feeling really freaked. I mean, you hear all about date rape, but guys never think it will happen to them. And there I was, in this car with a guy who was so much bigger and stronger than me. I'd never have imagined …"

His voice drifted off and he shuddered. Riley was worried.

Might he shut down as his memories became more frightening?

"Try to relax," she said again. "Take it slowly."

Murray gulped hard.

"Well, I pretended to finish my beer, then put the can in the cup holder. It's still there, maybe."

Riley hoped so. It could be a crucial piece of evidence.

"Go on," she said.

Murray twisted about uncomfortably.

"By the time we got to my house and pulled into my garage, I was really out of it. I barely understood what was going on. I'm not sure if I can remember …"

"Please try," Bill said.

Murray's face tightened as he tried to focus his memory.

"As soon as I turned off the car engine, I went absolutely limp. I was still conscious, but it was like I didn't have any control over my body. Dane unbuckled my shoulder harness and dragged me out of the car like I was a limp rag. I think I may have tried to ask what he was doing, but I'm not sure any words came out."

Riley tried to visualize what he was saying.

I really need to see that garage, she thought.

Murray continued, "He let me down in a heap on the floor. Then he set up an aluminum ladder we keep in the garage. He put something over my head and around my neck. It took me a few seconds to realize it was a noose. But I couldn't even struggle by then. He pulled me by the rope up the ladder, then swung the other end of the rope over a rafter. He tied the rope in place and pulled the ladder out from under me."

Murray groaned at the terrible memory.

"After he was gone, I somehow managed to get my feet back on the ladder. Then I cut the rope with something …"

He glanced around as if trying to see what he had used. "Was it garden shears?"

Riley waited while the boy collected his memories again.

"Yes," he said. "It must have been the garden shears. Then I must have passed out because I woke up on the floor of the garage."

He seemed confused, as though he had lost track of the story again.

"How did you get out of the garage?" Bill asked.

"There was an opening, I think. Yes, that's it. The door wasn't closed all the way. I managed to crawl out and into the street. Then car lights …"

He stopped again, breathing hard. Then he continued, "Car lights coming toward me and I heard a horn and I thought I was going to get run over."

He stopped talking for a long moment.

"That's it. That's all I can remember. The next thing I knew, I was … here."

At last, tears welled up in his eyes and a sob forced its way out of his throat. The doctor stepped over to the bed.

"That's enough," he said to Riley and Bill. "You've got to leave right now."

Riley didn't have to be told twice. She knew perfectly well that the doctor was right. She and Bill left the hospital room.

As they left the hospital, Riley realized that she was shaking.

It was from empathy with the young man's horror.

It was also from fear that someone else might soon be less lucky.

We've got no time to lose, she thought.

CHAPTER TWENTY

Riley was anxious to get a look at the garage where Murray had almost died. Maybe at the crime scene she would be able to get into the mind of this killer. That often worked for her, and they badly needed some kind of insight if they were going to stop this one before he killed again. So that's where she and Bill were headed next.

As Bill drove, Riley realized that she needed psychological input from Mike Nevins. She called him and told him about the interview with Murray.

"You guys did good work," Mike said.

"Maybe," Riley said. "But I get the feeling he's repressing a lot."

"You can count on it."

Mike paused for a moment.

Then he said, "I'll tell you what—I'll go over to the hospital and interview him myself. I'll take a sketch artist along."

"Do you really think you'll be able to get a description of the suspect?" she asked.

"I'll try."

"Great. Let me know how it works out."

Riley felt relieved as she ended the call. She knew that a skilled psychologist like Mike could get a lot more information out of the young man than she and Bill had managed to do.

Meanwhile, there was plenty else to think about.

"Where do you think we are with the case?" Riley asked Bill.

Bill shook his head as he drove.

"I don't know, Riley. About all we've got so far is a big guy with a high-pitched voice and an eastern accent who drives a pickup. He seems to work at some kind of job that he needs a pickup for. And he's not a Byars student."

"It's a good guess that he lives somewhere in DC," Riley said.

"Yeah, but where does that get us? It doesn't sound like Murray ever saw the pickup, so we don't know the make or year or anything else about it. How many pickups do you think there are in a city with more than a half a million people?"

Riley didn't reply. But she couldn't help but agree with Bill. They didn't have a lot to go on so far. She hoped Mike would have some success with the sketch artist.

As they drove up to Murray Rossum's home, Riley was a bit surprised that it wasn't larger. Murray had talked about using it to impress the suspect, but it didn't strike Riley as especially impressive. It was a much bigger townhouse than her own, but a townhouse nonetheless. It hardly seemed like a mansion.

They had been told that the garage entrance was on a street behind the house, so they drove around to the back. From what Riley could see of the house from behind, she realized that it was much, much larger than it had looked from the front. But she still couldn't get an idea of its true scale.

Bill parked in the driveway, where he and Riley were greeted by Trey Beeler, head of the BAU's forensic unit. Riley and Bill had worked with him a lot over the years. It looked like Trey and his team of three were just finishing up their work at the crime scene.

Trey walked toward them grinning.

"Murder, eh?" he said. "Sure looks like suicide to me."

Riley was sure that Trey had heard about all the trouble she had gotten into about this case. Now he was teasing her about it.

"Looks like murder to me," she said. "And I haven't even gotten a look at the crime scene yet."

Trey chuckled grimly.

"Well, you should know. You're the one with the legendary instincts. I guess that's why you're bringing in the big bucks."

He was still teasing Riley. She didn't know what Trey's salary was, but she doubted that she was making as much as he was. With all his medical degrees, he was a notch above her in the BAU food chain. But she wasn't going to start bantering with him about it right now. She wasn't in the mood for it.

"What have you got so far?" Riley asked him.

"We're just finishing up," Trey said. "Come on, I'll show you."

He led Riley and Bill toward an open garage door. She saw that another one of the big doors was raised a little—just as Murray had said.

That's how he got out, she remembered.

Riley scanned the driveway from the door to the street, where Murray had crawled to safety.

It must have been a desperate effort, she realized. *It would be a long crawl for a drugged and wounded boy.*

Then she and Bill followed Trey into the garage.

It was startlingly big inside. It reminded Riley of the nightmares she'd been having in which the Penningtons' garage had become impossibly vast. Three cars were parked there—a BMW, a Mercedes, and a Lincoln. Beside the Lincoln there was still enough space for another car.

An aluminum ladder was standing near the wall, which was lined with shelves filled with garden tools. A piece of rope was still tied to an overhead beam. On the floor lay a length of rope with a severed noose. A pair of garden shears was also lying there.

Since Trey and his team hadn't yet broken down the scene, Riley was sure that everything was exactly where it had been when Murray had escaped. The Lincoln's passenger door was standing open. Riley peered inside.

"What have you gotten from in here?" Riley asked Trey.

"Lots of fingerprints and fiber and DNA. It's going to be very hard to analyze and sort through. God knows how many people have been in and out of this car."

Riley saw an open beer can in the driver's cup holder.

She remembered what Murray had said.

I pretended to finish my beer, then put the can in the cup holder.

Riley lifted the beer can. It felt like it was about three-quarters full.

She told Trey, "Be sure to get a full analysis of the contents of this can."

"We're planning on that," Trey said. "What do you expect to find?" he asked.

"Alprazolam—and lots of it."

Riley took a few long, slow breaths. Now it was time to mentally recreate just what had happened here—from the killer's point of view, if possible.

She climbed into the car and sat in the passenger seat.

She took herself back to the moment when Murray had pulled into the garage. He'd surely been driving erratically, even dangerously, by the time they'd gotten here. The killer had probably been scared they'd get in an accident. He might well have breathed a sigh of relief when Murray turned off the ignition.

Then Murray went limp, and it was time for the killer to act.

Riley imagined the killer unfastening the shoulder harness and pulling Murray away from the wheel ...

"Like I was a limp rag," Riley remembered Murray saying.

The killer was big and strong, and Murray was just a little guy. The killer lifted Murray with no effort at all. Meanwhile, Murray's mouth was moving and he was moaning, but he couldn't struggle or protest.

Riley climbed out of the car, retracing the killer's movements.

First the killer lowered Murray's limp body to the garage floor. Then he needed a ladder.

Riley looked around.

Over there, she thought, noticing a space on the wall next to the shelves.

Riley walked over to where the ladder might have been leaning and continued to think out the killer's movements.

He moved the ladder and set it up—not where it was now, but a couple of feet away.

But where did the rope come from? Riley wondered.

Maybe he found it in the garage, but Riley doubted it. It was more likely that he had it with him the whole time. He must have carried it in a satchel or something. The crude noose was probably already tied.

Riley imagined the killer looping the rope around Murray's neck and pulling the noose tight. He hauled Murray up the ladder and tied the end of the rope around the beam. Finally he climbed down the ladder and pulled it out from under Murray.

Riley stepped back and tried to take in the scene.

How did the killer feel when he saw Murray kicking, his fingers fumbling feebly with the rope around his neck?

Elation?

Euphoria?

Or a quieter satisfaction?

Again, Riley's instincts seemed to be failing her. She just couldn't get a strong feeling about the scene.

The only emotion that she could register was the drugged terror of Murray himself.

She noticed that Bill was watching her with great interest, undoubtedly expecting her usual keen insights to emerge.

But Riley was getting nothing.

The killer was still a void, an absence.

She felt nothing about him at all.

She walked to the slightly raised door and crawled under it into the daylight.

This was where Murray had crawled out. And this had to be how the killer had left.

She looked slowly all around.

How did the killer get away from here?

And where did he go?

She had no idea.

He must be out there somewhere, she thought.

But she didn't feel it. She had no sense of him at all.

Was this monster so powerful that he could block her usual skills?

The thought gave her chills.

Bill and Trey had come out of the garage and joined her.

"Did you get anything?" Bill asked.

Riley sighed, deeply disappointed with herself.

"Come on," she told Bill. "Let's get back to the BAU."

CHAPTER TWENTY ONE

When Riley and Bill got back to the BAU, they were greeted in the hall by an unusually enthusiastic Brent Meredith.

"We got Trey Beeler's preliminary forensics report," he said. "Nothing useful has turned up in the garage so far. He confirmed that the beer was loaded with alprazolam as you expected. Fingerprints don't match anyone in our database. They're still running DNA samples."

"So nothing there for us to work with?" Bill asked.

"No, but I just got a call from Mike Nevins," Meredith said. "He wants to talk to the team. I think he's got something for us."

That was quick, Riley thought.

She hoped that Mike's interview with Murray Rossum had turned up something new.

Riley and Bill followed Meredith into the conference room, where Craig Huang and Lucy Vargas were already waiting. Meredith dialed Mike Nevins's number and put him on speakerphone.

"I've had some success," Mike told the team. "Murray was able to remember a lot more about what the killer looked like. The composite sketch artist was able to make a good drawing. I'll email it to all of you right now."

A moment later, all five of the people in the conference room were looking at the drawing on their cell phones.

"Excellent," Meredith said to Mike. "This is a terrific image."

Riley more than agreed. It was unusually vivid for a suspect drawing. Dane—if that was his real name—had a broad, strong face. His hair was thick and shaggy, and heavy eyebrows hung over a pair of rather beady eyes. His nose appeared to be thick and rounded. But Riley thought that his most striking feature was his mouth. His thin lips were slightly twisted, as if in a permanently mocking expression.

It seemed that Mike's skills had really activated Murray's memory. She wondered if the psychiatrist had used a little hypnosis.

At the same time, something started nagging at her.

Was the image *too* good, too vivid?

She knew that sometimes victims of such a terrible trauma could confabulate, seemingly remember things that hadn't happened.

Riley tried to dismiss her doubts. After all, Mike was awfully good at his job.

"Did he remember anything else?" Bill asked Mike.

"Yes. The attacker mentioned to Murray that he was dating somebody."

"A guy?" Riley asked, remembering the flirtatious nature of Murray's encounter with the killer.

"No, a girl. A Byars student. Her name is Patience. Murray doesn't think he said a last name."

Patience! Riley thought.

Did parents really name their daughters Patience these days? Hadn't that name gone out of style along with Gilbert and Sullivan?

Still, it was a valuable tip. It might even be the key to solving the case.

"By the way," Mike added, "Murray is being released from the hospital tomorrow. He's going home."

Riley was surprised. The boy had looked so terribly weak and frail in his hospital bed.

"Isn't that a bit early?" Riley asked.

Mike paused for a moment.

"I thought so at first," Mike said. "But he really wants to go home. He's been in touch with his father, who's in Germany right now. His father contacted the hospital and ordered his release. The truth is, I think it's all right. They're hiring home nursing care. The boy will get all the care he needs. He's not badly injured physically, and he'll probably do better emotionally at home."

Riley realized that Mike was probably right. And after glimpsing the house, Riley was sure that the security there was excellent. The family would surely beef it up when Murray got home. He'd be much safer there than in the hospital.

"Thanks for the great work, Mike," Meredith said.

"Glad to help," Mike said. "Let me know how things go, and if I can do anything else."

They ended the call.

Meredith proceeded to give orders.

"Agent Huang, go to the Pi Delta Beta frat house. Talk to the guys there, see if they can remember anything about the guy Murray left with. Find out if anybody knew him."

"I'm on it," Huang said eagerly.

He got up and left the room.

"Paige and Jeffreys, head straight over to Byars College. You shouldn't have any trouble finding a girl with a name like Patience."

Lucy spoke up a bit shyly.

"May I go with Agents Paige and Jeffreys?" she asked.

Meredith smiled. Riley felt herself smile too. Because Lucy was new at the BAU, Riley knew that she was anxious to make her mark as an agent. And Riley and Bill both enjoyed working with her.

"Absolutely," Meredith said. "The three of you, go right now."

As the three agents stood up to leave, Meredith added sternly, "And come back with some results!"

*

A little while later, Riley, Bill, and Lucy arrived on the Byars campus, which looked as cold and inhospitable as ever. They went to the dean's office, where the secretary greeted them in her usual icy manner.

She picked up a manila folder off her desk.

"Here's as much information as I could put together," she said. "All the records we have of any students, staff, and graduates who may have had mental health problems."

Then she added with a supercilious look, "It's a pretty small file. We don't have many such problems here at Byars."

She handed the folder to Bill and sat back with her arms folded. It was a silent gesture inviting Bill, Riley, and Lucy to leave.

Instead, the three agents stood and looked at her—their own silent way of telling her that they needed to talk to the dean again.

The secretary let out an irritated sigh. Then she got up and opened the dean's door and announced the visitors.

The dean came out, looking as unhappy as usual to see them.

"Back already!" he grumbled. "What sort of nonsense are you going to trouble me about this time?"

Riley said, "Sir, we're sorry to inform you that another of your students has been attacked. His name is Murray Rossum."

Autrey's eyes widened with alarm. Riley could see that he immediately recognized the name. Doubtless he regarded the Rossums as important and influential—hardly the kind of family he wanted any trouble with.

"Good heavens!" he said. "What's the boy's condition?"

"He survived, but just barely," Bill said. "He was able to give a very good description of his attacker."

Riley showed him a printout of the composite sketch.

"Have you seen this young man?" she asked. "He might go by the name of Dane."

Autrey barely glanced at the sketch and said, "Never seen him before in my life. Is that all you wanted to know?"

"You need to put up this picture all over the campus," she said.

Autrey rolled his eyes with exasperation.

"Now look here," he said. "I just got finished putting out a warning that has the campus in a near-panic. And now—"

Riley interrupted.

"You need to do this. It's a matter of life and death."

Autrey took the sketch and looked at it more carefully through his reading glasses.

"Calls himself Dane, you say? He's definitely not one of our students."

"We don't believe he is," Bill said.

Autrey scowled.

"Well, we'll put a stop to this, I assure you. I'll make sure that campus security watches out for him. He's got a lot of nerve, coming around here and pestering my students."

"Pestering"? Riley thought.

It was obvious that the dean still couldn't bring himself to utter the word "murder."

Autrey handed the sketch to his secretary.

"Miss Engstrand, make copies of this and make sure it's posted in all the appropriate places."

Then he turned back to Riley, Bill, and Lucy.

"Now if you'll excuse me, you're once again interrupting my very busy schedule."

Lucy interrupted him before he could go back to his office.

"We need one other thing, sir. According to Murray, his attacker said that he was dating a girl here at Byars. Her first name is Patience. We don't know her last name."

Autrey squinted.

"Patience. Yes, that name rings a bell. Miss Engstrand, could you check?"

The secretary typed on her computer.

"Her name is Patience Romero," she said. "A Mexican girl, from Mexico City. Here's her picture."

Bill, Riley, and Lucy surrounded the computer screen.

The girl was conventionally pretty—light-skinned and blonde.

Riley was briefly surprised. Patience didn't look at all Mexican to her. But she immediately felt ashamed of herself for her stereotypical assumptions. The very idea that there was a standard Mexican "look"—why would she think such a thing?

But when she glanced at Lucy, she couldn't help noticing the Mexican-American agent's richly colored dark skin and thick black hair. Riley also observed an odd expression on Lucy's face as she looked at Patience's picture.

Does Lucy know this girl? Riley wondered.

If so, she wasn't saying so.

"We need to talk to this girl," Bill said. "How can we get in touch with her?"

The secretary brought up the girl's class schedule.

She said, "Her psychology class is ending in just a few minutes. If you hurry right over to Howard Hall, you should be able to catch her coming out of the building."

The secretary gave directions, and Riley, Bill, and Lucy headed straight over to the ivy-covered old building.

A group of students was coming out. Yet again, Riley noticed a strange lack of camaraderie among the students—no playfulness, no idle chatter. Each one of them seemed isolated and determined to get to the next class as quickly as possible.

With her pale good looks, Patience Romero was easy to spot. The three agents approached her, showing their badges.

Bill said, "I'm Special Agent Bill Jeffreys, with the FBI. These are agents Paige and Vargas. Could we go someplace and talk?"

The girl didn't reply right away. Riley saw that she was staring at Lucy, who was staring back at her.

Finally the girl said, "We can talk at the student union, I guess. Come on, I'll take you there."

As they walked toward the union, Riley continued to feel a palpable tension between Lucy and the young student.

What's going on here? Riley wondered.

CHAPTER TWENTY TWO

Lucy Vargas half-wished she hadn't come along today. She felt very uncomfortable as she walked toward the student union with Agents Paige and Jeffreys and Patience Romero.

Nevertheless, Lucy knew she had to handle it like a professional.

If I can't deal with this, how am I supposed to do my job? she asked herself.

The three agents followed the girl into the old building. They all sat down in chairs around a table in the common area. Now Patience was smiling brightly at Agents Paige and Jeffreys and carefully avoiding eye contact with Lucy.

"Isn't this a wonderful school?" Patience said. "It's one of the best, you know. It's not easy to get accepted here. And it's very expensive. But my family can afford it. My father is a very important man here at the Embassy ..."

The girl went on talking with barely a trace of a Hispanic accent, not giving anyone a chance to speak. As she talked, she occasionally fluffed her blond hair with the fingers of one hand. Her other hand rested on the table, displaying an impressive diamond ring.

Lucy could see the perplexity in her colleagues' faces. After all, Patience Romero was so busy bragging about her family background that they couldn't even ask any questions.

But Lucy understood the situation perfectly.

It was a cultural thing, a class thing.

Having been born and raised in the US, Lucy seldom had to deal with this kind of situation.

But Lucy's Mexican-born mother had told her about it.

It was called *malinchismo*—an almost obsessive identification with North American or European culture. Even the girl's non-Hispanic name, Patience, reflected this attitude. She was obviously proud of her blonde hair and pale complexion—signs of a purely European ancestry.

And in Lucy's much darker face, a girl like this would see everything that she held in disdain. Lucy understood that she was a lowly *india* as far as Patience was concerned—someone with indigenous roots. As far as a proud, pale *güera* like Patience was concerned, Lucy ought to be in a position of servitude.

She didn't like it at all that Lucy had a badge and authority.

So she was determined to acknowledge Lucy's presence as little as possible.

Even so, all this boasting was really directed at Lucy. Patience was asserting her cultural superiority.

Finally, Riley managed to interrupt the girl's self-centered flow of words.

"Patience, I'm sure you've heard that some Byars students have been murdered. We're here to ask you some questions."

Now the girl looked positively annoyed.

"Well, of course I know nothing about that," she said in a haughty tone.

Lucy saw Riley and Bill glance at each other. She wished she could explain to them what was going on. She knew that Patience didn't want to discuss anything as serious as murder at her superior school in front of an *india.*

Maybe I should just get up and leave, she thought. *They might get more information without me here.*

But no, she couldn't do that. It would be completely unprofessional. She had to do her best to participate. But how?

Bill asked, "Do you know a student named Murray Rossum?"

The girl rolled her eyes.

"I don't think so. Should I?"

Lucy forced herself to speak.

"He was attacked at home last night. He was almost killed."

Patience's blue eyes flashed at Lucy with indignation.

"Why would I know anything about that?" she snapped at Lucy. "I don't know why you're asking me these questions."

Lucy felt herself starting to get angry now.

Didn't she understand that this was no time for snobbery?

"Murray mentioned your name," Lucy said.

Riley brought up the composite sketch on her cell phone and showed it to Patience.

"Murray's attacker looked something like this," Riley said. "He might go by the name of Dane. He's not a student here and he drives a pickup truck. He told Murray he was dating you."

Patience let out a short, sarcastic laugh.

"Really? He's not a student and he drives a truck, and—"

She pointed to the sketch.

"And he looks like *that?* I don't think so. And I'm not sure what you're accusing me of."

Bill looked completely baffled.

"We're not accusing you of anything," he said.

"We just want to know if you know this man," Riley said. "Are you sure?"

Patience waved the picture away.

"Oh, I'm sure, all right. And if you don't mind, I've got to go. I've got another class right now. My grades are excellent, and—"

Then glaring at Lucy again, she added, "And my family expects a lot from me."

Patience got up from her seat to leave.

Lucy was starting to feel a new emotion that surprised her.

It was panic.

This girl could be in serious danger, and she was ignoring it out of pique.

Before Patience could leave the table, Lucy said, "Patience, this is serious. A murderer is stalking students on this campus. If someone who looks like the guy in this sketch approaches you, you need to call for help right away. And don't walk on the campus alone."

The girl picked up her books.

"I know how to stay out of trouble," she said to Lucy. "I can take care of myself, thank you."

Then she strode out of the cafeteria.

Bill and Riley were looking at each other, dumbstruck.

"What was that all about?" Bill asked.

Lucy sighed bitterly.

"I'll explain it to you on the way back to Quantico," she said.

Lucy and Agents Paige and Jeffreys got up from the table and headed back toward the car. Lucy's worry was mounting.

If anything happened to Patience Romero, how could she help blaming herself?

*

Riley was feeling discouraged by the time she got home that afternoon. April was already home from school and greeted her in the living room.

"Is Jilly home?" Riley asked.

"Upstairs doing homework. She's really digging into her classes now."

Riley drew a sigh of relief. At least things seemed to be going well at home for now.

"How's the case going?" April asked.

"I'm not sure, April," Riley said.

"Well, you're getting lots of help, right? I mean, you've even got Lucy working with you."

Riley didn't reply. She knew that April was fond of Lucy. But Lucy had run into some trouble this afternoon during the interview with Patience Romero. Lucy had explained to Riley and Bill that it was some kind of Mexican class thing.

What had she called it?

Oh, yes, she remembered. *Malinchismo.*

It seemed to be based on an old Mexican legend about a Spaniard and a native girl.

Riley knew that the problem they'd had this morning wasn't Lucy's fault—not in the least. But Lucy was blaming herself and taking it hard. Riley was afraid that Lucy was going to have trouble getting back in the game.

"You look so worried," April said. "Is there anything I can do to help?"

Riley was touched by her daughter's concern.

"As a matter of fact, maybe there is," Riley said. "Let's go have a chat with Tiffany."

Riley and her daughter went up to Riley's bedroom office. They called Tiffany for a video chat.

"Mom's working real hard on the case," April told Tiffany.

"I'm so glad," Tiffany said.

"She's got some questions for you," April said.

Riley showed Tiffany the composite sketch.

Riley said, "I don't suppose you spent a lot of time on the Byars campus. But I need to know if this face looks familiar to you."

Tiffany peered at the picture.

"Is this the man who killed my sister?" she asked.

"We think it could be," Riley said.

Tiffany shuddered.

"I don't think I've ever seen him. I think I'd remember that face."

"Are you sure?" April asked.

Riley added, "He seems to call himself Dane."

Tiffany squinted and looked closer.

"I don't remember the name, either," Tiffany said. "But I guess he *could* be the odd guy that Lois told me about. Was he a student?"

"We don't think so," Riley said.

"Then I guess he wasn't that guy."

Riley thought for a moment about what else she should ask.

"Did your sister ever mention a boy named Murray Rossum?" she said.

"I don't think so. Why?"

"It's just one of the names that came up," Riley said. She was only asking to make sure she wasn't leaving any loose ends.

A silence fell.

Riley couldn't think of any more questions to ask Tiffany.

"That's all for now," Riley said. "You've been a great help."

Tiffany's face saddened.

"I haven't been any help at all," she said. "I've just been feeling so helpless about all this. I feel terrible."

Before Riley could reply, April spoke up.

"Don't let yourself feel that way, Tiffany. Do you hear me? None of this is your fault. I know what it's like to want to blame yourself for things you can't help. But you can't let yourself do that. Just keep telling yourself it's not your fault."

Riley smiled. April was telling Tiffany exactly what she needed to hear. Riley had been sure she would. That was exactly why she had included April in this conversation.

Tiffany nodded and said, "OK."

"It's true," April said. "Just don't forget it."

They ended the video chat, and Riley put her arm around April's shoulder.

"You handled that really well," Riley said.

"I didn't do anything really," April said, blushing.

"Yes, you did. You know you did."

April laughed a little. "Yeah, I guess I kind of did. Well, I'm going downstairs to help Gabriela get dinner ready. I'm sure you've got work to do."

April hugged her mother and left the room.

Riley sat at her desk for a moment, trying to collect her thoughts. Then she got on the phone and called Craig Huang.

"How did things go at the frat house today?" she asked.

"We came up with nothing," Huang said. "We showed the sketch to all the guys, told them what had happened to Murray. Nobody recognized the guy in the sketch. Nobody could remember anything about the guy Murray left with."

Riley was startled.

"How is that possible?" Riley asked.

Huang sounded defensive.

"Don't blame me, I'm just the messenger. They said lots of people come and go at their parties. Whoever it was, he didn't stand out."

Riley doubted that Huang had asked the right questions. Maybe he wasn't growing into his job as well as she'd thought. But there was no point in taking him to task about it now. She thanked him and ended the call.

Then she started going over whatever information she could bring up on her computer—reports on the deaths, newspaper stories, and pictures of the victims.

It looked like plenty of information.

So why did she feel that she and the team were making no progress at all?

This isn't going to be easy, Riley thought.

*

Riley was fast asleep when she felt a hand shake her shoulder.

"Mom! Mom! Wake up!"

Riley opened her eyes and saw pale sunlight pouring through her bedroom window.

It was early morning and she had slept through the night. At least she hadn't been in the middle of any nightmares. Not that she could recall.

"What is it?" Riley asked. "What's the matter?"

"Tiffany just called. Do you remember that girl we talked to at Byars, Piper Durst?"

Riley struggled to get her thoughts together.

"Lois's friend," she said, groggily remembering a video chat with a girl named Piper.

April's face was lit up with excitement.

"Right," she said. "Well, Piper called Tiffany this morning. Piper says that her boyfriend thinks he saw the guy in the sketch. That's good news, right?"

Riley sat up in bed.

"It could be," she said.

"So what are you going to do?" April asked.

"I'm going to call Bill and Lucy. The three of us need to head right over to Byars to talk to the boyfriend."

April was bouncing up and down.

"Can I go too?" she said.

"No way," Riley said.

April slumped with disappointment.

"Aw, Mom."

"You've got school today. Now go downstairs and eat some breakfast. And please make sure that Jilly gets off to school all right."

April left the room grumbling mildly. Riley knew that Gabriela would see to it that both girls got fed and off to school, but she wanted to encourage April to take on responsibility. She was proud of the way her daughter was growing up.

Riley scrambled around, putting on clothes.

This might be it, she thought. *This might be just the break we need.*

CHAPTER TWENTY THREE

Riley sent a hasty text message to both Bill and Lucy.

We might have a good lead at Byars. I'll pick you up.

Then she drove to get them. Both had apartments in the town of Quantico near the BAU base.

Bill was standing out front when she got there.

"What have you found out?" he asked as he got into the car.

"Someone thinks he spotted the guy in the drawing. And the truck. Let's get Lucy and go over everything."

Lucy's apartment was just a few blocks away. The young agent came out as soon as they pulled up in front, but she was silent as she climbed into the back seat. Riley could see that she was looking glum.

"First things first," Riley said to her. "I know you're unhappy about what happened yesterday. But it won't be your last interview that goes badly, believe me. This time it wasn't your fault. The next time, it's liable to be a real screw-up on your part. We've all been through it, so get used to it. It's time to get back on the horse."

Riley could see Lucy smile in the rearview mirror.

"OK, boss," she said. "I hear you."

Bill chuckled with approval.

"Well, I'm glad we've got that cleared up," he said. "Now who are we rushing off to see?"

"Lois Pennington's sister got a call this morning from Piper Durst, a friend of Lois's. We've talked to Piper before and she didn't know anything helpful, except that Lois told her about some rather odd guy. But it turns out that maybe her boyfriend has found out something. We're going to talk to him."

"So the kids on campus are finally coming through with something," Lucy said.

"About time," Bill added.

As Riley drove toward the city, she said, "Let's talk about where we are in the case. What do we know at this point?"

After a moment, Lucy said, "Well, I think maybe we're getting an idea of the killer's range of activity. Not only have all the victims been Byars students, they've all lived fairly close to DC."

At least all the victims we know about, Riley thought.

But she didn't say so aloud.

Bill said, "Now that he's attacked a male victim, I think we can be pretty sure he's bisexual."

"Not necessarily," Lucy said. "Not *bi,* anyway."

Riley was surprised, and she sensed that Bill was surprised as well.

"What do you mean?" Riley asked.

Lucy mulled it over for a moment.

"I think maybe he's a closeted homosexual," she said. "Think about it. He targets girls—he's trying to prove to himself that he's straight. But he can't stick with that scenario. He finally targets a boy. When he does, he doesn't finish the job. He doesn't even stay there to make sure the victim is dead. But all the girls wind up dead. To me, that suggests a deep-seated misogyny, along with repressed erotic feelings toward men."

Riley glanced at Bill, who was glancing at her. They smiled at each other.

She's definitely back in the game, Riley thought.

It was a pretty good effort at profiling, given how little they knew so far. And Riley couldn't think of anything better.

Nevertheless, something was still nagging at her—an unshaped feeling that things were off somehow.

It felt as if they were forming theories out of thin air, basing them on unreliable assumptions and information.

Her instincts weren't telling her much these days. But her gut did seem to be warning her not to jump to any conclusions.

Riley suspected that she'd better pay attention to that feeling.

*

When Riley, Bill, and Lucy arrived on campus, they headed straight to the commons room in the student union, where they had agreed to meet Piper and her boyfriend. Piper got up from a table and invited them to sit down. Riley introduced the girl to Bill and Lucy.

"But where's your friend?" Riley asked Piper.

Piper looked around, seeming surprised that her boyfriend wasn't there.

"Where *is* he?" she muttered.

Then her eyes lighted on a young man across the room. He was standing idly staring at a vending machine. Piper rolled her eyes and walked over to him. Riley couldn't hear what they were saying, but she could tell that Piper was trying to coax him back over to the table.

It seemed as though the kid wasn't eager to cooperate.

But why? Riley wondered.

Soon Piper and the boy came back over to the table and sat down.

"This is Kenneth—Kenneth Mohl," Piper said. "My boyfriend."

Kenneth nodded his head but avoided making eye contact.

They immediately struck Riley as an odd couple. Piper was robust, full-figured, and outgoing. Kenneth was skinny, awkward, and withdrawn, perhaps painfully shy.

What were these two kids doing together?

But then Riley remembered some of her own ill-fated, ill-advised college relationships. She couldn't look back on them without wondering …

What was I thinking?

Piper would probably look back on this and other early relationships and wonder the same thing.

Piper patted Kenneth on the shoulder.

"Kenneth saw the guy in the sketch. Didn't you, Kenneth?"

Kenneth shrugged.

"I dunno. Maybe. I saw somebody."

"Please tell us what you can," Riley said.

Kenneth sat hunched over for a moment.

Then he said, "OK, it's like this. Yesterday afternoon, the college staff put up copies of the sketch all over the campus. I didn't bother to look at it right away. I was walking through Howard Hall when I saw this guy standing at a bulletin board. He was looking at the picture. He looked really, really interested in it. Then he saw me coming toward him, and he walked away."

Kenneth paused.

"Tell them what happened next," Piper urged.

"Well, I looked at the picture myself. And I realized that the guy looked a whole lot like the face in the sketch, and in the description that went with it. You know, a big guy, athletic, with shaggy hair. I hurried out of the building to see if I could get a better look at him. I saw him going away toward the parking lot. He got into a pickup truck and drove off."

Riley felt a tingle of excitement.

A pickup truck!

According to Murray, the guy who called himself Dane said

that he drove a pickup truck. But as far as Riley knew, that information hadn't been made public.

Riley sensed that Bill and Lucy were also excited.

"Can you describe the pickup?" Bill asked.

"Yeah," Kenneth said. "It was a Ford, kind of beat-up looking. It was pretty old—maybe from the 1990s."

Riley was surprised at this detail. Kenneth seemed to be a much better witness than she'd expected from his behavior.

"Can you remember anything else?" Lucy asked.

The boy gulped a little.

"Not exactly, but …"

He produced a small piece of paper. With shaking fingers, he handed it to Riley.

"I wrote this down," he said.

Riley took the note. She almost gasped with surprise. It was a license plate number.

"This is a great help," she said to Kenneth.

Kenneth's eyes darted nervously among the three agents.

"Do you think so?" he said. "I mean, I've never done anything like …"

He couldn't seem to finish his thought. But now at last, Riley thought she understood what was bothering him. Kenneth was not only shy but truly sensitive—and also smart. He knew that what he was doing was serious and consequential. He wasn't used to making a difference, especially when it came to something as dire as murder. It made him uncomfortable.

In Riley's experience, the best witnesses were sometimes like him—unsure of themselves and deeply concerned about what their actions might lead to.

"You did exactly the right thing," Riley said.

Riley, Bill, and Lucy all thanked both Piper and Kenneth, who headed out for their next classes. Riley then got Sam Flores on the phone and read the license plate number to him. She told him that the vehicle was probably a Ford pickup from the 1990s.

"How long will it take you to find out who the truck is registered to?" Riley asked.

Flores replied in a classic geek manner.

"Give me exactly forty-nine seconds," he said.

Riley smiled at Lucy and Bill.

"He's getting it," she told him.

Hardly half a minute passed before Flores got back on the

phone.

"The truck is registered to a guy named Pike Tozer. He lives in DC at ten-twenty Beal View Drive. He's a licensed electrician, but he doesn't seem to work with a company. Probably a handyman who gets called in from time to time for minor repairs."

Riley ended the call and told Lucy and Bill what Flores had said.

"What are we waiting for?" Lucy asked. "Let's go to his house and pick him up."

But Riley knew that it might be a wasted trip. They might not catch Pike Tozer at home.

"I've got a better idea," Riley said.

The three agents headed straight for the dean's office, where the secretary greeted them in her usual chilly manner.

"Dean Autrey isn't in his office," she said.

The dean's door was open, and Riley could see that nobody was inside.

She's telling the truth for once, Riley realized.

"That's OK," Riley said. "I'm sure you can help us. Does Byars College hire independent contractors for minor repairs? For example, electrical work?"

The woman frowned. The idea of being in any way helpful seemed to be positively repugnant to her. Riley guessed that she was under orders from Dean Autrey to give the FBI as little information as possible.

Nevertheless, she replied, "Yes, our wiring is very old. Someday we'll have to have the whole campus completely redone. But we don't have the funds right now. We hire freelance electricians to troubleshoot."

"Do you ever hire an electrician named Pike Tozer?" Riley asked.

The woman continued to frown silently.

Riley said in a mock-charming voice, "Miss Engstrand, I hope this doesn't have to become difficult."

The woman made a low grumbling sound. She obviously understood Riley's meaning—that the threat of a subpoena was still very real. She picked up her phone and made a call. Riley felt pretty sure that she was calling the maintenance department.

She asked, "Do we happen to hire an electrician named Pike Tozer?"

She listened for a moment, then ended the call without another word.

She glared at the agents silently.

Then she said, "Mr. Tozer is working on campus right now. You'll find him in the basement of Olmsted Hall."

"Would you be so kind as to tell us where we can find Olmsted Hall?" Riley asked.

The woman growled again and handed Riley a flyer with a map of the campus.

A moment later, Riley, Bill, and Lucy were headed across the campus.

Lucy was practically bursting with excitement.

"This is it," she said. "I can feel it in my bones."

Riley was pleased that Lucy had pulled herself out of her funk.

Riley, too, felt suddenly hopeful.

They walked across the campus to Olmsted Hall, a majestic, ivy-covered brick building with a clock tower. In a small parking lot alongside the building, Riley saw a few cars. Among them was a beat-up Ford pickup truck.

Things are looking up, Riley thought.

Riley, Lucy, and Bill walked into the building. They saw a professorial-looking man with a bow tie walking down the hall.

"Excuse me," Riley called out. "Could you tell us how to get to the basement?"

The man looked puzzled.

But when Riley pulled out her badge, he pointed.

"Turn left at the end of this hall. The basement door is at the end of that corridor."

When they got to the door, the three agents looked at each other. Riley knew what they all were thinking.

Is this going to be easy or hard?

Riley opened the door. A flight of steps led down to a damp, gloomy basement.

"This is the FBI," she called out. "We're looking for Pike Tozer."

No one answered.

But Riley's instincts had kicked in.

She could feel in her gut that he was down there.

CHAPTER TWENTY FOUR

Lucy's heart was pounding as she and Agents Paige and Jeffreys stood at the top of the basement stairs.

This is it, she thought.

The suspect was surely down there.

And maybe, just maybe, this was going to be her chance to make up for her poor handling of the interview with Patience yesterday.

Agent Paige called down again, "Is Pike Tozer there? Is anybody?"

Again there was no answer. The only sound was the low, rattling growl of the building's furnace.

Lucy silently signed to the others that she would go first. She started to draw her weapon. Agent Paige touched her hand to stop her.

Does she know something I don't know? Lucy wondered.

Then Agent Paige herself went down the stairs, and Agent Jeffreys followed close behind her.

Keeping her hand near her weapon, Lucy followed them downstairs. The huge furnace dominated much of the basement. Watching carefully, they made their way around it.

On the far side of the basement, they found him.

He had a breaker box open and was poking at the wiring with some sort of professional tool.

He was also wearing a pair of headphones.

Lucy fought down an embarrassed sigh.

So that was why he didn't reply.

He couldn't hear Agent Paige.

Agent Paige had saved her from making a ridiculous scene by charging down here with her weapon drawn.

Again and again, Agent Paige daunted and surprised her. Somehow, while they'd still been at the top of the stairs, Agent Paige had known the suspect wasn't immediately dangerous. Lucy hoped that someday she'd have instincts like Agent Paige's. It might take her years, but she was determined to develop those skills.

So far, the man hadn't even noticed that he had company.

Agent Paige said his name in a louder voice.

This time he jumped with alarm. He fumbled with his

headphones and took them off.

All three agents took out their badges, and Agent Paige told him who they were.

"What's this all about?" the man asked in a deep gravelly voice.

Agent Paige showed him the flyer with the picture on it.

"We're looking for this man," she said.

Lucy's eyes darted between the man and the sketch.

Sure enough, they looked remarkably alike—the same unruly hair, broad face, dark eyes. Lucy thought his mouth looked a little different from the sketch—less sneering somehow. His nose was different too. But she was sure that those were minor details.

This is our man, she thought.

The man looked at the sketch, his eyes shifting about uncertainly.

"Yeah, I saw that posted over at Howard Hall. I don't think I've seen him. I'll be sure to call the FBI if I do."

He turned his attention back to his work—or maybe he just pretended to, Lucy thought.

Agent Jeffreys said, "We'd like to ask you a few questions."

The man shook his head as he poked at the wires.

"Look, I'm really busy," he said. "Could we do this later?"

Lucy said, "It would be better if you'd come with us."

The man looked at all three agents.

He appeared to be surprised.

But was he really?

Lucy doubted it.

Scared is probably more like it, she thought.

"Wait a minute," he said. "Am I a suspect?"

He looked more closely at the sketch.

"Do you really think I look like this guy? Because I don't see it."

Lucy was sure he was lying. How could he or anybody else look at that sketch and not see the resemblance?

Agent Paige asked, "Can you account for your whereabouts Monday during the early morning?"

Agent Jeffreys added, "What about the early morning hours of the Sunday before last?"

The man stood silent for a moment. Then he shrugged.

"Home asleep, I guess," he said.

"Can you prove it?" Agent Jeffreys asked.

The man forced a smile.

"Prove what? That I was asleep?"

His smile disappeared.

"Sounds like I'd better get a lawyer," he said.

Lucy stepped forward.

"You might want to do that," she said.

She was about to tell him he was under arrest when Agent Paige tugged her by the sleeve. She turned and looked at Agent Paige, who shook her head slightly.

Lucy could hardly believe it.

Were they going to let this guy get away?

Agent Paige said, "Sorry to trouble you, Mr. Tozer. Please let us know if you see the person in the sketch."

Lucy followed Agents Paige and Jeffreys up the stairs and out of the building.

As they walked toward the car, Lucy protested, "Why aren't we taking him in?"

"Because he's not our guy," Agent Jeffreys said.

Lucy was growing more baffled by the second.

"He's got to be," Lucy said, trotting along to keep up with the others. "What about the pickup?"

"Coincidence," Agent Jeffreys said.

Lucy was starting to get angry now.

"I don't believe in coincidences!" she blurted.

She regretted the words as soon as they were out.

Agents Paige and Jeffreys both stopped walking and looked at her sternly.

"You'd better *start* believing in coincidences," Agent Paige said. "Because they happen from time to time. They're going to be part of your job."

Lucy sputtered, "But he looked so much like the sketch."

"Not the nose," Agent Paige said. "It's much thinner."

"But that's just a detail," Lucy said.

"Not a small detail," Agent Jeffreys said. "The sketch artist drew a nose that was practically bulbous. Murray must have been very specific. It's not likely that he would have been that wrong about it."

Lucy didn't know what to say. But the truth was starting to sink in. She'd misread the whole situation.

Agent Paige smiled a little.

"What about the guy's accent?" she asked. "Where would you

say he was from?"

"The South," Lucy said. "The very deep South, I'd say. Alabama or Mississippi or someplace like that."

Agent Paige said, "When I talked to Murray, he was sure that his attacker came from somewhere north—Boston or New York, he said. How would you describe his voice otherwise?"

Lucy remembered the impression she'd gotten with the first words he'd said.

"Really deep, and kind of rough."

Agent Paige said, "Murray told me his voice was high-pitched, odd-sounding for a guy his size."

Agent Jeffreys chuckled a little as they neared the car.

He said, "Of course, he *could* have cleverly disguised both his accent and his voice—either when he was talking to Murray or to us. What do you think of that theory, Agent Vargas?"

The whole thing was becoming clearer to her.

"Not likely," she said. "If he were going to disguise his voice, surely he'd also have gone to the trouble to *look* different."

"You're catching on," Agent Paige said.

Lucy felt herself flush with embarrassment.

"Agent Paige, Agent Jeffreys, I—"

Agent Paige interrupted her with a peal of laughter.

"If you apologize, I'm going to slap you silly. You're not making mistakes. You're learning. Maybe I'll tell you all the goofs *I* made back in my days as a rookie. You've got nothing on me."

Agent Jeffreys laughed too.

"I'm sure as hell never going to tell you the dumb stuff *I* did. Hell, I still make my share of goofs."

Lucy joined in their laughter, feeling a bit encouraged.

Just then, Agent Paige's phone buzzed.

Agent Paige looked at it and said, "It's a text message from Murray Rossum. He wants me to come to his house."

"What about?" Lucy asked.

"I don't know," Agent Paige replied. "But he said just me. Do you two have something else to cover here?"

Lucy looked at Agent Jeffreys. He nodded and said, "Sure."

"We can keep showing that picture around," Lucy said.

Agent Paige got in the car and drove off.

CHAPTER TWENTY FIVE

The text message Riley got from Murray Rossum was very short.

Plz come 2 see me.

Riley hoped that maybe the injured boy had remembered some important detail. She hurried to meet with him.

When she got out of the car in front of the townhouse, Riley once again felt oddly underwhelmed by the place. It was big but very plain, hardly the kind of home she'd expect for a family involved in international real estate. At least from outside, it didn't compare with Representative Hazel Webber's estate in Maryland or Andrew Farrell's mansion in Georgia.

She was greeted at the door by a tall, muscular, dour-looking woman. The woman's formal pantsuit was tuxedo-like, except that she was wearing a red blouse with its collar unbuttoned and no tie.

"I'm Maude Huntsinger, the Rossums' butler," she said stiffly. "May I ask the nature of your business?"

A female butler? Riley thought.

Then she felt slightly shocked by her own telltale prejudice. The assumption that butlers had to be male had gotten stuck in her mind somehow. Of course, there was no reason to think anything of the kind.

Riley produced her badge and introduced herself.

"I'm here to speak with Murray Rossum," Riley said. "I believe he is expecting me."

The woman seemed to be genuinely surprised.

"It's the first I've heard of it," she said.

Riley showed her the text message.

"Please wait a moment," the woman said.

She disappeared inside the house. Riley waited on the bare front stoop. She was beginning to feel impatient when the woman finally returned.

The butler said, "Agent Paige, you may come talk to him."

Riley followed the woman inside. Right away she was stunned by her surroundings. The townhouse's modest facade masked a truly vast, contemporary interior. All the walls and floors were white, except for a massive black marble fireplace. A single gigantic abstract painting loomed in the hallway—the work of some famous artist she'd never heard of, Riley figured.

A couple of sturdy men in black suits were talking into wrist microphones while watching Riley closely. Weapons bulged from under their jackets. Riley guessed that they were part of the extra security that had been hired to protect Murray. They looked more like US Secret Service agents than conventional security guards. They were surely expensive, and Riley hoped they were worth the money.

She asked the butler, "Why does Murray want to see me?"

"It's hard to say," the woman replied.

After a pause, she added in a softer tone, "We've been worried about young Master Rossum. He doesn't want to see anybody—barely even the household staff. He shuts himself up in his room or wanders through the house by himself. We see very little of him. He hasn't been himself at all."

Riley followed the woman up a staircase made of polished wooden steps with scarcely any visible means of support. The only railing was against the wall. Riley wondered if anybody had ever tumbled off the open side of the stairs. It struck her as a strange design choice.

A white-clad nurse was stationed in the hallway on the second floor. She looked out of place, as if she had nothing to do.

The butler opened the door to Murray's bedroom and announced his guest. She ushered Riley inside and left, closing the door behind her.

Murray was lying in a massive bed in the middle of a vast, barren room. He had pulled the covers up under his chin.

"Thanks for coming," he said quietly.

He didn't suggest that Riley sit down. In fact, there wasn't a chair anywhere in sight. Riley felt stranded and uncomfortable.

"Why did you want to see me alone?" Riley asked.

"I'm not sure," Murray said.

He thought for a moment.

"I've been scared to death ever since … it happened. For some reason, I can't trust anybody—not even people who are here to protect and care for me. Not even people I've known all my life."

He hesitated, then added, "I know this is weird, but you're the only person I've met that I feel like I can trust. I don't know why."

Riley didn't say anything. But she thought she did understand why. Trust was often a casualty of the kind of trauma Murray had been through. Riley knew this from dealing with people who had suffered from PTSD, and from her own experience with it.

She found it oddly touching that Murray seemed to trust her alone.

She also knew that it was completely unhelpful.

"What can you tell me?" Murray asked in a quietly desperate tone. "Please say you're making progress. Tell me you're about to catch the guy who did this."

Riley's spirits sank a little. Now she understood why Murray had sent her a message. It was solely because he wanted her to personally reassure him. She couldn't bring herself to lie, to say that they expected to close the case at any moment.

"Murray, we're doing everything we can," Riley said. "Anyway, you're as safe as can be here. Nobody can possibly harm you."

Tears welled up in Murray's eyes.

"Why can't I believe that?" he asked in a choked voice.

"Believe it or not, I've got some idea how you feel," Riley said. "But you've got to trust the people who are trying to help you. You've got armed security people watching you day and night. Your butler, Maude, is obviously very dedicated. And I saw a nurse just outside who—"

Murray interrupted her sharply.

"I don't like her. There's something not right about her. I'm firing her. I want her out of here today."

The boy's paranoia was starting to shock Riley.

"I'm not sure that's wise," Riley said.

Murray didn't reply for a moment. A tear trickled down his face.

"I keep having flashbacks," he said. "The noose choking me, trying to cut myself loose, crawling away. The fear keeps coming back in waves. I feel like it's getting worse, not better."

"It will get better," Riley said.

He was shaking now.

"Yeah, Dr. Nevins and the other doctors said that it would. But they also said—I might remember things. Bad things."

Riley studied his face closely.

"Are you—remembering things?" she asked. "Things you didn't remember before?"

"Sometimes. Almost. It comes in flashes. But I don't know. Dr. Nevins warned me that I might remember things that didn't happen at all."

"It's called 'confabulation,'" Riley said.

"Yeah, that's what he called it. But there's one thing …"

He swallowed hard.

"I think—when we were still at the frat house at the party—he didn't want to come to my house right away. He wanted to go someplace else."

Riley felt a tingle of expectation.

"Where?"

"That's what I can't remember. I think maybe he wanted to go to another party and I didn't want to go there for some reason, and that's why we decided to come here."

Riley stepped closer to the bed and looked closely at him. She knew better than to push him too hard. If she stressed him, his mind might shut down on the memory forever.

"Try to relax," she said. "Close your eyes and breathe deep. See if it comes back to you."

Murray shut his eyes for a moment. Then they snapped open.

"I can't shut my eyes," he said. "That's when the flashbacks get really bad."

Riley fought down a sigh. She really didn't have the expertise to handle a situation like this.

She said, "Maybe you'll remember, sometime when you're not trying to remember. If you do, please call me, OK?"

Murray's eyes widened with alarm.

"You're not leaving, are you?" he asked.

Riley felt more and more uneasy.

"I've got to go, Murray. I've got to find the person who did this to you. And when I do … things will be better. I promise."

She could tell by his expression that he didn't believe her.

"I can't stay here," she said. "I'll tell you what. I'm going to station an FBI agent here to help keep you safe."

Murray turned away from her and pulled the covers tightly around him.

"Go," he said in a muffled voice.

Riley wished she could make him understand.

"Murray—"

"Just go."

He still made no reply. Riley hesitated for a moment, then left the room. Both the butler and the nurse were standing outside.

The expression on the butler's face was softer now, and full of concern.

"How is he?" she asked.

Riley didn't know what to say. She shook her head silently. She looked at the nurse, remembering what Murray had said about her.

"I don't like her. There's something not right about her."

But Riley didn't see anything sinister about the nurse. She just looked like a professional who wanted to do her job. Instead, she'd been exiled to this hallway. And soon she wouldn't be here at all.

There was just one more thing Riley wanted to do before she rejoined Bill and Lucy on campus.

She turned to the butler and said, "Could you show me around the house?"

"Certainly," the woman said.

One by one, the butler showed Riley the spacious upstairs rooms, including two bathrooms that were larger than Riley's own bedroom. Riley detected a pervasive feeling of loneliness.

So much space, and only Murray here, she thought.

Small wonder, she thought, that he considered bringing a total stranger here. Surely it hadn't been just about sex. Murray must have been positively desperate for companionship—any kind of human contact at all.

She remembered Mike Nevins telling her that Murray's father was in Germany right now. How constantly did the man travel? Riley also knew that the Rossums had homes all over the world. Did the father ever spend time here?

And what about Murray's mother? Riley didn't know anything about her, except that she had little or no contact with her son.

Riley worried more and more about Murray. She found it hard to believe that coming home from the hospital had been a good idea.

Riley followed the butler back downstairs. Riley looked all around. Again, she was struck by the white, elegant barrenness of the place. It didn't look lived in at all—as if it had been set up for a photo shoot and nothing more.

Finally Riley and the butler got to the back of the house. Through large glass doors, Riley saw a glass-sheltered patio with a lengthy swimming pool. The patio was walled all around, and it seemed secure enough against intruders. Riley couldn't imagine how anyone could get in.

Riley couldn't see the garage, which she knew was beyond the patio. When she'd seen it, the garage itself had seemed secure enough. It was only courtesy of Murray's trust and debilitation that the attacker had been able to get in at all.

As they made their way back through the house, Riley again saw efficient-looking security guards moving about.

She asked the butler, "Aside from these guards, how is the security here?"

The butler pointed to cameras above them.

"Every square inch of this place is covered. And you can't see it, but there's a wall with razor wire all around the house. This place is practically a fortress."

Riley thanked the butler for her help.

She added, "I told Murray that I would add an FBI agent to your staff. I will have Special Agent Craig Huang report to you."

The woman smiled stiffly and nodded.

Riley simply turned and left. Everything about her visit had left her feeling deeply uneasy. It didn't feel right to leave Murray in such isolation. But there was nothing she could do about it.

*

That evening after dinner, Riley went to her bedroom office and sat at her computer, poring yet again over what they knew about this case. Her mind kept coming up blank.

She got up and paced back and forth, still getting nowhere.

I need more room to think, she thought.

She left the bedroom and headed downstairs. She could hear the television in the family room in the back of the house. She figured that both Jilly and April were there, and possibly Ryan as well. Gabriela had probably gone downstairs for the night.

She muttered aloud to herself.

"Why can't I do it? Why aren't I getting it?"

Normally this far into a case, she'd have gotten a strong feeling for the killer himself—a moment of insight when she sensed his thoughts and obsessions. Those moments were always terrifying. But she needed them, depended on them. Without them she'd get nowhere.

Still pacing, she tried to put herself in the mind of the killer.

"Who are you?" she asked herself aloud. "*Where* are you?"

She couldn't bring herself to say aloud the most important question:

When are you going to kill next?

The only images that came to mind were the victims.

She could vividly picture all the girls—Deanna Webber, Cory Linz, Constance Yoh, Lois Pennington. She could imagine their drugged horror as a killer placed nooses around their necks.

And then there was Murray …

She could feel what he felt, just as she had when she'd been in the Rossums' garage. She was able to experience every moment of Murray's terror and confusion—the shocking realization that he could die, his frantic efforts to free himself from the noose, and finally his escape down the driveway.

What she *couldn't* get was any sense at all of the killer's feelings.

Only the terror of the victim.

"Why?" she murmured aloud. "Why? Why?"

The sound of Ryan's voice broke into her thoughts.

"Riley, what are you doing?"

Riley turned and saw that Ryan had come into the living room. She sighed miserably.

"Ryan, I'm stuck. I'm getting nowhere on this case."

Ryan stepped toward her and took her hand.

"You need to take a step back from it," he said. "You need to relax. Come on back to the family room. The girls and I are watching a funny movie."

Riley let go of his hand.

"I can't, Ryan. I've got to find this killer."

She resumed her pacing, aware that Ryan was still standing there silently.

She had to focus.

Then she heard the front door open. She saw that Ryan had put on his coat.

"Where are you going?" Riley asked.

"Back to my place. There's no point in my staying here. Even when you're home, you're really somewhere else. Just like it was before."

Riley stared at him. Ryan had spent whole nights away lately. How could he accuse her of not really being here?

"What about the girls?" Riley asked.

Ryan was going out the door.

"Go spend some time with them," he said in a tight, angry voice. "They miss you—even more than I do."

Ryan closed the door behind him and was gone.

Riley was stunned.

Was Ryan right? Was she shutting out everyone who cared about her? If so, what could she possibly do about it?

Nothing, she thought. *It's my job.*

She stood there in her living room alone, feeling helpless. Was she letting her job ruin her personal life? She'd faced problems juggling her responsibilities many times before.

She walked through the dining room to the doorway of the family room. The girls were watching TV and giggling. April looked around and saw her.

"Hey, Mom, she called, "come watch this with us."

Riley wanted to rush in and sit with them. She would love to giggle over something.

What's wrong with me? she wondered.

Surely she was flawed in some deep, terrible way.

Whatever was wrong, she couldn't let it get the best of her and her relationships.

She was determined to do better. After this case was over, she would spend more time with her girls. Maybe she would even patch things up with Ryan.

But for now a single thought sent her back to work.

How much time do I have before someone else gets killed?

CHAPTER TWENTY SIX

When she decided to take a morning walk, Patience did think about Monday's encounter with the three FBI agents. How silly it all seemed now! The weather hadn't been this nice in a long time, and she wouldn't let their warning stop her from doing as she pleased.

She smiled and thought, *Nobody's going to get murdered on a day like this.*

She took a long, deep breath of the clean, brisk morning air. True, it was a bit chilly outside—chillier than she'd been used to back in Mexico. But it wasn't nearly as cold as it had been lately. Tomorrow it was likely to get colder again.

So after her morning literature class, she'd bundled herself up and gone out for a walk. She headed off campus toward her favorite cafe. When she got there and peeked through the front door, she saw that there was a long line of customers. She knew it would be less busy shortly. She'd come back later.

Meanwhile, she strolled on to a little nearby park. She was pleased to see no one around. She'd gotten here at a good time. Local office workers would surely come around later to have lunch under the trees, taking advantage of the change in the weather.

She went straight to her favorite spot in the park—a white metal arbor arch with facing benches. She wiped off a spot on a bench with a tissue and sat down, smoothing her coat.

As she looked around, she remembered how the place had looked when she'd first come to Byars last August. Flowering vines had decorated the trellis arching overhead. It had reminded her of an arbor back in her family's hacienda outside of Mexico City. That one was covered with flowers all the time, while today this one was tangled with dried-up vines.

She wished Papá had sent her to a school where it was warmer. Someplace with a beach would have been much nicer. But Papá's heart had been set on sending her to Byars. He'd said she'd meet the right sort of people there. It would be good for her future.

In fact, she had met some students from good families. She'd also had too many encounters with poorer sorts of people. For example, on Monday there had been those FBI agents.

What business did they have asking her all those questions, anyway?

Especially that ill-bred Mexican girl—Agent Vargas, her name was.

The girl had obviously thought she was superior because she was a real FBI agent. And the older agents, the man and the woman, had made no effort to put her in her place. They ought to know better.

But they'd probably never heard that old Mexican saying:

"No tiene la culpa el indio sino el que lo hace compadre." It's not the fault of the *indio,* but of the one who makes him a *compadre.*

That girl—Agent Vargas—simply didn't know how she should behave.

Patience closed her eyes and tried to imagine that she was home. But the images just wouldn't come, not with this chill in the air.

Then she heard a voice.

"I've brought you your favorite."

She smiled. She knew right away who it was. She opened her eyes and saw him standing in front of her—that boy she had talked with before. He was holding two steaming cups from the café.

"Mapache!" she said.

It was a name she'd made up for him. She still had no idea what his real name was. That seemed odd, especially since he'd asked her on a date the last time she'd seen him. She'd politely refused. He was an odd boy, after all, not really her type. And what if he didn't come from a suitable family?

He'd seemed hurt when she turned him down. Patience was glad to see that he still wanted to be friends.

He handed her one of the cups. He didn't need to tell her what he'd bought her. She knew that it was delicious hot chocolate with a sprinkle of cinnamon. She patted the bench next to her, and he sat down.

"Are you going to tell me what your name is today?" she asked.

"I think I like having you call me Mapache," he said.

Patience giggled a little. Little did he know that *mapache* meant raccoon. Patience called him that because his big dark eyes reminded her of a raccoon. It certainly wasn't very flattering. She hoped he never found out what it meant.

"So what's on your mind today?" the boy asked.

His voice made her feel a little warmer. Not many people took

146

much interest in what she thought or felt these days. And the hot chocolate was delicious.

"Have you heard about the so-called murders?" she asked.

"Murders? I'd heard about some suicides."

"Yes, suicides—that's probably what they really are. A lot of panic over nothing. Some of the kids here can't handle the pressure. My papá would be furious if I ever tried to commit suicide."

The boy looked surprised.

"Furious?" he asked. "Wouldn't he be sad?"

The question took Patience slightly aback. She didn't know what to say. Sadness was in short supply in her family. For that matter, so was happiness. Papá wasn't exactly a warm man. Would he be sad if she died?

No, he'd probably just be offended, she thought.

Papá angered quite easily, and she did her best to keep from angering him. It was hard work keeping him happy. He expected a lot from her.

"Well, there's a big fuss about it on campus these days," she said. "Everybody's all scared and everything. Is this really the first you've heard of it?"

"Yeah."

"Wow, you haven't been around much lately," she said.

"I've been away for a couple of days."

Patience wondered yet again whether he was a student or not. She'd asked him a couple of times, and he'd only smiled. He seemed to enjoy being a man of mystery. The truth was, she also found it to be kind of fun.

"The FBI even came around and talked to me," she said. "They were really rude. Have you seen the flyer around campus, the face of the man they think is a killer?"

The boy shook his head.

She drank a bit more of the hot chocolate, then said, "Well, they say he's a big guy, and I think he's rather ugly, at least from looking at his picture. But the agents had some kind of idea that I'd been dating him! And he drives a pickup truck! Can you imagine?"

She tossed her head indignantly.

"I called Papá and told him—"

She paused. Had she already told this boy how important Papá was? Well, it wouldn't hurt to say so again.

"Papá is a very high-ranking official at the Mexican embassy. He's got a lot of influence. And he was simply furious that the

147

agents would bother me like that. He got in touch with Dean Autrey, who called me into his office just to apologize. It would never happen again, he said."

She took another sip of the hot chocolate.

"What do you miss most about Mexico?" the boy asked.

Patience thought for a moment.

"I suppose it's Rosa, my *niñera*—that means nanny. She's taken care of me for as long as I can remember."

She looked at her hot chocolate. It reminded her of how Rosa served her delicious hot *atole* whenever she felt down. That whole world seemed far away.

Patience said, "Really, Rosa has been more of a mother to me than my mamá …"

She felt like she was babbling now, hardly paying attention to what she was saying. After a while, she noticed that she was feeling oddly lightheaded. She didn't know why. But it wasn't a bad feeling.

She went on and on about what a shock it was to live in the United States, how wonderful Mexico was, how beautiful the family's hacienda was, and how much she missed Rosa and her delicious *atole*.

It felt good to let all these feelings out.

It also felt a little weird. She didn't usually go on and on like this.

Before too long, her dizziness was really bothering her.

The cup fell from her hand, spilling the last drops of the hot chocolate.

"I'm not feeling well," she said. "Could you please help me get back to the school?"

"Certainly," the boy said. "Just a moment."

He stood up and started fumbling with something. Her vision was blurry now, and she couldn't see what it was.

He took her hand and helped her to her feet. Her legs turned rubbery, and she almost fell, but he supported her.

Something isn't right, she thought.

The world was spinning, and she could barely tell up from down.

The boy was putting something around her neck—something that was rough against her skin. Whatever it was, it now was supporting her, holding her upright. Her vision cleared just a little and she realized …

I'm standing on the bench.

Then she felt a push, and her body dropped off the bench, and the thing jerked painfully tight around her neck, and she was dangling in midair.

She tried to ask ...

"Why?"

But she was gagging and choking now and she couldn't breathe.

And then ...

... where was she?

Why, she was in Mexico, sitting under the arbor arch with all the beautiful flowers, and Rosa had just brought her a cup of hot sweet *atole* to make her feel better, and ...

The world went black.

CHAPTER TWENTY SEVEN

Riley was in the Byars library when her phone buzzed. It was a text message from Meredith telling her to call him right away.

Riley's heart sank. This was going to be bad news. She could feel it her gut.

At that moment she was interviewing Byars's chief librarian, asking if she'd seen anything or anyone suspicious—especially someone who looked like the composite sketch. Lucy and Bill were elsewhere on campus conducting similar interviews with college personnel—secretaries, janitors, groundskeepers, and anyone else who might have noticed something amiss. They had all come back to the campus that morning, determined to turn up some clue before another student was murdered.

Riley turned away from the librarian and called Meredith.

He said, "Agent Paige, there's been another murder."

Riley almost groaned aloud. They had failed to find the killer and he had struck again.

"Where?" she said. "When?"

"The body was found just now in Witmer Park. It's just a short walk from campus."

"Another hanging?" Riley asked.

"That's right. Another Byars student. Her name is Patience Romero."

Riley was jolted by the name.

The girl we talked to on Monday!

"We'll head straight over there," Riley told Meredith. "Who's on the scene?"

"Somebody called nine-one-one," he replied. "They've got the area secured."

They ended the call, and Riley brought the park up on her phone. She sent Bill and Lucy text messages telling them to meet her there. Then she trotted across the campus. At the edge of the campus, she converged with the other two agents.

"What's going on?" Bill asked. Lucy was also listening eagerly.

Riley remembered Lucy's distress after Monday's interview with Patience Romero. If the young agent still felt bad over how that had gone, this was definitely going to be hard on her.

But there was no way to break the news gently.

"There's a new victim," Riley said. "It's Patience Romero."

"Shit," Bill snapped.

Lucy gasped aloud.

"No!" she cried.

Riley simply nodded. She wanted to tell Lucy not to let it get to her. But she knew it would do no good.

They all hurried toward the park. By the time they got there, official vehicles had already parked along the street. Riley knew that reporters would also arrive soon.

She, Bill, and Lucy followed a path to where the police were roping off the murder scene. She and her colleagues all ducked under the tape.

The girl's body was still in place. It was a grotesque sight—a pretty blonde in pretty clothes hanging beneath an arched bower. Her lovely clothing was rumpled, and her hair was moving a little in the breeze.

That pampered, privileged life had been cut brutally short.

The setting, too, was bizarre. This area had been designed as a nice place to sit—a decorative arch with benches, put here for comfort, for a touch of class. Whoever had decided on this design touch could never have imagined this scene.

The police forensic team was already here, prowling the scene for clues. Standing next to the body examining it closely was someone Riley knew—Chief Medical Examiner Ashley Hill. They'd worked on cases together in the past.

Riley walked toward Ashley.

"What can you tell me?" she asked.

Ashley's voice sounded bitter.

"It looks like she had been dead for more than an hour before anybody found her. It looks like suicide. But of course, it's *supposed* to look like suicide. It's definitely not."

Not that she needed to be told, but Riley could see at a glance that Ashley was right. The rope was attached at the center of the arch. Whoever had tied it there must have been more agile or taller than this girl in her pretty clothes.

Riley remembered her worry from the night before. Now her worst fears were realized. She and her team had moved too slowly, and the killer was quickening his pace.

Riley turned to the head of the forensics team.

"Who found her?" she asked.

"That guy over there," the man said, pointing to a young man who stood gawking just beyond the police tape. Riley walked over to him.

"Tell me what happened," she said.

He pointed to a woman standing next to him.

"Pearl and I work at a bank near here. It was a nice day, so we decided to eat lunch here in the park. When we got here, we saw—"

Words failed him and he pointed to the body.

The woman said, "Leroy called nine-one-one right away."

"You did the right thing," Riley said. "Be sure that the police have your contact information."

Riley rejoined Bill and Lucy, who were watching as the body was being brought down. Riley heard the sound of approaching sirens.

Bill said, "What I really don't get is the motive. Why privileged students, all from one school? Is it some kind of a class thing? Is it because the kids are wealthy and the killer's jealous?"

Riley thought for a moment.

"I don't think so," she said. "I think it's someone who knows these victims or is drawn to them for some reason. Each victim is personal."

If only I knew why, she thought.

Lucy was still visibly upset, but Riley sensed that she wasn't going to let it get the best of her.

"It's like he's invisible," Lucy said. "We've got a drawing of him out all over the place, but nobody ever sees him. He came here and did this, but nobody saw him."

Riley mulled it over silently. It was dawning on her now that something must be very wrong with the sketch. She'd suspected it when she'd first seen it. It had looked, if anything, too detailed and vivid.

I should have listened to my instincts, she thought.

After all, she'd spent enough time with Murray to recognize the symptoms of false memory and confabulation. Through no fault of his own, the description he gave of the attacker could be very inaccurate. Now they had to start trying to figure out what he looked like all over again.

Trey Beeler, head of the BAU's forensic unit, arrived with his team. The last time Riley had seen him was at the Rossums' garage after Murray's near murder. The sirens she'd heard must have been from the team's vehicle speeding here from Quantico.

"Damn," Trey said to Riley. "I'd hoped we'd seen the last of this."

Riley noticed that one of the cops was gingerly picking up a paper cup from beneath the arch.

"May I see that?" she asked.

The cop handed it to her, and she saw that there were still a few drops inside that hadn't been spilled. She took it straight to Trey, who immediately understood.

"We'll check it," he said. "I'll bet good money that we'll find alprazolam."

Riley heard the sound of a raised voice beyond the police tape. She turned and saw Dean Autrey quailing before a taller, angry man. Riley couldn't hear what was being said, but she detected a Hispanic accent.

As she walked toward them, she noticed the man bore a certain resemblance to Patience. His hair and complexion were a little darker, but had the same aristocratic features.

Her father, Riley realized.

She ducked under the tape and approached them.

Patience's father was livid and shouting.

"Incompetent! I talked to you on the phone! I warned you!"

Autrey was muttering "I'm so sorry" over and over again.

Riley called out, "Señor Romero, could I have a word with you?"

She pulled out her badge.

"I'm Special Agent Riley Paige with the FBI, and—"

The man took a threatening step toward her. Riley could see that he was both grieving and angry—a strange and alarming mix of emotions.

"You!" he yelled at her. "You knew there was a killer, but you did nothing!"

"I understand you're upset. I just need to ask—"

"No!" Romero said, interrupting her again. He pointed to Autrey and shouted, "You FBI people are as incompetent as this *cabrón.* I've got nothing to say to you. I'm hiring my own investigator—and you'll be hearing from my lawyer."

He stormed away before Riley could reply. Autrey was left standing there, dumbstruck and ashen.

Discouraged, Riley rejoined Lucy and Bill.

"It doesn't sound like he's going to be very cooperative," Lucy said.

"I'm not sure I blame him," Riley said with a sigh. "Besides, I doubt very much that he knows anything that can help us. Come on, let's head back over to Quantico. Meredith will want a report."

As Riley, Bill, and Lucy left the park and headed toward their vehicle, reporters descended on them. Sinking into a state of despair, Riley blocked out their questions. Even so, she could hear them saying the same word over and over again.

"Why … why … why …"

That was the question that kept rattling through Riley's brain. *Why?*

CHAPTER TWENTY EIGHT

Riley's day didn't improve when she got home that evening. She had supper with April, Jilly, and Gabriela, but Ryan didn't show up. He hadn't been home since he'd left angrily last night.

He had moved in to be part of the family less than two weeks ago, but he was already backing away. April and Jilly said nothing about it over dinner, but Riley could see that they were sad and disappointed. They'd come to enjoy having Ryan around—and he'd been a great help to them lately, especially Jilly.

After dinner, Riley went to her bedroom office and called Ryan at his house.

"When are you coming back?" she asked. "Are you still mad at me?"

She heard a long sigh.

"It's not a matter of being mad at you. You're never really there, that's all. It's just like it used to be."

The words stabbed Riley in the heart.

"It's just like it used to be."

He obviously meant when their marriage had been falling apart before.

Was it happening all over again?

"I think you're being unfair to me," Riley said.

"Am I?"

A silence fell between them.

Ryan said, "Look, I just need some time and space."

Riley's wound deepened. That was exactly what he used to say when he was pulling away from her and April.

"The girls miss you," she said.

He didn't reply.

She said, "Could you at least talk to them? Tell them what's going on?"

"You're the one who needs to talk to them, Riley."

Riley felt a spasm of anger. He was doing it again—unloading the responsibility for everything that was wrong onto her.

Memories came flooding back of how ugly things had gotten between them. An especially dreadful possibility occurred to her. When they were married, he'd had affairs.

"Have you met somebody else?" she asked.

Ryan's voice sounded defensive.

"Why does that even matter?"

"You could just say yes or no."

"No. And anyway, it's beside the point. I need space—and whether you know it or not, you do too."

He said goodbye and hung up.

Riley sat there, stunned. She realized she was shaking.

But shaking from what?

Anger? Bitterness? Fear? Grief?

Whatever it was, she knew that she was directing it against herself. She wished she could blame Ryan for what was happening.

Why not? Wasn't this all his fault?

But somehow, she couldn't help feeling horribly in the wrong.

"Maybe he's right," she murmured aloud.

In any case, what was she supposed to do now? Ryan had said that she ought to talk to the girls. Perhaps she should. Who else was going to help them make sense of what was going on?

But somehow she couldn't do it.

And of course, the girls must have felt her absence.

She was driving them away.

She drove everyone she cared about away.

She thought about her one-time neighbor Blaine—a charming, handsome man, and she'd almost struck up a relationship with him. But poor Blaine had been badly beaten by a killer Riley was pursuing. He'd been so frightened that he moved away.

April, too, had experienced horrors no teen should suffer.

For that matter, so had Ryan—bound and held hostage by a maniac bent on revenge against Riley.

My fault, she thought miserably. *Or my job's fault.*

But what was the difference, really? Weren't she and her job one and the same? As long as that was true, how could she ever hope to have a meaningful relationship with anybody at all?

And now she was even doing her job badly.

Without her work, what was left?

Nothing, she thought.

Worst of all, other lives were in danger. She had no idea who the killer would attack next, but she knew it would be soon. She even felt fearful for Murray, so isolated in his vast house. Of course the security there was good and she could think of no rational reason why he might be in danger. Even so, she sensed some kind of desperate trouble hanging over him.

She needed a drink. She went downstairs, where she found

herself alone. Gabriela had gone down to her quarters and the girls were in their rooms doing homework.

Everything was exactly as it should be.

Everything except Riley.

She went to the kitchen cabinet and took out a glass and a bottle of bourbon.

She poured a strong shot and put the bottle back in the cabinet. She turned to leave the kitchen, but another impulse hit her. She took the bottle out again, and carried both it and the drink she had poured upstairs.

She sat down again in her bedroom office.

She felt herself slipping into a very dark place in her own mind. It was the place where her inner demons lived—demons of anger, violence, and cruelty.

There was only one other person in the world who understood that place as well as she did.

She swallowed the shot of bourbon at a gulp.

She went to her closet and took down a box from a shelf. Inside the box she found an all-too-familiar object—a gold chain bracelet.

She sat down at her desk and fingered the bracelet.

"Shane the Chain," she whispered. His nickname signified his preference for killing with chains.

Shane Hatcher had a matching chain that he wore as a token of their dark friendship.

Riley had never worn hers.

Her inner darkness seemed to deepen.

Why not? she thought bitterly.

She poured another shot and gulped it down, gathering her nerve.

Then she unfastened the clasp and put the chain on her wrist for the very first time. It felt strange and heavy, and it seemed to emit an electric charge. It sparkled as she turned it in the light from her desk lamp. She rather liked having it on.

Once again, a tiny inscription on one of the links caught her eye.

"face8ecaf"

She'd long since cracked the riddle of the inscription. It meant "face to face," and it was suggestive of a mirror. Hatcher, after all, was a sort of mirror—a mirror in which Riley could see everything about herself that truly terrified her.

The letters were also an address.

She turned toward her computer, opened her video chat program, and typed in the characters.

She expected Hatcher's face to appear, to hear his sinister purr of a voice.

Instead, there was no answer.

She tried it again.

Nothing.

There's got to be some way to reach him, she thought.

She poured another drink, telling herself to drink more slowly. She had to stay coherent, at least for a while longer.

She ran an internet search on Hatcher's name. The results were perfectly predictable—mostly news stories about his escape from Sing Sing, and how he was still at large and high on the FBI's most wanted list. She found absolutely nothing that might help her contact him.

Then a new idea occurred to her.

There was one person who might be able to help.

She typed in the video address for Van Roff. A few seconds later, she was face to face with the hulking technician.

"Rufus!" he said, trying to revive his old joke. "How's Cancún?"

Riley didn't laugh.

"I need some help, Van," she said. "And this is really, really something we must keep between ourselves."

Van Roff's eyes widened with interest.

"Name it," he said.

"Have you ever heard of Shane Hatcher?"

Van Roff's mouth dropped open.

"Jesus, who the hell hasn't?"

"I'm trying to contact him."

Van's face turned pale.

"Agent Paige, I don't know about this."

"It's important."

"I'm sure it must be, but—"

"But what?"

Van was looking truly worried now.

"Agent Paige, whether you know it or not, your friendship or kinship or whatever the hell it is with Shane the Chain is something of an FBI legend. Everybody says it's dangerous. They think it's crazy that you're mixed up with him. Everybody's scared of him—I mean truly petrified. From what I know about him, *I'm* scared of

158

him."

Riley was startled. Van wasn't the type to get squeamish. He usually relished breaking the rules.

"Van, I just want you to find him. I'm not asking you to actually deal with him personally."

Van shook his head.

"I get that. It's not the point. Agent Paige, I like you. I like working with you. Hell, I admire you. But when you play with Hatcher, you're playing with fire. For your sake, I just can't be a part of it."

Riley could hardly believe her ears.

Van, you picked a hell of a time to get principled, she thought.

But she didn't say so aloud.

"Van, I wish you'd—"

"No. That's all I've got to say, just no. This is too crazy even for me. Look, I'm going to hang up now. I'm going to forget we ever had this conversation. If anybody asks me about it, I'll deny it ever happened. You'd better do the same."

Van Roff ended the call.

Riley just sat there staring at the computer screen, feeling desperately alone.

She swallowed another drink, then poured another.

*

Riley was in darkness again—the deep darkness of a vast garage. She heard her own footsteps echoing through the darkness.

She knew what to expect next—or she thought she did.

She was about to see one of the victims hanging in a pool of light, surrounded by framed family pictures.

Instead, a rustic cabin appeared in the midst of the darkness.

She recognized the place right away.

It was her father's cabin up in the Appalachian Mountains.

The front door to the place slowly opened.

An embittered-looking old man came out, wearing the full dress uniform of a Marine colonel.

It was Riley's father. She was surprised to see him in his uniform. Hadn't he retired from the military many years ago?

Then she realized ...

... her father had died last October.

He was walking away from the house, heading into the

159

surrounding darkness, not looking at Riley.

"Daddy," Riley called out.

He stopped walking but still didn't look at her.

"I thought you were dead," Riley said.

"I am," her father growled. "That's why I'm leaving."

He pointed to the cabin.

"That's your place now," he said. "I left it to you. You'd damn well better start taking care of it."

Riley remembered—Daddy had left the cabin to her in his will. She didn't know why. She had nothing but bitter memories of the place. She hadn't even gone there since he'd died. She didn't know why he hadn't left it to her older half-sister.

"You should have left it to Wendy," Riley said.

"What do you care about her?" Daddy said.

Riley didn't know what to say. The truth was, she hadn't seen Wendy in many years. She'd talked to Wendy once on the phone after Daddy died. It hadn't been pleasant.

"Wendy was with you when you died," Riley said. "You used to beat her black and blue, but still she took care of you at the end. She was kind to you. I never was. She deserved something from you. You should have left her the cabin."

Daddy let out a growl of a laugh.

"Yeah, well, life sure is unfair, isn't it?"

He pointed to the cabin.

"Anyway, it's not mine anymore, it's yours. If you don't go in there and fix things up, you'll be lost. Nobody in the world can help you."

With a snarl he added, "Not that I give a damn."

He turned away from her and walked off into the surrounding darkness.

Riley stood facing the cabin.

I've got to go in there, she told herself.

But she felt paralyzed.

She couldn't move from her spot.

And she was terrified—as terrified as she could remember ever being.

Riley awoke at the sound of a knock at the door. Morning light was shining in through the windows. She realized that she'd fallen asleep at her desk and had been there all night.

She managed to grunt, "Come in."

April poked her head inside.

"Jilly and I have had breakfast already. We're on our way to school."

"OK," Riley said.

April didn't leave. She looked at Riley with concern. Riley was sure that she noticed the near-empty bourbon bottle sitting right beside her.

"Are you OK?" April asked.

Riley managed to smile weakly.

"I'm fine," she said. "You kids hurry along."

April left, closing the door behind her.

Riley's head was splitting. She needed to clean herself up a bit, then go downstairs and get some coffee. But before she could get up from her chair, her phone rang. It was Bill.

He said, "I just want to talk over what we're going to do today."

Riley didn't reply.

Bill said, "I can't help but feel like the killer's right under our noses, hiding in plain sight. I'm thinking maybe you and Lucy and I should interview the electrician again—Pike Tozer. We may have been wrong about him. I can find out if he's going to be working on campus today. If not, we can find out where he'll be and—"

Riley interrupted.

"I'm not coming in today."

"What?"

Riley struggled to find the right words.

But there were no right words.

"I can't, Bill. Not today."

"What the hell's going on?"

Riley struggled against her tears.

"You and Lucy go. I won't be any good to you today. You'll do better without me."

A silence fell.

Then Bill asked, "Have you been drinking?"

Riley couldn't bring herself to reply.

"Jesus," Bill said. He sounded angry now. "OK, take today off, get yourself together. Let me know when you're ready to get back to work."

Bill hung up.

Riley sat there miserably, still determined not to cry, trying to decide what to do.

Then she remembered the dream she'd just awakened from, and something her father had said.

"If you don't go in there and fix things up, you'll be lost. Nobody in the world can help you."

She also remembered her terror as she'd stood outside the cabin.

I've got to face it, she thought.

Riley got up from her desk and headed for the bathroom.

CHAPTER TWENTY NINE

The effects of Riley's hangover lifted as she drove through the Shenandoah Valley. But her dread remained.

As always, she was struck by the beauty of Virginia farmland. She'd always had a special liking for this country in this kind of weather—the thinning blanket of snow, the starkness of the trees without leaves, the monochromatic grayness of it all.

Still, she couldn't quite bring herself to enjoy it.

It had always been like this during her rare visits to her father when he'd still been alive—a feeling that things were going to be ugly between them.

And of course, that feeling had always been right.

But why now? she wondered.

Her father wasn't there anymore—not there to fight or argue or engage in his own unique talent for cruelty.

So why was she so apprehensive?

Then she realized—she dreaded his very absence.

Irrationally, she feared that his disembodied cruelty might still have a life of its own up there, still haunting the place.

As she turned off the highway and made her way up into the Appalachian Mountains, there was more remaining snow on the ground than down below. She also saw some ice on the streams that she drove by, but the back roads were clear.

She passed through one last little town, then followed a dirt road that wound its way upward among bare trees and occasional boulders. This was the only part of the drive where the snow hadn't been cleared. But even so, the driving wasn't very difficult.

The road ended at the cabin—the sturdy wooden structure that she'd seen in last night's dream. As she pulled to a stop, she was startled to see that her father's battered old utility vehicle was still there, covered with a layer of snow. Wood was still stacked near the tree stump in front of the cabin—wood he had cut for heat and cooking through the winter. He'd never had a chance to use it all up.

More weeds than usual were poking up through the snow. Riley knew that the weeds would overrun the place in the spring. She needed to do something with the place before then.

As she got out of the car, she half-expected her father to come walking down from the wooded hills behind the place. He might be carrying a couple of freshly shot squirrels, which he would sling into a basket that was still beside the front door.

But of course he wouldn't be here now.

She stood by her car and looked all around. The cabin was surrounded by deep forest. She knew that her deed to the place included some thirty acres that backed up to National Forest property. She had no idea if the land had any value, hadn't given it any thought.

Why did he leave it to me? she wondered yet again. *Why not to Wendy?*

Poor Wendy. Riley couldn't help but pity her. When Wendy was young Daddy had beat her whenever he was annoyed, and she had finally run away. And yet at the end, Wendy was at his deathbed and had arranged his funeral.

She'd come back to him like a loyal dog.

Riley, by contrast, hadn't even gone to his funeral.

She walked to the cabin door and found that it was locked. That would have been unusual when her father was still alive. In this out-of-the-way place, there was no need to worry about intruders.

Fortunately she had the key. The lawyer who had settled the estate had mailed it to her after she signed and returned the necessary papers.

She turned the key, but hesitated before opening the door.

She remembered that spasm of terrible fear she'd felt in her dream last night at the prospect of going inside.

She felt some of that fear again.

Going in there seemed momentous somehow.

But she gathered her courage, opened the door, and stepped inside.

It was dim in the cabin. The only light was coming in through the small windows. She was struck by the familiar warm and pleasant woody smell from the pine paneling. The place looked a bit more rundown now, but she didn't see much that had actually changed. What was missing was the enormous, fierce vitality of her father's presence.

But that vitality had been on the wane during her last visit.

She looked at the stool where he'd been sitting when she last came in here. Grizzled and stooped, his face pasty and pale despite the heat from the wood-burning stove, he'd been deftly skinning a dead squirrel. Several naked squirrel carcasses had been piled up next to him.

She'd known at a glance that he was deathly ill. He coughed all through their visit, sometimes uncontrollably. But he wouldn't talk about it. The visit had been grim enough without such talk. They'd even come to blows. In his weakened state, she'd defeated him easily.

She remembered what she'd said to him after that—the last words she ever spoke to him.

"I don't hate you, Daddy."

The words weren't the least bit conciliatory. They were harsh and cruel. She'd known it when she'd said them. They'd crushed him with a feeling of his own failure.

Although he'd beaten Wendy, he had saved his worst for Riley. Instead of laying a hand on her, he'd demeaned, belittled, and insulted her in every way he could. He'd hoped to make her as unfeeling as himself—and invulnerable to any kind of hurt.

He'd failed, of course.

Now she said it aloud.

"I don't hate you, Daddy."

In her mind, she could see his devastated face when she'd said those words.

It served him right, she thought.

But she also felt a lingering pang of guilt.

She pushed the feeling away and reminded herself that she was here for a reason.

She was here *"to fix things up"*—or so Daddy had said in last night's dream.

She still didn't know what needed fixing or how.

There was a roll-top desk next to a wall. Riley had never looked inside it. She opened the desk, and the first thing that caught her eye took her by surprise.

It was a framed picture of herself and Wendy and their mother. Riley looked like she must have been about four, and Wendy in her teens. Both girls and their mother looked happy.

When were we ever happy? Riley thought.

She couldn't remember.

Instead, painful memories came flooding back.

She remembered her despair when Wendy left home for good. Riley had only been five, and Wendy had been fifteen. She hadn't seen her sister since. How old was Wendy now?

Oh, yes, she thought. *Fifty.*

What did she look like now?

What had her life been like?

Riley had no idea.

Worse was the memory of her mother's death, which happened a year after Wendy's disappearance.

Suddenly it felt as though it had all happened yesterday.

Mommy had taken her to a candy store. She'd been spoiling six-year-old Riley, buying her all the candy she wanted.

But then a man with a gun and a nylon stocking over his head demanded Mommy's money.

She'd been too terrified to comply, too terrified to move.

The man shot Mommy, who died at Riley's feet.

Riley trembled all over at the memory.

Daddy had never forgiven Riley—as if a six-year-old could possibly have saved Mommy's life.

And somehow, deep inside, Riley had always accepted the blame.

Riley rummaged around in the desk. Its drawers and compartments were stuffed with receipts and lists and such. But poking out of one compartment was a folded piece of paper. It looked almost as if it were intended to be found.

Riley took it out and unfolded it.

What she saw took her breath away.

It was an unsent letter written to her.

It began …

Dear Riley

The rest of the letter consisted of crossed-out beginnings of sentences.

~~You never were much of a~~
~~I've always known you'd never~~
~~Ever since you were little you've failed to~~
~~I've always been disappointed that~~
~~I don't know why I ever hoped that you~~

There were at least twenty more cross-outs. But at the end, the one-word signature was not crossed out.

Dad

Riley understood perfectly.

Her father had written exactly the letter he'd intended to write.

And he'd left it here for Riley to find.

A sob exploded out of Riley's throat. Her tears fell on the paper, smudging the ink.

This was it—the thing she had come here to find.

In a letter that said precisely nothing, her father had succeeded in saying everything there was to say about their relationship—not just their mutual hatred, but the mysterious kinship they'd shared.

No, it wasn't love.

There wasn't a word for their dark and powerful bond.

So it could only be communicated in crossed-out words.

Riley collected herself and folded the letter and put it in her pocket.

She looked around the cabin.

"Goodbye, Daddy," she said.

She knew that she was saying goodbye to the cabin too. She had no need to come here anymore. She'd give the place to Wendy if she'd take it. If not, Riley would sell it and put the money in the bank. It would be a good way to start a college fund for the girls.

She walked to the door and opened it.

She almost collapsed from shock at what she saw.

Standing outside, facing her with a sinister smile, was Shane Hatcher.

CHAPTER THIRTY

Shane Hatcher always cut a disturbing figure, with his dark and knowing smile, his sturdily built frame, and dusky features. But suddenly turning up here was even more alarming to Riley than his other unannounced appearances.

"Riley Paige," Hatcher said. "Fancy finding you here."

As usual, he was taunting her, feigning surprise.

How did he get here? Riley wondered.

Then she noticed a car parked a short distance down the road. She realized that he'd followed her here, perhaps all the way from home. Overcome by her father's letter, she hadn't heard the car's approach.

"It's been too long," Hatcher said.

"It hasn't been long enough," Riley said in a grim, tight voice.

In fact, it had been just about a month since they'd met face to face.

Hatcher tilted his head in an expression of mock self-pity.

"Oh, Riley, that's not a very nice thing to say. It's seemed like a long time to me. I've felt neglected."

Then he added with a sarcastic chuckle, "I *do* have feelings, you know."

"What are you doing here?" Riley asked.

Hatcher shrugged.

"I was under the impression you wanted to talk."

Now Riley understood. Hatcher had seen her attempt to contact him, but had decided to ignore the call. He'd preferred to meet her under his own sinister terms—face to face and in the flesh. And now here she was, all alone in the mountains with the most dangerous man she'd ever known.

But she knew that the danger he posed to her wasn't likely to be physical.

Like her father's cruelty, it went much deeper than that.

Hatcher put his hands in his pockets, striking a casual pose as he looked all around.

"Nice place," he said. "This is the first time I've come here."

His smile broadened a little.

"I'd love to have met your father. I'm sure we'd have had a lot in common."

Riley felt a chill deep inside. Had she ever talked to Hatcher about her father? She didn't think so. But she knew that Hatcher had researched her life obsessively.

Hatcher added, "I didn't dare show up here when he was still alive, though. He'd have known who I was in an instant—I'm sure you told him about me. He wouldn't have called the cops, even if he'd had a phone, and I'm pretty sure he didn't. No, he'd have just blown me away, shot me like a squirrel. Can't say I'd blame him."

For a fleeting moment, Riley wondered—how did Hatcher know that her father hunted squirrels?

But of course, it was just common sense. After all, her father had hunted for subsistence. And there was never a scarcity of small game to kill and eat.

"Care to show me the place?" he asked. "It must have a lot of significance for you. A lot of history."

"I never lived here," Riley said.

"No, you spent your earliest years in Slippery Rock, about ninety miles from here. It's a nice town, I spent a couple of days there just to check it out. But then your family moved to Lanton, where you wound up going to college. I've been there too. Not as nice as Slippery Rock, bigger, less personal. You weren't happy there, were you?"

Riley felt queasy now. It was uncanny that he knew she'd been unhappy about the move to Lanton. She'd only been a little girl back then.

He knew her much too well for comfort.

Hatcher continued, "Anyway, your roots are truly here. Here with your father—or rather his ghost. He made you what you are, after all. Ever the ex-Marine, that strong and angry man who told you that you were worthless time and time again—and yet who taught you your true worth. You even look like him."

Riley almost blurted …

"How do you know?"

But of course, he'd had no trouble finding a picture of her father. "Aren't you going to invite me inside?" Hatcher asked.

Without waiting for a reply, he strode past Riley into the house. Riley followed him. He sat down on the stool where Daddy used to skin his squirrels. He looked around the place with an expression of keen interest.

"So this is your inheritance," he said. "You're a person of property, such as it is. What are you going to do with this place?"

"I'm thinking about giving it to my sister," Riley said.

"Oh, yes, Wendy. Have you asked her if she wants it?"

"Not yet."

Hatcher smirked knowingly.

"She won't want it."

Riley's jaw clenched. She realized that he was right. Wendy would want nothing to do with this place. To get rid of it, she'd have to sell it. Hatcher's intuition was nothing short of terrifying.

"Can we just get down to business?" Riley said.

"Certainly. But you know I'm going to want a favor in return."

Riley shuddered slightly.

"What do you want this time?"

"Oh, we'll settle on that later."

It was a familiar story between them. Hatcher always wanted something in return for his insights. Riley had always granted those favors, but the price could be high.

Hatcher seldom wanted anything less than a piece of her soul.

"Sit down," Hatcher said. "Let's go over things."

Riley sat in an uncomfortable wicker chair facing him.

"So," Hatcher said, "you're looking for a killer who hangs his victims. But he drugs them first. With alprazolam."

He's certainly done his homework, Riley thought.

She was sure that the media had made no mention of the drug alprazolam. But however he managed it, Hatcher's research resources seemed to be as good as her own. She knew he had a fortune stashed away, and a growing network of criminal colleagues. Among them was surely at least one hacker—some brilliant geek with fewer scruples than even Van Roff. Hatcher could access any official records he desired—the police, the FBI, Byars College. And he didn't have to worry about the Constitution or any other legal issues.

Hatcher crossed his arms and kept talking.

"Let's see—who have you come into contact with so far? Of course there have been the victims' families—Lois Pennington's parents, Representative Webber, the Linzes. Then there was that dead-end trip to Georgia—I could have told you that Kirk Farrell really did kill himself. And isn't his father a bastard though?"

Riley didn't reply.

"And of course, there are various other people you've met along the way—butlers and bodyguards and nurses and such. There's Dean Autrey—unctuous little prick, isn't he?—and his tight-ass secretary. Too bad about Patience Romero, though. I hear that her father isn't taking her death at all well. So sad."

Riley's patience was wearing thin. So were her nerves. But Hatcher didn't seem to care.

"What about that Pike Tozer fellow?" he asked. "Do you think you may have eliminated him too quickly?"

Riley kept silent. She wasn't about to tell him that Bill and Lucy were planning to interview Tozer again today.

Hatcher paused for a moment, then spoke more pensively.

"Tell me, Riley. Don't you love Oscar Wilde? Such a wit, eh? 'I can resist everything except temptation.' I personally think he's terribly underrated. He wasn't just wisecracks and witticisms. Few people appreciate the philosophical power of his best works—*De Profundis,* for example. He wrote that in prison, you know. I suppose that's why I feel such a kinship with him."

Riley wasn't surprised at Hatcher's literary knowledge. She knew that he'd given himself an astonishing education during his years behind bars. But she had no idea where he might be going with all this talk about Oscar Wilde.

Hatcher tilted his head back, as if trying to remember something.

"And such a penetrating grasp of human nature. 'It is absurd to divide people into good and bad. People are either charming or tedious.' So true, so true. Did I ever tell you that I find you quite charming, Riley? For that matter, so am I. Not a tedious bone in our bodies, either one of us."

He leaned toward Riley.

"Oscar also said something about the weak—people who are weak. It was really quite brilliant, and terribly true and honest. Odd that I can't remember. Do you happen to know it?"

"No," Riley said.

Hatcher locked gazes with her.

"I wonder—of all the people you've talked to so far, do any strike you as especially weak?"

When Riley made no reply, Hatcher patted his knees and got to his feet.

"Well. It was lovely having this chat, catching up. Let's do it again soon."

Riley stood up too.

"You haven't told me anything," she said.

Hatcher chuckled.

"Oh, I have. It's got a slow fuse, that's all. You'll understand before long. But will it be soon enough? Will somebody else die before you get it? That's not my problem. Anyway, I've got to get back to work, and so do you, I imagine."

He shrugged.

"Or maybe you'd like to hang around here for a while, bask in your memories. Tell me, did Daddy ever sing to you?"

Riley's anger was rising. She'd never heard her father sing a note in her life. But what business was it of Hatcher's?

Then Hatcher sang in a remarkably good voice.

You're the end of the rainbow,
My pot of gold ...

"Stop it," Riley growled.
But Hatcher kept on singing.

You're Daddy's Little Girl
To have and to hold ...

Abruptly, he stopped singing and smiled darkly. He was looking at her wrist.

"Wearing my gift, I see," he said.

With a jolt, Riley realized that he was talking about the gold chain.

She remembered what she'd told Hatcher the last time they'd met:

"I'll never wear it."

But she'd put it on for the first time late last night.

And for some reason, she hadn't taken it off.

Hatcher purred, "This brings me to the favor I want. This one's easy. Keep on wearing it."

He turned away and silently left the cabin. Badly shaken, Riley sat back down in the wicker chair. In a few moments, she heard Hatcher's car start and drive away.

Riley looked at the bracelet on her wrist.

She desperately wanted to take it off, in defiance of Hatcher.

But for some reason, she couldn't.

She wondered if she ever could.

But she couldn't waste time thinking about that now.

She had a case to solve.

CHAPTER THIRTY ONE

When Riley left the cabin and drove down the winding road to the highway, she had to make a decision about where to go next. Not home. She wanted to get back into this case but she wasn't sure how.

Bill and Lucy were on the Byars campus, rechecking every lead. She didn't think she could add anything to their efforts. She could drive to Quantico and bug Flores about turning up more information on Byars students. Or tracking down the woman who had told Cory Linz that the Webber girl had hung herself. That woman seemed to have disappeared from the earth. Riley could only hope that she had been paid off and was enjoying a comfortable life somewhere.

She knew that Flores had reached dead ends in both cases, and she actually had nothing new for him to work from.

She needed to think, perhaps to finally get some sense of this killer. She pulled into the parking lot in front of a little café and sat in the car for a moment. She closed her eyes and reached mentally for the killer's mind.

All she felt was fear. All she saw was the terrified faces of the girls who had died and the boy who had escaped. She finally shook her head and gave it up.

Riley drew a deep sigh and went inside the café. She sat alone in a booth and ordered coffee and a Danish. When her order came, she sipped her coffee and considered what she knew.

Hatcher must have told her something useful. But what was it?

"It's got a slow fuse," Hatcher had said.

Riley sighed. It was too typical of Hatcher, teasing her along like that. She didn't have time for a "slow fuse"—not when a murderer was out there getting ready to strike again. She had to figure out what he was getting at fast.

She replayed the conversation in her head.

"Don't you love Oscar Wilde?" he'd said.

Then he'd rattled off a couple of quotes—something about resisting temptation, something else about people being charming or tedious. Then finally there was a quote that Hatcher couldn't quite remember—or so he pretended. Nothing ever escaped Hatcher's steel trap of a mind. Riley was sure that he remembered it perfectly.

Something about "the weak."

"It was really quite brilliant, and terribly true and honest."

She got out her cell phone and ran a search for "Oscar Wilde," "quotes," and "weak."

In a matter of seconds she found it ...

"The worst form of tyranny the world has ever known is the tyranny of the weak over the strong. It is the only tyranny that lasts."

Riley felt a chill of understanding.

The quote obviously resonated with Hatcher—and it did with her as well.

Weakness and evil were strongly linked in her mind. The killers she hunted down were typically weak deep down. So were the politicians and bosses who so often thwarted her. The underhanded BAU bureaucrat Carl Walder came to mind.

But Hatcher surely meant something very specific.

The killer she was now looking for was especially marked by weakness.

But who could it be?

So far, the only viable suspect they had was that electrician, Pike Tozer.

Did he strike Riley as a weak man?

Physically, no—he seemed quite strong, in fact.

But Riley realized that she hadn't gotten much of a sense of his character. She also remembered that Bill and Lucy intended to interview him again. Maybe they'd found out something important.

Riley called Bill.

"I'm back on the job," she said. "I'm sorry about my lapse this morning."

"It's OK," Bill said.

"Did you and Lucy talk to Pike Tozer again?"

Bill's voice sounded discouraged.

"Yeah, we tracked him down. He gave us an airtight alibi for yesterday morning. He was working on a job on campus, and he's got witnesses to back him up. He definitely didn't kill Patience Romero."

Riley took a sip of her coffee.

"Something's not right, Bill," she said.

"Tell me about it. That composite drawing must be way off. Nobody recognizes that face."

Riley thought for a moment.

She closed her eyes.

Those words went through her mind again.

"The tyranny of the weak ... the only tyranny that lasts."

Had she encountered anyone during the last few days who was noticeably weak?

Then something started to occur to her.

Who have I met who isn't *weak?*

Weak people had surrounded her—including non-suspects.

Deep in her gut an idea started to take shape.

Her eyes snapped open.

She told Bill, "You and Lucy keep working the Byars campus. I've got somewhere else to go. We'll meet up later."

"When?"

"It'll be maybe three hours."

Bill sounded surprised.

"Three hours?"

Riley felt embarrassed. Of course Bill had no idea where she was right now.

"I'm out of town," she said. "I'll explain it to you later."

They ended the call. Riley paid the bill, left the café, and started to drive.

*

Riley's intuition was in full gear when she pulled into the visitor's parking lot at Franklin Pierce High School. She didn't yet know exactly where her gut was leading, but she had a pretty good idea how to get there.

Riley barged in through the front entrance, where she was greeted by an alarmed-looking receptionist.

"May I help you?" the woman asked.

Riley flashed her badge and introduced herself.

"I need to know where I can find Tiffany Pennington," Riley said. "I've got to talk to her."

The woman checked her computer.

"She's in gym class. I can call her out of class for you."

"I know where the gym is," Riley said, barreling past her down the hall.

Riley burst in through the gym doors. Girls were playing volleyball—Tiffany and April among them.

April looked at her mother with alarm.

"Mom! What are you doing here?"

Riley showed her badge to the gym teacher.

"I need to talk to Tiffany," she said. "In the hall. Right now."

The stunned gym teacher nodded and sent Tiffany out with Riley. April followed.

"Mom, what's going on? Have you lost your mind?"

Riley didn't reply. She seized Tiffany by the shoulders.

"Tiffany, you've *got* to be forgetting something. There's something you haven't told me."

Tiffany looked alarmed.

"What do you mean?"

Riley took a deep breath to calm herself.

"Lois's friend Piper said something about a strange guy. Lois told Piper she didn't know whether to like him or feel sorry for him."

Tiffany nodded dumbly.

"Tiffany, your sister *must* have told you something about him. Think!"

Tiffany's eyes widened.

"I think I *do* remember something. Oh my god!"

Riley held her breath as she waited for the next words.

"Yeah, Lois mentioned some guy in her poetry class. She said he was a nice guy, but small and skinny, and his eyes were a little creepy. He had really big eyes, she said."

Tears welled up in Tiffany's eyes.

"I'm sorry I didn't remember before. How could I have forgotten? I was so stressed out."

Riley smiled and patted Tiffany on the shoulder.

"That's OK," she said. "You told me exactly what I need to know."

Riley left Tiffany and her daughter in the hallway and hurried back to her car. She sat in the car and called Dean Autrey's office at Byars. She got the dean's secretary on the phone.

"Miss Engstrand, Lois Pennington was taking a poetry class when she died. I need you to tell me who the students were in that class."

A few moments later, the agitated secretary was reading off names to Riley.

At first she didn't recognize any of them. But then came the tenth name and Riley tingled all over.

It was Murray Rossum.

176

CHAPTER THIRTY TWO

When Riley parked in front of Murray Rossum's townhouse, Bill and Lucy were already waiting in their car. They all hurried up to the front entrance, where they were met by the female butler, Maude Huntsinger. When they said they had to see Murray, the butler sternly refused.

"The young master gave me strict instructions," she said. "He wants to be alone. Nobody in the staff is supposed to bother him for the rest of the day."

Riley and Bill exchanged anxious looks.

Bill said, "Ma'am, this is extremely important."

"I understand, sir, but Master Rossum was very clear."

Suddenly, to her own surprise, Riley blurted out, "I think something is very wrong in this house."

The butler's eyes widened.

Then she said to Riley, "Only you."

Riley shook her head. "No, I need my colleagues."

The woman's face softened. Riley could see that she cared about Murray. Riley had to use that genuine feeling to get into this house without taking time to get a warrant.

"We've got to see him right now," Riley said. "All three of us."

Then the butler nodded and said, "Come with me."

Riley, Bill, and Lucy followed her into the house, where a couple of security men were still on duty. They continued up the stairs. There was no nurse waiting outside Murray's bedroom this time.

The butler knocked on the bedroom door.

"Master Murray, Agent Paige is here again."

Cautiously she added, "And two other agents. They really need to talk to you."

No answer came.

The butler knocked more sharply.

"Master Murray, I'm sorry to disturb you, but this is important."

Riley could see a trace of panic in the woman's face.

Riley whispered to her, "Ma'am, we've got to go in there."

The butler hesitated. Riley guessed that she'd never barged into a room in this house without permission. But in her worry, she was reconsidering her usual ways.

Maude Huntsinger opened the door. Riley stepped inside, followed by the others.

The bed was unmade, but Murray wasn't in it.

The vast, cavernous bedroom was entirely empty. There was no furniture to hide behind. The butler looked under the bed.

"This is impossible," the butler said with a gasp.

Riley and her colleagues spread across the room. Riley saw that the door to the adjoining bathroom was open. She looked inside and saw no one.

"I don't understand," the butler said. "He must be somewhere in the house."

The butler took out her walkie-talkie and called other personnel throughout the house. She also called Agent Huang, whom Riley knew to be in the house monitoring security screens.

"No one has seen him," the woman said, her voice trembling with alarm.

Riley looked around. Her eyes fell on a panel that looked different from the rest of the wall. It had a small keyhole.

"What's this?" Riley asked.

"The door to his wardrobe closet," the butler said. "His dressing room. It's always locked. Nobody in the staff has a key. I haven't been in there for years."

Riley looked around some more. Her eyes fell upon the bed.

She remembered how crumpled and pathetic he had looked the last time she'd seen him.

"I can't shut my eyes," he'd said. *"That's when the flashbacks get really bad."*

Riley shuddered as she remembered the quote:

"The worst form of tyranny the world has ever known is the tyranny of the weak over the strong."

Had she ever in her life met a person as palpably weak as Murray Rossum?

Riley pounded on the wall and called Murray's name.

There was still no answer.

Riley looked at Maude Huntsinger.

"We don't have time to get a warrant," she said. "We have to know if Murray is inside."

The woman was sputtering with confusion.

"But without the young master's permission … or his father's …"

Riley interrupted sharply.

"I don't have time to argue."

The woman nodded.

"I understand," she said. "Do what you have to do."

Bill hurled himself against the wall to no effect. The panel rattled, but didn't open.

Riley drew her weapon, aimed at the lock, and fired into it at an angle that would prevent the bullet from striking anyone inside. The damaged door then slid effortlessly open.

It room was dark, but some of the light from the bedroom spilled inside. The first thing that struck Riley about the room was its size.

This is a closet? she thought.

She could tell at a glance that it was bigger than her own bedroom.

She found a switch and turned on a light.

Murray wasn't here.

Riley stepped inside. Lucy and Bill followed close behind her.

Both sides of the room were lined with expensive clothes and shoes. At the far end of the room was a big mirror. In the very middle of the room stood a desk covered with papers.

The next thing that caught Riley's eye was a large bulletin board hanging at one side. Her mouth gaped with horror at what she saw pinned up on it.

Photographs of young women were carefully arranged under slips of paper with their names …

DEANNA … CORY … CONSTANCE … LOIS … PATIENCE …

They were pictures of the girls who had been murdered.

He must have taken the photos with his cell phone without the girls' knowledge, then printed them out and posted them here. Riley recognized all the names—except for one. At the top on the far right was the name *RACHEL*. There were no photographs under it.

"It's him," Lucy said with a gasp. "Murray's the killer."

Then came a hoarse outcry of horror from Maude Huntsinger.

"My God! No! It's impossible!"

But Riley knew that it was true.

Riley heard Bill's voice behind her say, "Riley, you'd better look at this."

She turned and saw him standing at the table reading the pieces of paper. Riley joined him and saw that they were all unsent letters that began with the victims' names.

Dear Deanna ... Dear Cory ... Dear Constance ...
She picked up the letter that began "Dear Patience." It began ...

I don't understand. You like me but you don't like me. You say I'm nice, but you don't want to go out with me. This happens to me again and again. Girls don't want a boy who's "nice." But this time it hurts more than it has before. Because you're special to me, Patience. And do you think I don't know what "mapache" means?
...

The rest of the letter was a mess, with illegible passages and countless cross-outs.

It reminded Riley of her father's letter—with one important difference.

By saying precisely nothing, her father had said exactly what he'd wanted to say. He'd signed his non-letter "Dad." But this letter had no signature. It was hopelessly unfinished. Murray had no idea how to put into words what he wanted to say. In the end, the only way he knew how to communicate his feelings was murder.

Riley picked up the letter Murray had started writing to a girl named Rachel. It was much the same, filled with self-pity and bafflement at why the girl somehow both liked and didn't like him. One crossed-out phrase seized her attention ...

I know I'm not a big strong guy, but ...

Riley stopped reading right there.

She murmured aloud, "'The tyranny of the weak over the strong.'"

The veil had lifted from her eyes.

Now she understood what her instincts had tried to tell her all along.

Every time she had tried to get into the mind of the killer, she'd found herself in Murray's mind. She'd sensed some kind of danger hovering around Murray. She had thought it was because he'd been a victim. Because he could still be in danger.

But the danger wasn't *to* Murray.

It was *from* Murray.

And now, at long last, she could slip into Murray's mind and feel what he'd felt, think what he'd thought.

In the bed ... lying there ... his eyes pleading with her ...

looking so pathetic …

He was gloating!

And he'd played her completely, just as he'd played his victims.

He'd carried his deception out as fully as he possibly could—even faking his own attempted murder.

Murray Rossum *was* his weakness.

His weakness was his obsession—and his power.

Murray killed out of weakness.

His weakness of character made it possible for him to kill. His physical weakness forced him to drug his victims.

Shane Hatcher had figured it out already. He knew that the truth was right under Riley's nose. So what had kept Riley from getting the message?

It was my pity, Riley realized.

She'd let compassion cloud her instincts.

By his very weakness, Murray had tyrannized Riley's judgment.

Riley looked again at the bulletin board.

Why weren't there any photographs under Rachel's name? He'd surely stalked her, taking pictures of her—pictures that must be in his cell phone. Why hadn't he printed them and posted them?

Riley realized with a shudder …

Because he hasn't killed her—yet.

Riley turned to Lucy, whose mouth was hanging open with shock.

"Agent Vargas, call Byars College right now. Talk to Dean Autrey. The school must have some kind of campus alerts app. Have the dean broadcast a warning and a photo of Murray to all the cell phones on campus. Tell him to personally contact and warn every single student at Byars named Rachel. Tell him that one of those girls is in immediate danger. Autrey might give you some resistance. Don't take no for an answer!"

Lucy nodded, took out her cell phone, and went right to work.

Riley turned toward the butler, who was sobbing uncontrollably.

"Where is he?" Riley demanded. "Where is he right now?"

"I don't know!" the butler cried. "I have no idea!"

"Is he in the house?" Bill asked.

"I said I don't know!"

Riley called Craig Huang, who was in the basement watching

181

security monitors.

"Agent Huang, do you know whether Murray is in the house?"

"Huh?" Huang asked.

Riley understood his confusion. He'd thought his job was to watch for intruders, not to keep track of Murray.

"I need to know if he left the house," Riley said.

"No. He couldn't have. I've been watching the entrances like a hawk. Windows too."

"Have you got recordings?"

"Yes, but—"

"Go over them. Right now. We're coming right down."

Riley ended the call.

"Take us to Agent Huang," Riley told the butler.

The woman led them down a back stairway that wound floor by floor to the basement. The basement was a maze, with rooms for utilities and supply storage, and also servants' quarters and rest areas for servants who didn't live in the house.

Riley asked the butler to open a door to one of the storage rooms. Riley could see at a glance that there were no windows. She guessed that there weren't windows anyplace else in the basement. The place was built like a bunker.

"Does Murray ever come down here?" Riley asked the butler.

"No. The basement is for servants only. He'd feel out of place here. And the servants wouldn't like it."

Not true if he's got an accomplice, Riley thought.

Maybe somebody was hiding him.

Was she going to have to arrest the whole staff?

And what if he wasn't in the house at all?

If so, they were wasting valuable time.

They went into the security room, where Agent Huang was watching a bank of computer monitors.

"I've just gone over the recordings," Huang said. "I'm sure he hasn't left the house."

The group stood silently thinking for a moment.

Then Lucy said, "It's what we've been saying about the killer all along. Nobody notices him on campus. People can't even see him in his own house. He's like the Invisible Man or something."

A realization seemed to be dawning on the butler.

"Yes—he *can* be like that," she said.

"What do you mean?" Riley asked.

"This may sound crazy, but … sometimes he just seems to

182

disappear. He'll be in the house, but nobody will know where he is for long periods. A few times I noticed ..."

She paused.

"I'll see him leave his bedroom. Then I won't see him at all for a long while. It's as if he vanishes into thin air. Then he reappears again, seemingly out of nowhere."

Lucy was pacing and looking around.

"That reminds me of something," she said. "A few years ago, I went on a trip with my family to the town in Mexico we originally came from. It's an old town, dating way back to colonial times. Back during the Mexican War of Independence, the townspeople dug all kinds of escape tunnels among the houses. The entrances were well camouflaged."

That's it! Riley thought.

"Where do you see him just before he disappears?" she said to the butler.

"I'll show you," the butler said.

CHAPTER THIRTY THREE

As they followed the butler, Riley felt in her gut that Lucy had hit upon the truth. Murray must have left the house through some kind of secret exit. The house was old enough to have been built when a man could hide that sort of thing if he owned enough property in the area.

She was glad for Lucy. After all, the young agent had gone through some setbacks lately and had been down on herself. Riley decided to let her take charge for the moment.

The group arrived at the bottom of the back stairs that led down to the basement.

The butler pointed up the stairs.

"It has happened just a few times, and I'm not even positive about it. When I'm up on the second floor doing something, I'll see him leave his room and head down this staircase. I think he's going to the kitchen or maybe out to the pool. But after that I don't see him at all. I don't know where he goes."

Looking eager and alert, Lucy crept slowly up the stairs, knocking on the wall as she went. The others followed her.

At the first landing, Riley could hear a hollow sound as Lucy knocked on a panel.

"Here it is!" Lucy said, knocking again.

The sound was definitely different from the wall beside it.

"But how does it open?" Bill asked.

Lucy pressed firmly and evenly with both hands. It took some effort, but when she leaned her body into it the panel slipped back a few inches. Then Lucy was able to slide it open. Lying before them, down a short flight of steps, was a concrete tunnel.

Riley asked the butler, "Did you know anything about this?"

The woman shook her head, mouth agape.

"It must have been here for years and years, ever since the house was first built," she said. "Murray's great-grandfather built this place. Nobody ever breathed a word about it to me."

Lucy flicked a switch that turned on a light. It was a bare bulb hanging from the tunnel ceiling by a bare cord. Riley could see that the tunnel took a sharp turn a short distance up ahead.

Where does it lead? she wondered.

And what had it been built for?

Riley, Bill, and Lucy drew their weapons.

"I want to come," the butler said. "I want to see where it goes."

Riley hesitated. But she knew that they might need the woman's knowledge of the family history.

"Come on," Riley said. "But stay behind us."

They all crept into the tunnel. When they reached the sharp turn, Riley saw that the tunnel extended for a couple of hundred feet, lit here and there by hanging light bulbs. There was no sign of Murray or anybody else up ahead.

After another turn, Riley and her companions found themselves facing a locked door.

"Do you have a key?" Riley whispered to the butler.

"I'll see," the woman said.

She took out a key ring with a vast array of keys and tried them one by one. None worked.

Bill started to aim his pistol at the lock, but Riley stopped him. She didn't want to make any more noise than was necessary.

She reached into her handbag for the flat tension wrench of her lock-picking kit. She inserted the wrench into the lock, then groped and twisted it until the lock rotated. When she turned the doorknob the door swung open.

Riley and her companions found themselves in another basement.

"Do you know where we are?" Riley asked the butler.

"I'm not sure."

They moved silently up the basement stairs. The door opened into the ground floor of a narrow house—obviously smaller than Murray's home, but expensive-looking just the same.

The butler gasped.

"Why, this house belongs to the older Master Rossum—Murray's father! He sometimes uses this house for important visitors, special friends. I had no idea the two houses were connected. They're not even on the same street."

With guns still drawn, Bill and Lucy went upstairs. Riley made a quick check of the kitchen and bathroom that adjoined the living room. No one else was there.

"All clear," Bill said, as he and Lucy came back down the stairs. "Nice place," he added.

Riley found it easy to guess just what the tunnel had been built for. The family patriarchs—perhaps for three generations—had used it as a route to carry on sexual trysts. It allowed them to slip out of the house without anybody noticing, especially their wives.

The tunnel made it possible to discreetly meet a woman in the house where they were now.

A mistress, perhaps?

Maybe, Riley figured, but the rendezvous were likely much more casual—prostitutes, call girls, or other men's wives.

Doubtless the secret had been passed down from each father to each son all the way to Murray.

And now Murray was putting the house and tunnel to a use that his forebears surely hadn't anticipated.

He was sneaking away from his own home to commit murder.

Riley shuddered. He had to be found.

"I need Murray's cell phone number," she said to the butler.

The butler immediately told her.

Riley whipped out her own cell phone and called Sam Flores, the technician.

"Sam, I need you to do a GPS search right now. We're looking for Murray Rossum."

Sam sounded surprised.

"The kid who almost got killed?"

"He's our killer, Sam. And he's after somebody else right now."

She told Sam the number and waited for a few moments.

"Damn," Sam said. "He's a clever bastard. He's disabled his GPS system. I have no idea where he is."

Riley ended the call. Then she called Dean Autrey and put him on speakerphone. Autrey sounded worried, and much more cooperative than he had been in the past. Riley figured that the horrible reality of the situation had finally sunk in.

"Have you reached out to all your students named Rachel?" Riley asked.

"I've tried. We've got seven Rachels. We were able to warn all of them except three."

Riley felt a surge of adrenaline.

"Give us their full names and contact information," she told Autrey. "We've got to find them—and fast."

CHAPTER THIRTY FOUR

Bill moved through the front door of the apartment building and up the stairs quickly. He, Riley, and Lucy had split up. A girl named Rachel was in serious danger, but three Byars students named Rachel hadn't responded to the campus warning. GPS tracking had located all of them in the neighborhood around the Byars campus.

The one he was looking for, Rachel Reeves, was definitely here—or at least he'd tracked her cell phone here. His own cell phone indicated that she was upstairs.

But was she the right Rachel?

If so, was she in immediate danger?

It was a desperate situation. The girl might have been murdered already. Or there might be only seconds to spare.

As Bill mounted the stairs, he heard music blaring from above. It sounded like it was coming from the third floor.

A party? Bill wondered.

It seemed likely, given that the building was full of students.

It was also possible that the killer was using it to cover the sounds of murder.

For the moment, the noise was to Bill's advantage. Nobody could hear him approaching. When he reached the third and top floor, he followed the GPS signal to apartment D.

The music inside was almost deafening.

Bill hesitated as he stood outside the door.

What should he do next?

In the heat of the situation, there hadn't been time to get warrants of any kind. Bill and his colleagues hadn't even known what premises they might need to search.

Should he knock on the door and announce himself?

No, he thought. *A girl might be getting killed in there.*

If he'd gotten the wrong girl, he'd just have to deal with the legal consequences later.

He drew his weapon. He doubted the killer himself would be armed. But a threat of deadly force might be necessary to stop a murder in progress.

He turned the doorknob. The door was unlocked and he pushed it open.

He almost choked from the smell of marijuana, and his eyes stung from the smoky haze. When his eyes adjusted, he saw seven stunned college-age youngsters, all of them looking thoroughly stoned.

Some were sitting on the floor, others on the stuffed furniture.

They raised their hands, their mouths gaping with alarm. Some of them staggered to their feet.

With a groan of discouragement, Bill holstered his weapon.

"Turn the music down!" he yelled.

A young man did so, then stared at Bill.

One of the other kids murmured, "Oh, man, this is so not cool."

"Tell me about it," said another. "We are so vigorously fucked."

Bill showed his FBI badge and introduced himself.

"I'm looking for someone named Rachel Reeves."

A freckled redhead sheepishly raised her hand.

"Please don't arrest me. My parents will freak out totally."

Bill looked straight at Rachel.

"Didn't you get the warning? The administration tried to contact all the students named Rachel."

"Yeah, I got it," Rachel said. "I'm safe here, thanks."

"Why didn't you respond?" Bill asked.

Rachel shrugged.

"I dunno. I don't even know this Murray What's-His-Name. What's the big deal?"

"Oh, I know him," another said. "A real dork."

"Me too," said yet another. "Who'd have figured he was some kind of killer?"

Bill was seething with anger and frustration. He felt like shaking Rachel Reeves.

"You brought me here on a wild goose chase," he said. "I could haul you in for obstruction—and a few other things. Meanwhile, another girl named Rachel is in danger right now. And instead of keeping her alive, here I am in a room with a bunch of stoned college kids."

The kids looked thoroughly chastened—not that it did any good.

"Never mind," Bill growled. "Enjoy your goddamn party."

He left the apartment and walked back down the stairs. He heard the apartment door close and the music start up again.

Bill hoped that either Riley or Lucy was having better luck.

I'd better check in with them, he thought, taking out his cell phone again.

CHAPTER THIRTY FIVE

Murray thought that Rachel looked bored. He knew she didn't much enjoy his company, although she did her best not to show it.

"Where are we going?" she asked Murray as they walked along.

"Someplace nice," Murray said. "You'll see."

It was chilly outside. Murray watched Rachel sip her hot chocolate, then took a sip of his own. The drug didn't seem to have affected her yet.

He was running out of time and he knew it. He'd seen the warning on his cell phone a little while ago. But he was sure that Rachel hadn't seen it—not yet. He'd met her just after a class, and he knew that she always turned her phone off during classes.

And he knew she wasn't going to check it now. He had easily snatched it out of her jacket pocket and tossed it aside a short distance back. So far, she hadn't noticed that it was missing. With luck, she wouldn't notice until it was too late.

He hoped he could squeeze in just one more retribution before the law closed in.

The noose is tightening, he thought.

He was amused by the metaphor.

He knew what it felt like to have a real noose tightening around his neck. His fake suicide attempt had been an excellent ruse. It had been especially effective with that woman, Agent Paige. How easy it had been to gain her sympathy and trust!

But all that was coming to an end.

Meanwhile, he had to keep some conversation going.

"Have I ever told you about my trips to the Greek islands?" he asked.

"No," the girl said. "Tell me."

He started telling her about the nude beaches in the Aegean— an entertaining story, he thought. But he could tell she wasn't at all interested.

She was being polite.

Rachel was like that—always polite.

All the girls were always polite.

He hated their politeness.

He wanted to be loved, wanted, desired.

But it never ever happened.

He was nice, they all told him.

That word "nice" was always the kiss of death.

Of course, it was only figuratively the kiss of death for Murray.

It was quite literally the kiss of death for the girls.

He kept on talking, keeping his eye on the girl. She still wasn't showing any effects of the drug. He hoped she didn't get too out of it before they reached his destination. It would be bad if she keeled right over as they walked. He was prepared for what was to come next, and the noose was tied and ready in his backpack.

Still, it seemed kind of crazy, taking this enormous risk when the law was closing in.

What the hell did he think he was doing?

Well, he wasn't thinking at all, of course.

He was following his urges, as he always did.

How could he do otherwise?

Anyway, he'd been lucky so far—lucky with Deanna, Cory, Constance, Lois, and Patience.

And he had a strong feeling that his luck was going to hold.

All he had to do was kill this one and get away.

He had a one-way plane ticket for a flight to Venezuela that left in an hour and a half.

If he could just slip away from the murder scene and get on that plane, he'd never come back.

What would become of him then, he didn't know. But he had all the resources he would ever need to live well wherever he went.

Oh, well, he told himself. *All good things must come to an end.*

He smiled as he thought …

Rachel's life, for example.

CHAPTER THIRTY SIX

Riley's pace quickened as she approached a quaint little brick building with shutters flanking the windows.

Had she located the right Rachel?

The letters on the awning said ROSEDALE BOUTIQUE INN. It wasn't far from campus, and it looked like many of the shops and residences in the area.

The GPS signal was definitely coming from here. Bill had just called to tell Riley that his own Rachel had been a dead end. He'd also said that he'd talked to Lucy, who was still following her own signal.

Guess there's a fifty-fifty chance, Riley figured.

She walked into the small lobby, where an elderly male concierge stood behind the desk. Riley produced her badge and introduced herself. He peered through thick glasses at the badge, as if not sure what to make of it.

Then she showed him a picture of Murray Rossum on her cell phone.

"Has this young man checked in here?" she asked.

"I wouldn't know," the man said, pointing to his eyes. "I'm not good with faces. Macular degeneration."

"His name is Murray Rossum."

The concierge peered closely at the register with a magnifying glass.

"No such guest," he said.

"He might not have used his real name," Riley said. "I think he may have brought a young woman here—a Byars student named Rachel Hawk."

The man's lip curled with disdain.

"So what if he did bring her here?" he said. "Ma'am, this is the twenty-first century."

"Sir, Murray Rossum's a serial killer," Riley said. "If he brought her here, it's likely that he's going to murder her. If he hasn't already."

The concierge's bushy gray eyebrows rose.

"A young man brought a girl in here just a little while ago," he said. "He signed in this morning by the name of Toby Seton."

He picked up his desk phone.

"I'll call his room," he said.

"No," Riley said. "I can't give him any warning. You've got to let me in the room right now."

The man wavered.

"Do you have a warrant?"

Riley stifled a groan of frustration. There simply hadn't been time for legal formalities.

"Sir, have you ever found a dead body hanging in one of your rooms? Because that's what may very well happen unless we stop it from happening."

His face grew paler. He picked up a set of keys and silently led Riley up the stairs. He turned the key in a room door and opened it.

Riley heard a girl's squeal of alarm and a boy yelling, "Holy shit!"

Two naked young people were cowering under a bed sheet. The boy definitely wasn't Murray Rossum. The room was small but comfortable.

"What the hell do you want?" the girl said.

Riley produced her badge and introduced herself.

The girl looked truly alarmed.

"Lady, I beg you, don't tell my parents about this. They'll have a fit. Toby came down from New York just to see me, and—"

Riley wasn't interested in her story.

"Are you Rachel Hawk?" she asked.

"Yeah, so what?"

"Haven't you checked your cell phone?"

The girl shook her head.

"Not lately. Why?"

"Byars has an excellent warning system," Riley said. "You should start using it."

The girl was reaching for her cell phone when Riley left the room and shut the door behind her. She heard a shrill screech of alarm as the girl found out what the warning had been. Of course, the warning wasn't of any use to the girl now.

Riley thanked the bewildered concierge for his help and left the building.

Where does this leave us? Riley asked herself as she walked away.

She and Bill had eliminated two Rachels. That meant that Lucy must be heading straight toward the true murder target—and into trouble.

Riley got on her phone to warn Lucy.

*

Rachel was feeling uneasy—and oddly lightheaded.

"Where are we going?" she asked Murray again.

"You'll see," he said again.

Murray resumed telling her all about his travels all over the world. Right now he was droning on and on about Paris.

He was leading her into an out-of-the-way area. The path was lined with shrubbery that probably bloomed in the spring, and bare tree branches crisscrossed overhead.

Rachel had never been here and didn't especially like it. The path was narrow and the area was somewhat tangled with vines. And today was uncomfortably chilly for such a walk. She gulped down the rest of the hot chocolate Murray had bought for her, but it didn't really help.

She was also feeling uncomfortable around Murray. For one thing, she found his stories to be boring and tedious.

So why didn't she come right out and tell him?

The answer was simple. She didn't want to hurt his feelings. The truth was, she felt more than a little sorry for him. She knew that he came from a wealthy family—far richer than hers. And he was a perfectly nice guy, which was pretty rare at Byars. Even so, he wasn't popular, and he didn't seem to have a girlfriend.

She certainly didn't want to be his girlfriend.

But she also didn't want to be cruel.

Her friends always told her that she was way too polite.

"You're a chump, Rachel," they said.

Her friends were right. It was a character flaw that left her vulnerable to odd and off-putting people.

She felt especially awkward around Murray. Once he had even turned up at her home in Bethesda while she was there one weekend. He said he wanted to take her to the movies. She told him that her family had made plans for her that day. It was a lie, and she'd immediately felt guilty about it. And Murray had looked terribly hurt.

She didn't want to make him feel like that again.

Shouldn't she put a stop to this?

Surely it was high time for her to stop being a chump, to show a little backbone.

It was time to tell him that she wanted to go back to the campus center.

If it hurt his feelings, there was nothing she could do about it.

But as soon as she opened her mouth to say something, she was seized by a sudden dizziness. Her knees went weak and she almost fell. The empty cup tumbled out of her hand.

Murray caught her by the arm.

"Are you OK?" he asked.

"I'm not sure," she said.

He led her toward a fallen log underneath some overhanging branches.

"Sit down here," he said.

She sat down. Her head was buzzing and reeling, and the world was spinning around her.

What's going on? she wondered.

Her thoughts were foggy, and she couldn't make sense of things.

But she had a vague feeling that she was in danger.

She had to get help.

She reached into her jacket pocket for her cell phone.

It wasn't there.

Had she left it back in her room?

No, she'd had it in class, she was sure of it. She'd turned it off before the lecture started.

Murray was still standing and rummaging through his backpack.

What's he doing?

As she struggled to think, a terrible memory formed in her mind.

Several Byars students had been murdered recently—drugged and hanged.

A sketch of the killer was posted everywhere.

She remembered the sketch and the description—a big man with thick, shaggy hair.

Murray didn't look at all like that.

He couldn't be the killer.

But he was. She knew that now.

She tried to get up from the log but dizziness overwhelmed her and she fell sideways.

She knew that she should be afraid. But she was too foggy and disoriented. And that was bad. Fear would help her. It would energize her so she could escape.

194

Now Murray was putting something around her neck.

I've got to get scared, she thought.

If she didn't, she knew she was going to die.

CHAPTER THIRTY SEVEN

Lucy's nerves were tingling as she moved along the path, following the GPS signal for Rachel Mackey's cell phone.

She'd just gotten off the phone with Agent Paige, who had told her that she and Agent Jeffreys had eliminated the other two Rachels.

Lucy now knew that she was tracking the true murder target.

Agents Paige and Jeffreys were on their way to join her. But from the looks of the GPS signal, Rachel wasn't far away. Lucy doubted that they'd arrive before she found the girl—and the killer as well.

It's going to be up to me, she thought. She hoped she was up to whatever awaited her.

But now, looking at the GPS instructions on her cell phone, something seemed to be wrong.

It looks like Rachel is right here, she thought.

Lucy stopped in her tracks and turned all around.

She saw nobody at all.

Then a glint of plastic caught her eye on the ground under a bush. She reached down and picked it up. It was a cell phone, the one she was tracking.

Rachel's cell phone! The killer must have taken it from her and tossed it away.

Lucy was seized by a wave of despair.

How long had it been since Murray and his victim were here?

How far away could they be?

She broke into a run along the path, winding her way between ornamental bushes until she came to a three-way fork.

Her eyes darted frantically among the three paths.

Murray must have continued along one of them.

But which?

There were footprints along all of them, some fresh, others older.

Which were the freshest?

Lucy's heart was pounding. She couldn't decide. Was she too agitated to think clearly?

Surely Agent Paige wouldn't have this problem!

Lucy took a long, slow breath, knelt down, and looked at the paths more carefully.

She simply couldn't see any difference.

She decided to follow the middle path and hope for the best.

She hurried along that way until she thought she heard a noise from her right.

She turned and thought she saw something move some distance off among the brush and branches.

"Murray Rossum!" she yelled.

Now she was sure that she detected another flash of movement.

Should she retrace her steps and follow the path to the right?

No, there wasn't time for that.

Lucy plunged through the thicket, lashed all over by twigs and branches.

She emerged into a clearing.

And there the girl was.

She was hanging by the neck from a rope looped over a bare tree branch. Her feet were dangling just a foot or two off the ground. It looked as though she had been pushed off a fallen log.

Her face was an unnatural shade of blue, almost as if she'd been painted.

Lucy saw no sign of movement.

Is she dead? Lucy wondered.

She reminded herself that the other victims had been drugged. Just because the girl wasn't struggling didn't necessarily mean she wasn't alive.

Just then she saw a figure moving away farther down a path.

"Murray!" she yelled.

He didn't stop, and Lucy had no time to pursue him. She ran to the hanging figure and wrapped her arms around the girl's hips, lifting her a little so that there was slack in the rope.

Just then the girl's body jerked and she coughed.

Rachel was still alive!

But how was Lucy going to get her down?

To untie the rope, she'd have to release her hold on the body. If she did, Rachel would be strangled anew—probably fatally.

Still barely conscious, Rachel let out a groan.

"Stay with me!" Lucy said sharply.

But she could see that the girl was slipping back into unconsciousness.

Lucy shook the body, but Rachel didn't respond.

She's dying! Lucy thought.

Keeping one arm wrapped around the girl's hips, Lucy released the other and reached up to try to loosen the noose.

It was still tight around her neck. Rachel's breathing was coming in hoarse, semi-conscious gasps. The blood flow was still cut off. Lucy felt hopelessly clumsy, clutching the body with one hand and fumbling with the knot with the other.

For a moment, Lucy thought she was loosening the knot.

Then, to her horror, she realized she'd tightened it instead.

Rachel was no longer breathing at all.

Lucy didn't dare keep trying to loosen it. She'd only make things worse.

She couldn't possibly save Rachel by herself.

Then, over the sound of her own heart beating, she thought she heard voices and footsteps.

"I'm here!" she yelled. "I've got her! Help me! She's not going to make it!"

Then she didn't hear anything at all.

Had her ears been playing tricks on her?

Then Agents Paige and Jeffreys burst into the clearing.

"She's alive!" Lucy yelled out to them. "I need help!"

Agent Jeffreys helped Lucy support the weight of the girl's body. They lifted her a bit higher.

Agent Paige clambered up onto the log, reached out, and loosened the noose. Then she slipped it off of the girl's neck.

Lucy and Agent Jeffreys carefully lowered the girl's body and stretched her out on the ground.

"Where is Murray Rossum?" Agent Paige asked.

Lucy pointed.

"Headed in that direction," she said. "You two go after him. I'll take care of Rachel."

Agents Paige and Jeffreys took off down the path as Lucy called for emergency medical care.

CHAPTER THIRTY EIGHT

Murray climbed a little way up into a tree that hung over the path. He was holding the spare noose he always kept with him. He'd thought he might have to use it for himself someday.

It was over now, and Murray knew it.

The path ended here, and there was no way for him to escape.

He'd seen the young agent coming after him. The only reason she hadn't followed him was to save the girl.

Murray smiled a little.

She had surely been too late for that.

He'd carried out one more act of retribution.

That was enough to satisfy him once and for all.

It had been a good game, a fine chase, and he'd enjoyed it.

He had especially enjoyed the sympathy he had gotten from that woman—Agent Paige.

How easy it had been to make her believe that he was a victim!

Of course, that was what he really was—a victim.

If people had cared about or tried to understand him, no one would have had to die.

The girls had brought their deaths on themselves.

And now he was going to finish everything on his own terms, nobody else's.

He worked his way out onto a branch and tied the rope to it. He placed the noose around his neck. He tightened the noose. Now all he had to do was step off into space. The fall probably wouldn't be enough to break his neck. But he would certainly be strangled to death.

He found himself hesitating.

But why?

He knew perfectly well that it had to end this way.

He had no reason to be afraid.

And yet …

… he was afraid.

He viscerally remembered that night in the garage when he'd faked his own suicide attempt. He found himself reliving the instinctive terror, the frantic thrashing and clutching as he'd fought to save himself.

He dreaded the thought of it happening again.

It seemed strange to be frightened of something he truly wanted to do.

But it couldn't be helped.

He stepped off the branch. He dropped a short way and hit the end of the rope with a painful jerk.

He couldn't breathe, and he immediately felt the loss of blood flow to his head.

And sure enough, his hands grabbed at the rope, and his feet kicked at nothing.

Then he saw that woman … Agent Paige.

Was it a hallucination?

He didn't know.

CHAPTER THIRTY NINE

As they rushed to find Murray Rossum, Riley and Bill had separated at a fork in the path. When Riley found her way into the clearing, she saw Murray.

He was a short distance ahead and above her, hanging from a rope attached to a tree limb.

He was kicking wildly and grasping at the rope with his hands.

Her first impulse was to rush forward and try to help him as they had done with Rachel.

It shouldn't be hard. She only needed to climb up to the branch where he was hanging, carefully hoist him up, and free him from the noose.

She took a couple of steps forward and reached out toward him.

As she did, she saw the bracelet that Shane Hatcher had given her.

It still felt heavy and unfamiliar on her wrist. She hadn't been able to defy his wish that she keep on wearing it.

She stopped in her tracks and watched Murray Rossum writhe. His eyes were bulging, and he was staring straight at her.

It was a desperate, imploring look.

But what did he want from her? To cut him down or let him die?

What was going on in his twisted mind?

He wanted to die. If he hadn't, he wouldn't have done this to himself.

And yet his body was still fighting for its life.

Riley remembered something from the Bible:

"The spirit is willing, but the flesh is weak."

Now she felt as though she understood.

Of all the killers Riley had pursued, Murray was possibly the weakest.

But now he was fighting one last battle against his own weakness.

And she herself was fighting her own battle: her own battle against weakness. The weakness of saving this boy's life.

Or of getting vengeance.

Vengeance for all the girls he had cruelly killed.

Vengeance for a justice system that would surely declare him insane.

Vengeance for the wealth that would buy him the world's best attorneys and set him free in a matter of years, if not months.

She stood and watched, and she fought her own battle.

Little by little, Murray's movements slowed, and his body calmed and slackened, and his eyes closed.

His face turned a weird bluish color right before her eyes.

Finally, he didn't move at all.

And neither did she.

A long, slow silence crept over her.

As she watched silently, Riley found herself remembering a question Shane Hatcher sometimes asked her …

"Are you already, or are you becoming?"

He had actually answered that question once.

"You're becoming. *You're becoming what you've always been deep down. Call it a monster or whatever you want. And it won't be long before you* are *that person."*

She still didn't understand exactly what Hatcher had meant.

But she shuddered at the thought that he'd been telling the truth.

At that moment, Bill appeared in the clearing.

Riley realized that he'd given up searching in the other direction and had come back to find her.

"My God," he murmured as he saw the body.

There was no longer any question that Murray Rossum was dead.

Bill stared straight into Riley's eyes.

She knew that he was silently asking her a question:

"Did you let this happen?"

By staring silently back, Riley told him the truth.

Bill nodded ever so slightly.

He was telling her that he understood.

And that he himself may have done the same.

"Let's cut him down," he said.

CHAPTER FORTY

Early the next morning, Riley was in her office at the BAU. Meredith had scheduled a meeting to review the case, and Riley wanted to put in some phone calls before that got started.

First she called her friend Danica Selves, the district medical examiner. She thanked Danica for her invaluable help in getting the case underway.

Next she dialed Mike Nevins's number.

He sounded excited to hear from her.

"I heard the news! It sounds like congratulations are in order!"

"I've got you to thank," Riley said. "Without your letter to Autrey, I'd never have gotten the case off the ground. I'm so glad you pitched in and helped."

Mike sounded a little sheepish.

"Yes, well … I'm not sure I did my best work this time around. I can't believe I interviewed that kid and didn't pick up on the fact that he was the killer."

"He had me fooled too," Riley said. "He was a weak man, and he did what weak people do best. He manipulated us, played on our sympathies."

"Well, he was damned good at it," Mike said. "Compassion's a tricky thing, isn't it? In our business, I mean. Too much of it clouds your judgment. Too little of it and you become a monster."

Riley winced at Mike's words.

They cut too close to home at the moment.

Shane Hatcher's words echoed again through her mind.

"You're becoming what you've always been deep down."

Riley thanked Mike again and ended the call.

There was one more phone call she wanted to make. She reminded herself that it was still very early morning in Seattle. But Van Roff didn't keep normal hours, and she doubted that he was asleep. And if he was asleep, he wouldn't mind if she woke him up.

She dialed his number. Like Mike Nevins, Van Roff had already heard the news.

"I couldn't have done it without your help, Van," she said.

"Think nothing of it. I'm always eager to bend the rules."

That reminded Riley of their last awkward phone call, when Van had refused to help her find Shane Hatcher. She felt the need to apologize for putting him on the spot like that.

"Van, about that other thing I asked you to do …"

"What thing? I've got no idea what you're talking about."

Riley smiled. It was Van's way of telling her not to worry about it.

Riley was still on the phone with Van when Bill poked his head into Riley's office.

He said, "Walder wants to see everybody in the conference room right now."

Bill disappeared again.

"Oh, shit," Riley said to Van.

"What's the matter?"

"It's the uber-boss. Through this whole case, I've disobeyed his orders even more than usual. Now I'm really in trouble."

"You'll bounce back," Van Roff said. "We troublemakers always do."

Riley thanked him again and headed for the conference room.

The whole team was there—Bill, Lucy, Craig Huang, Sam Flores, Brent Meredith, and Walder himself. To Riley's surprise, Walder's babyish, freckled face was beaming with joy.

"Excellent work, Paige," he said. "And to all the rest of you as well."

"Thanks, sir," Riley said, cautiously.

Then, almost chuckling at her own irony, she added, "Coming from you, that really means something."

Walder held court for a little while, heaping praises on everyone who was present. Riley found it to be an amazing performance. He seemed to have forgotten his fury about the multiple tricks and deceptions that Riley had pulled to get this case underway.

His capacity for denial was truly remarkable.

But of course, denial was part of how a weak man like Walder wielded his authority.

"The only tyranny that lasts," Riley reminded herself.

When he was gone, Meredith led the team in a routine debriefing. Murray Rossum was dead—a real suicide to follow four murders and another attempt, all faked up to look like suicides. Rachel Mackey was in the hospital, badly bruised but out of danger—at least physically. Riley knew that it would take her a long time to get over the emotional trauma.

If she ever gets over it, she thought.

As the meeting drew to a close, Bill jokingly asked, "Do you

204

think maybe we should touch base with Willis Autrey, just to reassure him that everything's OK?"

Meredith let forth a peal of rumbling laughter.

"I don't think so," he said. "I'm sure he never wants to hear from any of us ever again."

*

That afternoon, Riley got home just after the girls returned from school. She hadn't seen them since before they'd caught Murray Rossum. Riley hadn't returned home the night before until after the girls were in bed, and she'd left before they awoke this morning. Tiffany was there with April and Jilly. They all rushed to her as soon as she got through the front door.

"Did you find him?" April asked.

"Was it that guy in poetry class?" Tiffany wanted to know.

"Did you lock him up?" Jilly asked.

"We did find him," Riley told them. "It's all over now."

She took off her coat and sat on the sofa. The girls clustered around her.

"He's dead," she said. "He'll never hurt anyone else again."

Jilly asked, "Did you blow him away or what?"

Riley shook her head.

"He killed himself. Hanged himself. He knew the game was up."

Tiffany's eyes widened. Then she burst into tears.

"Oh, thank you, thank you!" Tiffany said to Riley. "Thanks for believing me in the first place."

April hugged Tiffany, comforting her.

Riley felt a pang at Tiffany's words. The truth was, she hadn't believed Tiffany right away—or her own daughter, either.

Next time I'll pay better heed, she thought.

"So tell us all about it!" Jilly said, bouncing with excitement. "How did you nail the guy?"

Riley sighed.

"I'm sorry, but I'm all tired out," she said. "I'll tell you some other time, real soon."

April said, "Tiffany's parents said she could stay the night. Is that OK, Mom?"

Riley smiled.

"Of course it's OK," she said.

Tiffany noticed the bracelet on Riley's wrist.

"That's pretty," she said. "Where did you get it?"

Riley felt an urge to tuck it under her sleeve. But it was too late to conceal it.

"It was a gift," Riley said.

"From an admirer?" April asked mischievously.

Riley shivered a little. Instead of answering the question, she said, "You kids go have a good time."

Chattering and giggling, the girls hurried off to the family room. Their cheerful voices warmed Riley's heart. Whatever her situation might be with Ryan, her girls were doing OK. April was helping Jilly settle in to her new life, and they were both helping Tiffany get over the trauma of her sister's death.

Riley was proud of them.

She heard Gabriela in the kitchen, singing a Guatemalan song as she fixed dinner. It felt good to be home.

Then Riley saw that there was a message on the answering machine.

It was from Ryan.

"Hey, gang. Sorry to be away lately, but I've got a lot of business here in DC. I'll come back when I can. Love to all."

The message ended with a beep.

Riley sighed. She had been trying to accept that Ryan was gone again, for good this time. But now what was going to happen?

It was terribly confusing.

*

Riley went up to her office. There was one more phone call she wanted to make. It was to her sister, Wendy. It was time to take care of some unfinished business.

Riley could hear Wendy gasp when she said who was calling.

"Riley!" she said. "What is it? Is something the matter?"

Riley was about to explain everything—how she felt that Daddy had made a mistake leaving the cabin to her, and how the cabin was Wendy's if she wanted it.

But suddenly it seemed wrong to try to resolve all this on the phone.

It's time to do some healing, Riley thought.

She said simply, "Let's get together and talk."

Wendy sounded surprised but pleased. They made plans to get

206

together on a weekend soon.

As soon as the call ended, Riley's cell phone buzzed.

It was an anonymous text message that read …

Sometimes the strong win.

Riley shuddered.

She knew right away who the message was from.

It was from Shane Hatcher, sending his congratulations.

She'd never gotten a text message from him before.

Should Riley reply?

She decided she shouldn't—and anyway, she didn't know what to say.

At least now Riley knew that she had another way to contact him.

But was that a good thing or a bad thing?

Riley didn't know.

ONCE COLD
(A Riley Paige Mystery—Book 8)

"A masterpiece of thriller and mystery! The author did a magnificent job developing characters with a psychological side that is so well described that we feel inside their minds, follow their fears and cheer for their success. The plot is very intelligent and will keep you entertained throughout the book. Full of twists, this book will keep you awake until the turn of the last page."
--Books and Movie Reviews, Roberto Mattos (re Once Gone)

ONCE COLD is book #8 in the bestselling Riley Paige mystery series, which begins with the #1 bestseller ONCE GONE (Book #1)—a free download with over 900 five star reviews!

There is one cold case that has plagued Special Agent Riley Paige for her entire career, dwelling at the corners of her consciousness, forcing her to return to it again and again. The only case she has never solved, she has finally put it out of her mind.

Until she gets a call from the murdered victim's mother.

It spurs Riley to face the case once again, and to not give up until she has found answers.

Yet Riley barely has time to catch her breath when she receives a lead for another cold case, one which, if possible, strikes an even deeper note within her. It is a lead that promises to solve the case of her own mother's killer.

And it comes from Shane Hatcher.

A dark psychological thriller with heart-pounding suspense, ONCE COLD is book #8 in a riveting new series—with a beloved new character—that will leave you turning pages late into the night.

Book #9 in the Riley Paige series will be available soon.

Blake Pierce

Blake Pierce is author of the bestselling RILEY PAGE mystery series, which includes seven books (and counting). Blake Pierce is also the author of the MACKENZIE WHITE mystery series, comprising five books (and counting); of the AVERY BLACK mystery series, comprising four books (and counting); and of the new KERI LOCKE mystery series.

An avid reader and lifelong fan of the mystery and thriller genres, Blake loves to hear from you, so please feel free to visit www.blakepierceauthor.com to learn more and stay in touch.

BOOKS BY BLAKE PIERCE

RILEY PAIGE MYSTERY SERIES
ONCE GONE (Book #1)
ONCE TAKEN (Book #2)
ONCE CRAVED (Book #3)
ONCE LURED (Book #4)
ONCE HUNTED (Book #5)
ONCE PINED (Book #6)
ONCE FORSAKEN (Book #7)
ONCE COLD (Book #8)

MACKENZIE WHITE MYSTERY SERIES
BEFORE HE KILLS (Book #1)
BEFORE HE SEES (Book #2)
BEFORE HE COVETS (Book #3)
BEFORE HE TAKES (Book #4)
BEFORE HE NEEDS (Book #5)

AVERY BLACK MYSTERY SERIES
CAUSE TO KILL (Book #1)
CAUSE TO RUN (Book #2)
CAUSE TO HIDE (Book #3)
CAUSE TO FEAR (Book #4)

Made in the USA
Middletown, DE
26 September 2021